A Love Unquenchable

Linen and Lace - Book Four

Rosie Chapel

First printing 2017
ISBN: 978-0-9954303-9-6

Ulfire Pty. Ltd.
P.O. Box 1481
South Perth
WA 6951
Australia

www.rosiechapel.com

Cover Artwork JF Holland

Cover Images Courtesy:
Period Images and Deposit Photos

Other Books by Rosie Chapel

The Hannah's Heirloom Sequence
The Pomegranate Tree - Hannah's Heirloom - Book One
Echoes of Stone and Fire - Hannah's Heirloom - Book Two
Embers of Destiny - Hannah's Heirloom - Book Three
Etched in Starlight - Hannah's Heirloom - Prequel
Hannah's Heirloom Trilogy - Compilation - Kindle only

Prelude to Fate

Regency Romances
Once Upon An Earl - Linen and Lace - Book One
To Unlock Her Heart - Linen and Lace - Book Two
Love on a Winter's Tide - Linen and Lace - Book Three
A Love Unquenchable - Linen and Lace - Book Four
A Hidden Rose - Linen and Lace - Book Five

His Fiery Hoyden - A Regency Novella

Contemporary Romance
Of Ruins and Romance
All At Once It's You

Anthologies
The Highway Man's Kiss - Once Upon A Love Anthology
Heart Rescued - Tales for the Season Anthology
Luck be a Pirate - Kiss My Luck Anthology
Finally Home - Tempting Fate Anthology
Love Kindled - Building Love Anthology - TBR Dec 2018

Dedication

To my wonderfully caring, supportive, patient, funny,
tenacious, and irrepressibly crazy Bards ~
this book is for you.
May your rails never stop rattling!

Acknowledgements

Thank you once again to Julie for this stunning cover.
My endless gratitude to Mum, Lilly, Amy and Joyce,
for caring enough to proofread my work.
Appreciation to the team at YM Zachary and JB Joseph PA
Editing Services, for refining my manuscript.

Although I recently updated the covers on my Regency series, I
remain forever grateful to my sister, Helen, who created the
gorgeous originals.

Some time ago I was involved in a weekend long author
takeover, following which several of us continued to chat as a
group. These people have become incredibly important to me
and, as they have been subject to all manner of snippets,
offering support and suggestions, I feel they deserve a mention
(in no particular order)
Amy, Lilly, Ani, Julie, Zesty, Bella, YM, JB, Shaan, Jade,
Alathia, Jeremy and Jon - thank you so much.

The Linen and Lace Clan

An exclusive club, only accessible to the fortuitous few. Those who - no matter their differences in money, title, background or position - marry for love. In an era when status, influence and wealth are bolstered under the guise of marriage, you are like rare gemstones - admired and envied. May your mutual respect, and true affection for one another, be the beacons by which you navigate the rough and the smooth of life's journey. Therefore, whether your clothing be of the cheapest linen or the finest lace, may the blend of either or both bring the richest and happiest union.

Author's Note

The quote from Shakespeare of which Duncan is reminded every time he sees Jessica is from *Hamlet* Act 2 Scene 2.

When I was trying to come up with the title for this book, I came across several quotes about love, and one, which resonated with me, was by of all people, Bruce Lee (possibly inspired by an earlier quote from Henry Ward Beecher). Yes, I know he wasn't even a figment of his grandparents' imaginations in the Regency era, but his words hold.

I hope you think so too.

"Love is like a friendship caught on fire.
In the beginning a flame, very pretty, often hot and fierce,
but still only light and flickering.
As love grows older, our hearts mature and our love becomes
as coals,
deep-burning and unquenchable."

Bruce Lee

A Love Unquenchable

Linen and Lace - Book Four

Chapter One

From her vantage point on the terrace, everything around her as far as the eye could see was painted in innumerable shades of white. Snow blanketed the landscape, muffling sound and, despite a wintry sun doing its best to warm the frigid air, all remained frozen. Jessica Drummond was mesmerised, she had never seen so much snow. Her whole life had been spent in London and, although the city experienced harsh winters, it was nothing like this. It simply took her breath away.

She had enjoyed a morning constitutional every day since her arrival, and there was no way she was going to let the snow stop her. Lifting the hood of her cloak over her head, and slipping cold hands into thick gloves, Jessica strode out across the glittering expanse of white. It was still early and the outdoor staff hadn't cleared the pathways, so she didn't know on what, precisely, she was walking. Hopefully she wasn't damaging precious garden beds.

Jessica followed, roughly, the same path she took every day, straight out into the Great Park and off into the wilds. She could walk for miles and see no one, relishing the utter nothingness of being on her own away from everything. She speculated whether this was something she inherited from their father who had loved being on board ship in the vast emptiness of the ocean. Odd really as she had lived her whole life in the centre of a bustling city always surrounded by people and noise, yet Jessica found the silence both a solace and a restorative.

The previous day had seen the wedding of her brother, Hugh, to Helena — sister of the Earl of Winchester, on whose estate she was currently staying. It had been a wonderful day, as had the week beforehand. It wouldn't be long before she

17

returned to London, but this short break had been splendid, just the place to unwind and let the cares of everyday life fall away.

The last couple of months had been fraught as the Drummond family's shipping company, Trentams, had been targeted by Lord Faversham, an unscrupulous earl, intent on taking the business by fair means or foul — although foul seemed his preferred *modus operandi*. After a lengthy investigation, his machinations were uncovered, but not before he had tried to kill Helena and Hugh, as well as causing damage to the shipyard itself. The man had obviously been taken by madness and, ultimately, his actions cost him his life.

Jessica, thankfully, had not been witness to Faversham's death, but she worked at Trentams and had been involved in the effort to reveal the perpetrator of the events leading to the final confrontation. Not only that but also the aftermath had been difficult; the repairs required for the two ships crippled by the earl's henchmen would be both costly and lengthy, the court case, never mind the not inconsequential injuries inflicted upon her own brother and his betrothed. Still, it was all in the past now and life had begun to move on.

All these things were running through Jessica's head when she paused, realising she had walked much further than intended. Disorientated, she spun around trying to assess where she was. It appeared to be the middle of nowhere. She could see her footsteps, a neat trail from the direction she had come and in the distance she could make out tendrils of smoke against the pale sky. That must be Whiteoaks — goodness she had come quite a way.

Shivering a little, Jessica was about to turn back, thoughts of a warm fire and a hot breakfast most inviting, when she heard an odd sound. Pushing back her hood, she stopped, listening carefully — nothing, all was still, not even the twitter of a bird broke the quiet. Shrugging, and presuming it had probably been the sound of snow slithering from the trees, she turned and began to head home.

She had barely taken two steps when she heard it, louder this time. There was no doubt; this definitely wasn't the sound of falling snow, more a sort of mewling cry. Jessica waited — on cue it came again, somewhere off to her right. Without pausing to think, she scuffed through the thick whiteness towards a copse of trees, well they were more like scrubby bushes, scarcely higher than she was tall but as she reached them, the noise stopped. Frustrated Jessica called softly,

"I'm here. Where are you? Let me help," she cooed, then, "gracious Jessica," she admonished herself, "how old are you? 'Tis likely an animal of some sort and it cannot understand what you're saying. Good thing no one is listening." She snorted on a giggle, biting her lip in realisation she was now talking to herself. Here, at the edge of the Great Park, the snow was much deeper; she was up to her knees and walking was difficult. Not one to let such a hindrance prevent her from discovering the source of the noise, Jessica simply pushed on into the copse, fighting her way through the briars, which caught at her cloak and tore at her hair.

"Dear me, this had better be worth it," she muttered, as she came to a small clearing. At the far side, apparently trapped in the same type of thorny bush she had just fought her way through, Jessica spied a furry bundle, definitely an animal of some sort. Suddenly aware it was no longer alone, the creature lifted its head, spotted the cloaked human and let out a pitiful howl. Jessica hurried over, falling to her knees next to the little mite, startled to see it was a dog. No more than a puppy, it was the scruffiest dog she had ever seen, although to be fair she hadn't seen many. The one or two owned by friends were all perfectly groomed, never made a sound and were hardly ever allowed to make an appearance.

She stroked its shaggy head, crooning softly while trying to work out how the dickens it had become stuck. All she could think was it had run into the bush, but realising it couldn't get through, tried to back out, its matted fur becoming caught in the sharp thorns — a most effective trap. Crouching closer, Jessica flipped the edges of her cloak over her shoulders, pushed up her sleeves in the hopes they wouldn't get torn, removed her gloves and began the painstaking task of untangling the wretched creature. It seemed to understand she was trying to help and stopped whimpering, instead just stared at her with huge, soulful brown eyes. Jessica trembled with cold and her teeth chattered, but she was determined not to abandon the tiny scrap, knowing it would perish in such icy temperatures.

It took a long time, and despite being as careful as possible, the barbs from the bushes raked along Jessica's arms, leaving angry scratches. Finally, after what felt like an age, she managed to free the puppy, lifting it away from the bush and into the relative warmth of her cloak.

"Now we must get you home," Jessica informed her grubby charge, who licked her chin before burrowing deeper into the folds of her cloak. Grinning to herself, Jessica rolled down her sleeves, shoved chilled hands into the warm gloves and wrestled her way back through the gnarly bushes, soon coming out onto the Great Park. "I expect people will be wondering where I am," she said to the puppy, "although perhaps they will assume I am still asleep." Jessica found her trail of footsteps and began the long walk home.

She was about halfway there when two horses appeared over a rise, thundering towards her and, for a moment, she felt quite frightened. Although most knew of Jessica's penchant for an early morning walk, today, what with rescuing the puppy, she had been out far longer than usual, had walked much further than she intended and was currently quite alone in the middle of a country estate. Then common sense reasserted itself. She surmised her mother had felt moved to comment on Jessica's tardiness, likely concerned her absence at the breakfast table would seem impolite to their hosts. "Oh bother, doubtless Mama has said something," she grumbled. "Anybody would think I was still a child not a grown woman of almost two and twenty."

She continued walking and, seconds later, the riders reined in alongside her. Jessica glanced at them, they seemed vaguely familiar but she could not be certain and so, not really knowing what to do, ignored them.

"Miss Drummond?" one of the men spoke, his voice gentle. Resignedly coming to a halt, Jessica raised her head, focussing on the kindly faced man addressing her. She nodded and he continued. "As we were saddling the horses, we came upon your brother in the courtyard, about to head out to find you. Apparently, you were missed at breakfast and he recalled seeing you set off for your walk well over two hours ago. I think he was worried for you in this cold weather."

"Oh, please don't tell me he asked you to help look for me?" She beseeched.

"He didn't need to, we offered. More snow's forecast, a city lady such as you might easily get lost hereabouts." The second man countered, derision in his tones.

Jessica spun to face him. "I have been walking this same path every day for a week now, *sir*. I think I can manage to find my way back despite the snow. Whiteoaks is just there," flinging her arm in its general direction. "I am sorry Nick felt the need to send out a search party, but as you can see I am absolutely fine and will be home forthwith." Jessica replied, rather more tartly than was warranted, bearing in mind these two men had been concerned enough to come and find her. She sighed, "I do beg your pardon, that was rude of me, but I have just spent the last I don't know how long trying to rescue this..." digging inside her cloak, Jessica withdrew a most bedraggled specimen, presenting her now snoring bundle to the two men. The one who had spoken first shouted with laughter, while his morose companion simply gawked.

"Where on earth did you find him, her, it?" The first man enquired mirth still twitching at his lips. "My name is Ralph Montgomery by the way," he added in introduction. Jessica, still unsure of their status, tried to drop a curtsy, rather difficult when you're holding a puppy, but she managed a sketchy one, to the continued amusement of Ralph.

"I am glad to make your acquaintance sir," she managed, through a jaw clenched in an attempt to stop her teeth chattering.

Ralph frowned and, realising Jessica was colder than she appeared, hurriedly dismounted.

"I think you should hop up behind me and we can get you home faster," noticing the slightly blue tinge to her lips and the shivers she couldn't quite suppress.

Jessica stared at him in horror. "N-no, p-please, I'm fine. I c-can walk. It w-won't take m-me long. M-maybe you could take the puppy though?" She stammered, optimistically.

"Come now, surely you are not afraid of a horse," the second man bit out. "Get on with you, Miss Drummond, 'tis too cold and too far for you to walk, puppy or not. We have call on our time today, time I have no thought to waste." His gaze bored into her and Jessica did not understand what she had done to cause such displeasure. She straightened her shoulders and glared back, their eyes clashing — glacial blue against fiery topaz.

"I beg your pardon, sir. I do not wish to keep you from your busy day and I apologise my brother saw fit to waste your time unnecessarily. Please, go, I can see the chimneys of Whiteoaks; I will make my own way." She turned to the man beside her, "thank you for your concern, *Mr Montgomery*," politely emphasising his name, deliberately excluding his angry friend. "Might you be so kind as to inform my brother I will not be long?" She tossed her head and began to stomp homewards. She knew she was behaving badly but whoever this man was, he seemed furious with her, for no reason she could think. Yes, he and Mr Montgomery had come to look for her, but there was no need to treat her like a naughty child. She didn't ask to be rescued and it wasn't her fault Nick didn't seem able to trust her to be on her own for more than ten minutes.

Jessica was tired, cold and hungry. She was covered in scratches from the briars and was worried about the puppy, which had not stirred since she had tucked him into her cloak. She knew she looked a mess, any number of twigs and leaves were likely stuck in her hair from her battle with the bushes and she did not need some self-righteous busybody telling her off.

What the two men did *not* know, which had they done, would probably have elicited a more sympathetic response, was that only a couple of years previously, Jessica had been tossed by her horse. She had been out riding with friends, when something had spooked her mare. The creature reared, throwing Jessica who had landed badly, breaking her leg and bruising her back. It took her a long time to heal and she had never plucked up the courage to get back on her horse. Thus, even knowing it would take her a good half an hour to get home, she much preferred to walk.

Seething with indignation, she didn't hear the heated exchange behind her, which began immediately she trudged away.

"Duncan, what the devil is the matter with you? Look at her, she is exhausted, and I know the creature she carries is a mere pup, but it will start to feel heavy long before she reaches Whiteoaks. I have never seen you take on so."

Duncan Barrington, couldn't explain himself either. He was not usually so churlish and certainly not with a young woman he had not yet met. There was just something about her that frustrated and intrigued him. When she lifted her head to look up at Ralph, Duncan had felt his world teeter. It was the most peculiar sensation but it made him want to take himself as far away from Miss Drummond as humanly possible. He conceded, however the young woman did look fatigued and to ignore her plight was just plain rude, something Duncan had rarely, if ever, been.

"Beg pardon, Ralph. I don't know what came over me. Mayhap I'm tired."

Something in Duncan's voice gave Ralph pause and he shot his friend a speculative glance, keenly aware that despite outward appearances, Duncan still struggled with trauma from the war and occasionally suffered from acute melancholia. Injured by canister shot on the battlefields of the Peninsula, Duncan had lain for over a day covered in mud, flies and the blood of his fallen comrades before he was found. A wound to his leg had proved less devastating than originally thought and had been saved by a clever military surgeon who, thankfully understood cleanliness, but the damage to Duncan's left arm had been so severe, the same surgeon had no alternative but to amputate below the elbow. Such injuries resulted in Duncan being discharged from the army, his life's ambition of being a career soldier cruelly snatched away.

It had taken a long time to come to terms with his disability and more than once, in his darkest hours, Duncan had contemplated taking his own life. Theo Elliott, doctor, friend and fellow Peninsula veteran, was wise to such thinking and had worked with Duncan, persuading him to talk about his time on the battlefield, drawing him out of his shell and making him appreciate what he did have rather than what he had lost. Giles, the Earl of Winchester and owner of Whiteoaks estate, knowing Duncan had always been clever with his hands, had offered him work as the estate carpenter, and to Duncan's surprise, he discovered a knack for working with wood, the loss of his lower left arm no impediment. The quiet of the workshop, along with the love and the support of his friends, had helped to heal his broken soul but to those he did not know he remained austere and remote.

Duncan, aware of Ralph's scrutiny, offered an apologetic smile and drew a calming breath.

"I know you have a meeting with the stewards this morning. Here, take Orion, I will walk with the girl since she seems incapable of getting on a horse." Duncan grunted as he dismounted. Ralph started to speak. "Fear not Montgomery, I'll apologise." Duncan appeased his friend. Ralph looked at him for a moment before he nodded and, taking Orion's rein, mounted Leon, his own stallion, and trotted off.

Chapter Two

Duncan stood, observing the rigid bearing of Miss Drummond as she marched, or tried to, towards Whiteoaks through the snow. Deliberately pushing aside the confusion of thoughts — pride, irritation and frustration — fighting for dominance in his head, he strode after her. He saw her look up at the sound of the two horses but, as they passed her with no sign of slowing, her shoulders sagged. He smiled grimly, so it appeared Miss Independence didn't want to be left to walk home alone after all.

"Miss Drummond," he called. She paused, half-turned, dithered but then carried on. "God's teeth she is a madam," he ground out under his breath. "Miss Drummond, please oblige your brother and wait for me."

Jessica stopped, shuffling her feet awkwardly as she waited for him to catch up.

"You should not have bothered, sir, I am quite capable of making my own way home. 'Tis clear you think me a waste of your time." Jessica, although attempting an air of vexation, sounded dejected, her tones pulling at something deep inside Duncan. Shaking it off, he forced a cheery note into his voice.

"Come now, no more of that talk. I am sorry I was brusque, I am feeling out of sorts today and should not have taken it out on you."

Jessica raised her head to look at him, eyes shimmering with tears. She blinked rapidly, refusing to let them fall, merely nodding an acknowledgement of his apology. As she did so, Duncan noticed she was still shivering; her skirts were wet from the knees down and the little of the one arm he could see was covered in scratches.

"Miss Drummond, are you hurt?" he inquired, rather more solicitously.

"No, 'tis but a few scrapes, I'm sure Lady Winchester will have something I can rub on them when I get home. I'm more worried about this poor scrap. He hasn't woken since I got him out of the b-briars and I-I'm afraid to ch-check in case he…" Jessica couldn't finish that thought. Her composure was quickly unravelling and she had absolutely no intention of weeping in front of this man who still seemed so very angry. Under normal circumstances, Jessica was a sunny soul, not much got her down and she never cried. She enjoyed her job at the shipyard, had a loving family and a small but close group of friends; her life was blessed and she appreciated all she had, but at this precise moment everything seemed too much. She just wanted to be where it was warm and for her mama to tell her everything was all right.

Duncan didn't really understand women. In fact, other than his mother and sister — who no longer lived in Oak Stanton, the hamlet attached to the Winchester Estate — the only other females he ever spent more than a brief interlude with, were Billie Trevallier, Grace Elliot and Tessa Montgomery — the latter two he had known since childhood. What he did understand, however, was fear and exhaustion, both of which were manifesting in the young woman standing before him.

"Might I check him…it?" he asked, gentling his tone and holding out his hand. Biting her lip anxiously, Jessica extracted the puppy from the depths of her cloak and handed it over. Wedging the creature between his bad arm and his body, Duncan ran his large hand over the dog, examining it carefully, concluding it was a female and was simply fast asleep. "He is actually a she and, she sleeps maybe more deeply than a pup ought, but I expect she has had a bit of a fright today."

Jessica smiled tentatively and Duncan could she was relieved. "Thank you, sir. I, too, am sorry my absence caused you to break your routine. It was never my aim to interfere in the running of the estate. I would surely have been back before anyone noticed, if not for… " she nodded at the puppy.

As he listened to her explain her delayed return, Duncan had the oddest notion that he would always notice her absence. Annoyed with himself for such distractions, he concentrated on hustling Jessica along.

Tucking the puppy into one of the enormous pockets of his riding coat, Duncan offered Jessica his arm, which she accepted gratefully, the two continuing their walk back to Whiteoaks. For want of something to pass the time, they began to chat, nothing of any substance just this and that. Duncan asked about London, and was interested to discover Jessica worked in the offices of her family's shipyard. He was amazed by her breadth of knowledge about the shipping industry, quite unexpected in a lady.

Jessica managed to wheedle a few titbits out of Duncan. He told her about the carpentry and answered all manner of questions about the estate and how it was run and without realising it, opened up to this inquisitive young woman, whose eyes kept fixing themselves on him while they talked, as though she could see right inside his soul. Ordinarily taciturn, he even found himself explaining how hesitant he had been when Theo Elliott first suggested he try woodwork.

"I was a soldier, what did I know of creating something functional from a piece of old wood? As long as I can remember I wanted to be in the army. It sounds far more glamorous than it really is, but I thrived on it and was well versed in military discipline, battle tactics and campaign strategies. None of which are of much use in a quiet village in the middle of Hampshire, especially when you only have full use of one arm." He shrugged, somewhat deprecatingly. "Thankfully Theo wasn't prepared to let me wallow in self-pity and, recalling I used to enjoy whittling wood, persuaded me to try."

Duncan paused, remembering how embarrassed he had been the first few times he attempted the tasks, until his naturally analytical mind took over and he began formulating better and more efficient methods of anchoring the wood, or manipulating it while he worked.

"I have to admit being rather surly and not particularly grateful when it was first proposed but, somewhere along the way, I forgot to be angry and realised not only was I enjoying the work but I was also managing to make solid, sturdy pieces of furniture. That wasn't enough, I wanted each piece to look good too and now, five years on, 'tis my whole world. To create something beautiful from a lump of unyielding wood is a skill I never expected to have..." he trailed off, astonished at how much he had revealed to this woman he did not know.

Jessica's naïve enthusiasm had crept under his defences and he was aware of an unusual lightness of being as they chatted. Somehow, she persuaded him to show her his workshops, which were situated behind the stables. He had no idea how she had done it, but, to his consternation, he found he was looking forward to it.

Too soon, or so it seemed to Duncan, they were on the edge of the Great Park and into the formal gardens, although currently the only delineation of such was the fence. Jessica disengaged herself and thanking him politely, a mischievous grin curving her lips, bobbed a curtsy and started for the house at a dead run.

"Miss Drummond," he called after her. She skidded to a halt and spun on her heel staring at him in puzzlement. Duncan, eyebrows raised, lifted the furry bundle out of his pocket.

Jessica gasped an apology. "Oh, I'm sorry, I'm so sorry. I was thinking about breakfast and not this poor little mite. What a horrible person I am." She dashed back, grabbed the wriggling puppy and without thinking brushed her lips to Duncan's cold cheek. "Thank you, sir, thank you. I don't believe you're quite as angry as you appear, are you?" Jessica smiled and fled, without so much as a backward glance. Duncan was rooted to the spot. He put his gloved hand to his cheek expecting to feel the warmth of her kiss right through the thick wool. A phrase from Shakespeare's *Hamlet* flickered through his mind, but was gone before he could pin down which one.

"The devil with her." He groused to no one in particular and stomped off to the kitchens, where Sarah was certain to have something tasty for him.

Meanwhile, Jessica rushed into the house to be met by Thomas, the Winchester's butler.

"I understand you found a puppy Miss Drummond," he stated in his usual unflappable manner.

"I did. How on earth did you know that?" she asked in astonishment, panting a little from her exertions.

"Mr Montgomery apprised us of your...errr...discovery and suggested we might like to bath the poor creature then get it warm and fed."

"Oh, you are quite the most wonderful man, Thomas, apparently it's a she," she gushed, handing over the wriggling puppy who, now totally fed up with being held, had apparently decided exploring her new and somewhat drier surrounds might be next on her list of how puppies get into trouble.

"Leave her with me Miss, we'll get her sorted and bring her to you later. If you pop into yonder room there's plenty of breakfast still to be had." Nodding towards the elegant dining room. "Give me your cloak, I'll make sure it gets dried too." He held out his hand.

Thankful, Jessica shrugged out of her heavy cloak and handed it over, flapping her gown, which was still damp and also rather muddy.

"Maybe I should change first," she muttered, "I don't wish to upset anyone else today."

Thomas took one look at her attire which was as bedraggled as the puppy, and smiled benignly, "I think that might be a good idea, Miss. We don't want you to come down with a chill." Jessica agreed wholeheartedly and fled up the stairs. Lucy, one of the maids, arrived almost immediately to assist her out of the wet dress, and into a fresh gown, then tidied her hair, removing the odd twig still caught in her tousled locks. Jessica's stomach rumbled loudly while Lucy was finishing up, causing the young maid to giggle and Jessica to blush.

"Go on with you Miss, I think you might feel better after a decent meal." Lucy gathered up the damp article of clothing and headed off to the kitchens as Jessica ran back down the stairs, the smell of hot food irresistible. She tumbled into the dining room, to find everyone, except Giles, sitting around the table. His wife, Billie, was sipping coffee, chatting gaily with the two mothers — the Dowager Lady Winchester and Mrs

Drummond. Nick Drummond was deep in conversation with Archie and Sybil Miller — friends of Hugh and Helena, and the last of the wedding guests still at Whiteoaks — the three laughing over something or other.

"Good morning everyone," Jessica said over-brightly. "I do apologise for causing concern. I...well...it was...you see..." she dried up seeing the expression on her mother's face, which could only be described as irritated. "Mama, please, I'm sorry, it's just..." as she spread her hands out in apology, her sleeves rolled back exposing the angry looking abrasions along her arms.

"Jessica, how did you come by those scratches?" consternation clear in Billie's voice. The others turned to stare at Jessica who, reading reproach in everyone's gaze, felt even more like a recalcitrant child.

"'Twas just the briars. I had to force my way through to reach a puppy." She looked at the faces of those around the table and felt those ridiculous tears forming again. "I couldn't leave it, it would have d-died. It's s-so s-small." Jessica scrubbed her face on her sleeve and Billie, wise to such emotions, asked Thomas to bring Jessica some breakfast before bustling her out, away from disapproving stares, to the cosy room at the end of one of the corridors. This was Billie's special room, not very large, it was equipped with a crackling fire, two chairs, a stone bench, a sink and so many bottles and jars, it would have taken Jessica all day to count them.

"Now, let me take a look at those marks."

Jessica submitted to an examination, unaware of how many ailments could result from a simple scratch. Billie cleaned her arms with some kind of liquid that stung when it came into contact with her skin, after which she smoothed balm over each graze. The ointment smelt quite strong but wasn't unpleasant. While she worked, Billie asked a few pertinent questions and Jessica's morning adventure spilled out, complete with her bafflement over her escort's attitude.

"He did apologise, but it was...well...I am unable to ride you see, which I think annoyed him, for we would have returned much more quickly on horseback. However, I don't think he was quite so upset by the time we reached home, he even promised to show me his workshops. That will be interesting, I love going into the yard to watch the men work on the ships. 'Tis a sight to behold."

Jessica paused — then, "Oh no, I didn't even get his name. My lady, I am quite the most bad-mannered person there ever was. Goodness me! Today started off so well, all that beautiful snow and such a pleasant walk and now look, I've run heedlessly into a bush, got all torn up — I've probably ruined my cloak — and to top it off, was rude to your friends." Jessica's voice rose as she realised how impolite she must have seemed to the gentleman who ensured her safe return to Whiteoaks.

Billie patted her knee in a motherly fashion, blithely ignoring the fact that Jessica was only a year or so younger than she.

"Jessica, please do not upset yourself. Ralph Montgomery and Duncan Barrington — yes..." as Jessica raised her eyebrow, "...that was who escorted you home — are perfectly capable of looking after themselves and I imagine by the time they found you, you were cold, hungry and maybe a little unnerved. I'm sure they understood your predicament." Billie assured Jessica comfortingly.

"Do you think so?"

Billie drew the girl into a warm hug. "I'm sure. Come now it's all over, Ralph and Duncan often ride first thing anyway, 'tis no hardship for them to cross the Great Park instead of the back fields. I expect Duncan was just a bit out of sorts, he'll likely have forgotten all about it the next time you see him."

"I don't suppose there'll be a next time, despite his offer," murmured Jessica.

She spoke so quietly, Billie wasn't sure she'd heard her, conscious of a mournful note in the girl's voice. Deciding not to question it for now, she checked to make sure she had cleaned all the cuts, coaxing Jessica into eating the huge plate of food Thomas had brought for her.

Freshly poached eggs, nicely crisped bacon and several slices of warm buttered toast were just what Jessica needed. Once she'd demolished that, she did feel better and her arms weren't stinging any more.

"Thank you, my lady, I am very grateful." Jessica said, earnestly, as she swallowed a last gulp of coffee.

"It is my pleasure to be able to help, and how many times must I ask you to call me Billie," she chastised gently.

"I will try, it's just you're...well...your status..." Jessica trailed off, uncertain how to phrase what she meant without causing offence. Billie was a member of the *ton* and society had its rules.

Billie grinned impishly, "I know, I am a countess and oh so very important, but I am also the sister-in-law of your sister-in-law which means we are related and so you can call me Billie. It would please me greatly if you would think of us as family," her rather convoluted explanation doing the trick.

"I should like that." Jessica whispered, blushing a little.

"Excellent! Now, let us go and find this puppy, it will no doubt need a name and a bed; something suitable for the latter I'm sure we can find in the stables." Billie suggested, leading Jessica along to the kitchens where the puppy was the centre of attention, its large brown eyes, floppy ears and massive paws drawing lots of silly cooing from the female staff.

To Jessica's surprise, her escort was now sitting at the huge table, eating a hearty breakfast. Standing at the edge of the room, half-hidden behind the circle of people, Jessica watched Duncan covertly, noticing his strong, yet grave features, his muscular shoulders and his beautiful hand. Large with long, slender fingers, the hand of an artist, she mused, as unbidden an image of him holding her hand popped into her mind, an image she found unexpectedly appealing. As she shook her head in an attempt to dismiss it, she caught Duncan's eye and he smiled, a sort of secret smile, one just for her and one that caused her heart to lurch. Unable to help herself, she responded in kind, a wholly unrestrained gesture and one that seemed to lift Duncan out of his dark mood.

His meal finished, Duncan pushed back his chair. "Ahhh, Miss Drummond. As you can see your charge is now wide awake and looking much brighter." He was so tall she had to tilt her head to look at him and as their glances met, a prickle of something indefinable ran through her. Her tongue refused to do her bidding and she felt like a simpleton for all she could do was stare at him. His eyes were quite the most piercing blue and she felt the strangest sensation — almost as though she was falling into them.

Duncan Barrington too, was beset by the oddest sensations. This unsettling woman, whose eyes were like rare gems, confused the very life out of him. He still wanted to take himself as far away from her as possible yet he was mesmerised by her. Their gazes locked, all sounds of the kitchen disappeared and it was as though they were completely alone.

The puppy yapped, its sharp little bark breaking the moment. Duncan noticed Jessica draw a shuddering breath and was intrigued by the mixture of emotions flickering across her expressive face. As he watched she appeared, deliberately, to push aside whatever troubled her, asking — maybe by way of distraction — whether she might hold the dog. Willing hands passed the creature over to her and seemingly recognising her rescuer, the little mite snuggled into Jessica's neck and promptly fell asleep.

Chapter Three

Duncan thanked Sarah for his breakfast, coming around the table to take his leave of the countess. Billie gave him a hug, which he returned as she thanked him for walking back with Jessica.

"'Twas naught, my lady. I'm glad she wasn't lost is all. We would have had her home more quickly, but she refused to get on either horse." Duncan shrugged, once again confounded by Jessica's reticence, putting it down to the quirks of city folk. He nodded to Jessica, who offered a sedate curtsy in return.

"Thank you again, Mr Barrington. I do hope your plans for the day were not ruined by my incautious conduct, and your willingness to show me around your workshop holds." Eager anticipation filled Jessica's voice and Duncan heard himself affirming her request at the same time as his brain told him it was a huge mistake. She smiled her delight and hurried out before he changed his mind.

Duncan, aware that something was shifting but unsure exactly what it was, watched her go, an odd expression on his face, one which Billie recognised immediately but decided, prudently, not to make mention of it quite yet. She merely grinned as Duncan left to start his day, the rest of the household went on with whatever they had been doing before a small and engaging little creature had ended up in their midst.

Once she had apologised, again, to everyone she could think of, Jessica, at Billie's request, enjoyed the rest of the day with her hostess. Fascinated by the herbal remedies created by the countess, Jessica had spent hours with her, taking copious notes and helping organise her stock. The two women were becoming fast friends and today, Billie's cheerful nature quickly dispelled any lingering discomfiture from Jessica's early morning sojourn. Recalling Jessica's earlier comment, and Duncan's reaction to her guest, Billie — in the guise of broadening Jessica's knowledge of the locale and its people —

relayed a fragment of the man's history, including how he came by his injury, while they were working. Unaware of her hostess' perception, Jessica chattered away, her guileless comments merely adding to Billie's suspicions.

The dog, tucked into a basket procured by Thomas, slept away the day, her gentle snores indication of a very relaxed puppy. Jessica kept glancing at her trying to come up with a name, without success. Billie had commented, that if the tyke's paws were anything to go by, she would be a good size when fully grown and Jessica wanted to be sure any name would reflect that. She kept ruminating over characters in books she had read, hoping something would jump out, but so far nothing seemed appropriate. Deciding it was best not to think too hard about it, she concentrated on the tasks at hand and the day flew by.

Later that evening, long after everyone else had retired; Jessica was wide-awake and sitting on the broad window-ledge in her bedchamber, admiring the landscape. The stark whiteness — broken here and there by ghostly silhouettes of trees, their branches glistening with rime — was stunningly beautiful. The sky was inky black but clear, the moon's soft glow simply adding to the mystery of the night.

Like her two brothers, Jessica loved the night sky and, on the few occasions she had successfully persuaded Hugh to let her accompany him on one of their ships, she usually spent the whole night on deck just watching the moon and the stars. She had always assumed it was because they were a sea faring family, but had discovered most of the women hereabouts felt the same, Helena especially. The sheer enormity of the heavens helped put most problems into perspective and she found it soothing.

This night, however, it wasn't working. Jessica was restless, her normally peaceful dreams invaded by a tall and brooding man whose presence disconcerted her, yet she did not know why and, although exhausted from all the excitement of the day, had not been able to sleep. Surmising a quick walk in the chill air might help, she dragged on her winter boots and pulled a heavy cloak over her nightgown. Padding quietly down the stairs and along the passageway at the rear of the kitchens, Jessica soon slipped out of the house and into the darkness.

As she walked past the stables, she could hear the horses shuffling around in their loose boxes, their soft nickering familiar and comforting. Crossing the courtyard she made her way to the long driveway and headed out towards the huge wrought iron gates, hoping that the time it took her to walk there and back would do the trick. Her boots crunching on the gravel sounded startlingly loud in the stillness, but didn't seem to disturb anyone and soon she was well away from the house. The gates weren't as far as she expected and so, to stretch out her walk, Jessica returned by way of a more circuitous route around the workshops and sheds.

Upon reaching the workshops closest to the main house, she noticed a light flickering in the window of one and, worried someone had left a fire burning, or worse a candle had fallen over, pushed open the door. There was a grating sound as it swung on its hinges and from within there was movement. Jessica bit down on a frightened squawk as a figure twisted to face her, his identity shielded by the light from the flames leaping in the hearth behind him, throwing his features into shadow.

"Hey! What are you doing?" she demanded, pleased she sounded annoyed, rather than scared. "Don't you *dare* steal from his Lordship." Forgetting she wasn't very tall and carried nothing with her that offered any protection, that it was the middle of the night and she was on her own, Jessica stormed into the room, the light of battle gleaming in her eyes. A muffled laugh reached her and she came to an abrupt halt just across the threshold. "You think this is funny!" she exclaimed, setting her hands on her hips. "Stealing is no laughing matter my good man, I think you ought to come with me." By now the figure was shaking with mirth, leaving Jessica perplexed. She knew she wasn't scary, but surely the threat of Giles should be enough to deter a would-be thief.

"Miss Drummond, what are you doing here? 'Tis the dead of night."

That voice — she knew that voice. "M-Mr Barrington?" she stuttered. The man came towards her, she backed away, still not certain, but he was by her side in two strides.

"Yes, 'tis me. This is my workshop. Why are you here?" his voice laced with humour also carried a hint of concern.

"I couldn't sleep, I find a walk will usually help quieten my mind. I was thinking about this m…" Jessica stopped. She couldn't tell him he was the one filling her thoughts, that every time she closed her eyes, his face floated into her head; his eyes, blue as the sea on a summer's day, staring at her until she lost all ability to think straight. She didn't know him and even though she had seen him from a distance around the estate, today was the first time they had spoken. He should not be affecting her this way, yet he was.

Duncan watched her, trying to read the kaleidoscope of emotions flitting across her lovely face. He did not know many women who would think to apprehend a thief in the middle of the night on a lonely estate — although actually, when he thought about it, he did know of three — but not this woman, she seemed so…delicate.

"You do realise, had I been of nefarious intent you could have been hurt or worse?" he asked.

Rubbing her forehead, Jessica simply stared up at him, unable to come up with a rational explanation for her actions. "I never gave that a thought. I just wanted to stop anyone damaging Lord Winchester's property. I suppose it was a bit silly wasn't it?" She gave a small sigh, "I seem to have lost all sense today; first this morning's…errr…incident and now this." She leaned against the doorjamb, "Maybe one day I will think before I act. My mother is constantly reminding me I am no longer a child," she admitted in tones that suggested this pearl of wisdom was not generally very well received.

Duncan chuckled. "I think you were rather brave, I cannot imagine many gentle born women thinking to thwart a burglar."

"Gentle born, Mr Barrington?" Unconsciously, Jessica lifted her head in proud correction. "I assumed you understood after our conversation this morning, we Drummonds are merchants. I am not gentle born."

"Ahhh, but then Miss Drummond…" he responded, inclining his head, "…to me, gentle born is nothing to do with a person's heritage, it is their mien, their nature which sets them apart."

"In that case, sir, anyone who knows me will attest I am far more hoyden than gentle born. I am sorry to disabuse you of so kind a notion." Jessica said ruefully. "Well, since I'm here and you're clearly not a burglar, might I ask you to show me what you do?"

Despite knowing that to show a young woman around his workshop in the dead of night without a chaperone was unwise, not to mention improper, Duncan gathered Miss Jessica Drummond had no intention of leaving until he acquiesced to her request. Swallowing on a humph, he stood aside allowing her to come right into the room.

Jessica looked around and, to her surprise, saw the workshop was far more spacious than she would have guessed. Opposite the door, the fire crackled in a massive hearth, either side of which, against the walls, stood a collection of shelves and benches. Three sizeable tables were placed randomly across the flagged floor and all manner of tools and equipment were scattered about, as were several pieces of furniture in varying stages of construction or repair. The smell of freshly sawn wood reminded Jessica of the workshops at Trentams and a wave of homesickness washed over her. Ignoring it, she said,

"Mr Barrington, I had no idea how much carpentry was required on a country estate. Do you work alone or…?" she left the sentence dangling, remembering what Billie had told her of Duncan's war injury and not wanting him to think she presumed him incapable.

He smiled slightly at her hesitation, "I am in charge of a dozen men. We provide anything required by his Lordship and make the furniture for all the tenant farmers, not to mention ongoing repairs. We're also responsible for maintenance of fences, carriage wheels and so on. 'Tis far too much for one."

"Incredible," she breathed, walking through the room, stroking the polished wood, turning an odd piece so she could study its design. Something on one of the side benches caught her attention, a few items, which didn't quite fit the scene. Going over, she picked one up. It was a horse, so flawlessly carved she expected it to gallop off into the moonlight.

"Mr Barrington, this is remarkable. Is it your work?" Looking over her shoulder at her host, who was watching her with an inscrutable expression. He nodded without speaking. "I cannot recall ever seeing anything quite as beautiful as this," she said, setting it down carefully and picking up the one next to it — a fox, just as intricately etched.

She counted eight, each as impressive as the first two, all animals, all perfectly rendered. That Duncan could accomplish something so exquisite with only one good hand was nothing short of astonishing. Enchanted, Jessica examined every one, running slender fingers over the tactile shapes, sensing the love that had gone into their creation. Placing the last one on the bench, she turned; Duncan was still watching her steadily, his earlier amusement replaced by a hint of wariness, his face guarded.

"Thank you for granting me the privilege of seeing your work, sir. Your artistry touches me." Jessica's hand hovered over her heart, the gesture drawing his gaze to her cloak, which had fallen open while she inspected his workshop. Duncan groaned; she obviously had no inkling her night attire left little to the imagination, her svelte figure clearly visible through the flimsy material.

"Are you in pain Mr Barrington?" Jessica asked anxiously, surprised at the sound.

"I think it would be prudent to fasten your cloak, Miss Drummond." Duncan's voice was strangled as he made a determined effort to drag his eyes from her body, only to be arrested by the way the candlelight caught the golden flecks in her eyes.

Puzzled, Jessica glanced down, then flushed bright red and yanked her cloak around her. Goodness what would he think of her? Surely, he didn't think she was flaunting herself? She was no better than a hussy. Humiliation radiated off her as these thoughts tumbled around her head.

"I...errr...s-sorry...hadn't..." once again her words bubbled out with little regard for intelligibility and, needing to put some distance between them, she prepared to flee.

Registering her panic and, for reasons he could not fathom, unwilling to let her run away because of him, Duncan reached out and took her hand.

"Please don't go."

Chapter Four

As they touched, something indefinable shimmered through Jessica, and her breath caught. She stared down at their clasped hands, up to Duncan's face then back to their hands and was visited by the most peculiar sentiment that although this was highly inappropriate, their hands fit together as though meant to do so and she never wanted him to let go.

"I thought you didn't like me," she whispered. "You were so angry with me." Her eyes, cloudy with bewilderment, held his. He rubbed his thumb over her palm, the gesture causing a frisson of warmth up her arm. She waited.

"I thought so too. Mayhap it was my head's way of protecting my heart, for I find myself in the most unexpected position of wishing I could kiss you." He admitted, quietly.

She cocked her head on one side, "So, pray tell, what's stopping you?" she took a step towards him but worry her behaviour bordered on the wanton, made her pause. Jessica knew she should be shocked by Duncan's confession; she also knew what was expected of young ladies, but had long presumed, since she rarely had a chance to meet anyone deemed eligible, an eventuality such as this would pass her by. "Oh, I beg your pardon, that was…rather I…errr…" she trailed off miserably aware of how gauche she sounded and, bowing her head turned once more to leave.

"Please don't go," he repeated, squeezing her hand, his fingers entwined in hers, the yearning in his voice causing her to do a slow about face. Jessica stared at him in the flickering light, tall and a little forbidding, his craggy features shadowed, and something inside her shifted. An almost imperceptible thrill stirred in her breast, as her free hand fluttered towards him, then dropped back to her side.

All was quiet.

Taking this as a sign, Duncan drew her closer, the desire to feel her against him outweighing the warnings in his head and any other consideration that should have stopped such behaviour. Out of the blue, he recalled the phrase, the quote which taunted him earlier; *doubt thou the stars are fire, doubt that the sun doth move, doubt truth to be a liar, but never doubt I love.* Maimed, not only in body, but also in soul, Duncan had long presumed his emotions just as crippled, yet these words resonated with him, making him feel more alive than he had since his return from the Peninsula. He shook his head trying to clear his mind, but never had he felt like this; it was as though she had somehow hypnotised him for, still holding her hand, he wrapped his other arm around her and brushed his lips lightly against hers.

Despite working in a shipyard where feminine sensitivities were largely ignored, Jessica remained a relatively naïve, not quite two and twenty year old, and kissing was a whole new experience for her. One of which she decided — as her body, acting of its own accord, moulded itself to Duncan's — she wholeheartedly approved. Lifting his head, Duncan started to speak, but Jessica didn't give him the chance to say what she feared, that his kiss was a mistake, that he was sorry and that she should leave. Instead she smoothed her fingers over his cheek and cupping the back of his head, brought his mouth back to hers.

He groaned and gave in, kissing her with sublime tenderness, his lips teasing over hers, promising so much more. As he felt Jessica respond, Duncan let their kiss deepen and although desperately trying not to let things spiral completely out of control, to kiss her wasn't enough; he needed to touch her skin, to stroke her hair and so he let go of her hand. Momentarily bereft, Jessica stiffened, but as his fingers began to explore the soft skin of her throat, trailing up her neck, to graze her ear and then entangle in her hair she forgot everything except the spell he was weaving around her.

Uncertain as to what part she should play in this heart-stopping tableau, Jessica floundered, but Duncan's caresses inspired her and tentatively, she let her hands wander randomly over his body. Even though it was the middle of winter, the room was warm and Duncan was wearing only his shirt, through which Jessica could feel his muscles flexing under the well-worn cotton. Fascinated, she traced them until her hand rested on his chest, the irregular thud of his heart pulsing under her fingers and she was inordinately pleased that it seemed as chaotic as her own.

His hand searching under the weight of her winter cloak, Duncan continued his magical dance, fingers skimming over Jessica, making her quiver with longing and tugging a soft whimper from her lips. Instantly Duncan stilled, breaking their kiss and lifting his head to gaze into her face.

"I'm sorry, did I hurt you? Alarm you?"

Jessica shook her head, "No, hurt or scared is the last thing I'm feeling, I simply couldn't help it. I blame your kiss, which by the way you've stopped." She accused and smiled impishly at him, stretching up her hand to push a lock of hair back off his face.

"Miss Drummond, this … I shouldn't have … advantage … what of your brother … your mother?" Duncan was at a loss both to form a coherent sentence and justify his actions, knowing that, had anyone a mind to check the lighted workshop, they would have come across a most compromising scene. His head refused to behave rationally when Jessica was near; all he wanted to do was kiss her. "You bewitch me." He finished, colouring a little at his confession.

"I bewitch you?" Jessica raised one eyebrow sceptically, thinking he mocked her. "Me? I think you are mixing me up with one of Society's beauties. I have nothing to bewitch anyone with."

Duncan gaped at her, truly perplexed, "Wait. I'm sorry, you think yourself less than pleasing to look at?"

"Well…" drawing out the word, "I suppose I'm not ugly, but neither am I especially pretty. My hair is mousy, my eyes are uninteresting and I'm of average height; in fact, I'm really quite ordinary and not in the slightest bit bewitching." Given her practical tones, it was clear Jessica believed what she was saying. It wasn't some trick to get Duncan to admire her; she genuinely thought she wasn't particularly attractive.

"Miss Drummond, you are quite stunningly beautiful. Your eyes are like gemstones and when they catch the light it is as though they have captured the sunset. Your hair is like ripened wheat shimmering under a summer sky and if you were any taller I wouldn't be able to do this…" he nestled her against him, fitting her to his much taller frame.

"Well, if you say so," she muttered against his shirt, sounding less than convinced.

"I most definitely do say so and, much as I would like to spend the rest of the night pointing out what else about you ensnares me, I think it might be sensible for you to find your bed." The thought of Jessica curled up under luxurious covers was nearly his undoing. His breathing became erratic and allowing ardour to take the upper hand, he stole another very satisfactory kiss.

"I don't want to go. I fear when I wake I will think this a dream." Jessica whispered against his cheek. Duncan didn't reply, he knew this couldn't happen again. She was a city lady, he a country carpenter. Their lives were so far removed from each other that under normal circumstances they would never have met. He knew she would walk out of his life, their paths never again to cross. It made his heart ache knowing once she returned to London she was forever lost to him, but he was old enough and wise enough to accept it would be so. That he had been given the chance to hold her, to kiss her, would warm him for a lifetime.

For a man who had never even considered taking a wife, the thought that another would marry Jessica was something Duncan could neither contemplate nor act upon. So, he kissed her one last time, gently guided her out through the door, escorting her across the dark courtyard and watched her walk away from him through the door to the main house. As she disappeared inside, Duncan resolved that for the few days left of her visit, he would take pains to avoid her as best he could.

Or so he thought, he just hadn't reckoned on Jessica.

The next morning Jessica, following a far more restful night than expected given what had happened, and a very filling breakfast, was sauntering across the courtyard to the herb garden when she spotted Duncan talking with Thomas and Samuel — the head gardener. Duncan had his back to her and she enjoyed being able to admire his soldierly physique, surreptitiously. Even if she hadn't known, his upright stance and rigid bearing told of his military background and she imagined him in full uniform, poised along with thousands of others preparing to march into battle. An image that made her shudder with horror, the outcome already known. Still, he had survived and maybe last night's interlude was the beginning of something with a much happier ending.

Deciding she might ask Duncan to show her his workshop officially, so she would be able to mention it without raising eyebrows, Jessica paused, and was contemplating just how to phrase her request, when Thomas noticed her standing there, acknowledging her presence with a grin.

"Good morning, Miss Drummond. Is there something I might get for you?"

"Good morning, Thomas. 'Tis Mr Barrington with whom I would appreciate a brief word, should he be able to spare a moment, once you have completed your business. Thank you for asking," she smiled brightly at the butler who had been so kind during her stay. Thomas nodded and after saying something Jessica couldn't quite hear to the other two, went back into the house, while Jessica waited patiently until Duncan and Samuel concluded their conversation. Samuel nodded at Jessica who beamed back — the two having already enjoyed one or two discussions about plants — before heading off to his beloved gardens, which were still buried under deep snow.

Duncan turned in her direction, but remained where he was; the distance between them wider than the oceans her brothers sailed across. Determined not to let his watchful demeanour bother her, Jessica offered a tentative smile.

"Mr Barrington, I came to ask whether you might have some time today or tomorrow to show me your workshops. Her ladyship tells me you have quite the gift and I am endlessly fascinated by anything created from wood. I realise furniture and ships are totally different in design and scale, but that simply adds to my interest." She spoke in formal tones so anyone overhearing her would never suspect that she had already seen everything Duncan was working on and then some. Duncan stared at her, seemingly puzzled at her inquiry until she dropped a slow wink, tugging a responding curve from his lips.

"It would be my pleasure, Miss Drummond. Would half an hour's time be suitable?"

Jessica dipped a neat curtsy, "Thank you, sir. I look forward to it."

Affirming he would meet her at that very spot, Duncan dashed off, ostensibly to ensure there was nothing to trip up the unwary visitor, in reality giving himself time to control his wayward thoughts. Jessica, in much the same state of ferment, went to find out what the puppy was up to, which proved a suitable distraction.

Half an hour later, to the second, Jessica was back, a little anxious, after his comments of the previous night, that when Duncan saw her in the pale light of the winter sun as opposed to flattering firelight he would see her as she really was — quite plain and uninteresting — conveniently forgetting this was not the first time they had met in daylight. Why this should bother her at all, she had yet to discern.

On cue, Duncan appeared from between the buildings and, offering her his good arm, strolled with her along to the workshop, encouraging her into comfortable chatter about ships and the building thereof. As they walked through the door, Jessica noticed another man working on one of the pieces of furniture.

"That's Nate," Duncan clarified. The two greeted each other, Nate smiling absently, his attention immediately refocussing on the item he was repairing. "We are all a bit like that," said Duncan, nodding at Nate, "we get caught up in our work often to the detriment of everything else around us."

"Which explains your presence here last evening," Jessica murmured for his ears only. Duncan squeezed her arm and proceeded to show her around the workshop as though she had never seen it before. She ooh'd and aah'd in all the right places and once again examined the carvings. In the morning light, they were even more lifelike and their intricacy took her breath away.

"Mr Barrington, these are extraordinary. I wonder, would I be able to commission you to carve a piece for me?" She held his gaze and he could not have said no even had he thought it prudent to do so.

"It would be an honour, Miss Drummond. Do you have a subject in mind?"

"A puppy, with large paws and floppy ears," she replied without hesitation.

"I think I might be able to manage that." Duncan smiled and it was all Jessica could do not to kiss him right there in front of Nate. She swallowed on a gulp and thanked him politely, before moving away to look at the furniture. A little while later, they came back out into the weak sunlight and Duncan, recalling her reticence the previous day, asked whether she would like to see the horses.

Jessica shook her head. "I would rather not, thank you, Mr Barrington, if it is all the same to you. I find horses rather unnerving. There was … it is because … only … I had an accident." Her words came out in a rush.

Duncan paused, waiting.

Jessica heaved a sigh and told him what had happened not so very long ago. She knew she sounded like a feeble milksop and that her fear was irrational, but try as she might she had not been able to overcome it.

Duncan felt his heart tighten as she tried to justify her panic, wishing he could kiss away her anxiety; instead of which he said, "I assure you, they are quite gentle and the stables are usually quiet at this time of day, mayhap seeing them so calm, will help alleviate your unease."

Jessica shot him a suspicious glance, trying to read his face. Duncan simply smiled and ushered her along. Before she knew it they were walking between the loose boxes of the Whiteoaks stables. There were several horses within and they seemed huge to Jessica, except Bronte whom she knew to be a favourite of Billie's. Oddly, with Duncan at her side Jessica didn't experience her usual qualms, but neither did she want to prolong her proximity to the noble creatures, however placid they seemed.

Sensing her disquiet, Duncan steered her towards the door. About to leave, he paused and looked down noticing, not for the first time, the luminous quality of her eyes and his breathing quickened. Wondering why they had stopped, Jessica turned to face him, an irrational desire to stroke her fingers over his cheek then entwine them into his dark reddish-brown hair, intruding into her already errant thoughts. All around them was tranquil, even the horses had ceased their shuffling.

Duncan leaned closer, his lips almost brushing her hair, then thought better of it and pulled away. Jessica reached up and did what she most desired, cool fingers teasing over his chiselled jaw, down his neck and skimming his throat feeling his rapid pulse. She smiled then and Duncan was lost, bending his head to hers, he kissed her with a passion that sent them reeling. His hand ghosted over her waist and up her spine, fingers following an invisible pattern, one which sent Jessica into a transport of delight, wresting a low sound from her lips, somewhere between a purr and a growl and she was powerless to prevent it.

Uncaring that it was the middle of the working day and that they were in full view of anyone entering the stables they let their ardour sweep them away.

Chapter Five

Some time later, they came back to earth, breathless, hearts pounding.

"Miss Drummond, I find myself incapable of restraint when it comes to you. God help us if your brother or Giles decide to come and find out what you are up to."

Jessica giggled, "I don't think they are bothered about me. I believe both are in the steward's office. Giles has been showing Nick one or two new methods he has employed in the administration of this estate, as he, Nick I mean, believes they will improve efficiency at Trentams. I did try to show interest but it became far too technical and I feared I should fall asleep, which would be rather impolite to our very generous host."

Duncan grinned, tucking a long curl back off her face, cupping her cheek as he did so before kissing her on the tip of her nose.

"I imagine such discussions might prove gruelling and we men tend to forget not everyone appreciates the minutiae of management. Nevertheless, I am risking your reputation and I cannot countenance such a thing. Mayhap we could take a stroll around the gardens. I think Samuel instructed the under-gardeners to clear the paths. I know 'tis cold still, but the day is brighter and we would be in full view of the household. Would you do me the honour?"

Jessica stood up on tiptoe and pressed her lips to his, revelling in his embrace for a moment longer, then nodded.

"I would be delighted to accompany you, Mr Barrington and please, call me Jessica. I rather think we have passed the formal address stage." Jessica gave him an arch look, making Duncan chuckle.

"Only if you might see your way to calling me Duncan." He replied and, ignoring his own advice, kissed Jessica until she was, once more, all of a whirl. Common sense finally prevailed and moments later, once sure they were presentable, the pair slipped out into the fresh air, looking to all the world as though they hadn't just been tempted to throw caution to the winds and make love on the floor of the stables.

They wandered aimlessly around the many pathways discussing all manner of things, finding conversation flowed easily between them and the time flew by. At some point the other guests, who declared themselves in dire need of a constitutional, joined them and their banter became more than a little lively. Lunch was announced and Duncan excused himself, saying he had things to which he should be attending. Billie gave him a hug, the relaxed familiarity between the countess and both her staff and friends, something Jessica found very appealing. Jessica dropped a curtsy and thanked him, courteously, for taking the time to show her the workshops and hoped they might meet again before she left for the city.

As Duncan walked away Billie noticed a wistful expression flit over Jessica's face and knew her suspicions were correct. Filing it away, the countess drew Jessica into a discussion about potential dog names, the puppy still being referred to as 'it' or 'she,' and it wasn't long before Jessica's natural exuberance reasserted itself and the rest of the day slipped away in laughter and fun.

The following afternoon, Jessica was in the garden with the puppy. Still nameless — for although her new mistress had finally come up with several possibilities, she simply could not decide — the creature was having a marvellous time chasing anything from the odd bird feather to snow. She kept tripping over her huge paws, making Jessica rock with laughter.

Duncan, having worked through the night again as well as all the morning was on his way home, hoping to snatch a few hours' sleep, when he was halted by a merry sound, echoing around the buildings. Following it, he came upon an unforgettable scene, one when he looked back on it later, recognised as the moment he stopped fighting his heart. Jessica, clad in a cloak of rich sable, sprawled on the crisp white ground, apparently oblivious to the fact her clothes were likely soaked from the snow, was still laughing, her flaxen hair tumbling around her shoulders and her cheeks pink from the chill air.

In front of her the puppy bounced about, kicking up the deep whiteness, covering Jessica in sparkling crystals, reminding Duncan of the winter sprite from a fairy tale his sister had loved to read when a child. Breath catching in his throat, he observed her for several minutes, spellbound, fixing the image in his head. Knowing he had to stop this madness, she was not destined for one such as he, Duncan quickly turned on his heel and stalked away, his boots scraping on the gravel path.

Distracted by the noise, Jessica lifted her head and saw a flash of coat tails as someone disappeared around the corner of the house. Intrigued, she scrambled up and ran lightly across the snow, spying Duncan striding towards the driveway.

"Mr Barrington!" she hailed him, her clear voice carrying in the stillness. Duncan ignored her and increased his pace. Puzzled, she started after him, calling his name one more time. He didn't respond, but the puppy, spotting another person with whom she could play, galloped along the drive. Hoisting her skirts, Jessica sprinted after both, all three arriving at the gate at the same moment. The puppy jumped up at Duncan who scratched her behind the ears, ruffling her fur to the dog's excited delight.

Jessica slithered to a standstill, "Duncan, did you not hear me?" she panted, somewhat breathless from her headlong dash, a cheerful smile curving her lips.

"I must get home, please excuse me," neither answering her question, nor looking at her, Duncan kept his focus on the dog. Nonplussed, Jessica felt a flicker of anger override her confusion.

"Oh, I do beg your pardon, *sir*. Once again I seem to have upset your plans by being so rude as to wish a moment of your very important time."

As his head jerked up, Duncan saw her smile falter, her bewilderment making his heart lurch, "Miss Drummond, you do not understand…"

She interrupted him, snapping, "I understand perfectly, Mr Barrington." Emphasising the formal address. "Have no fear I shall not interfere in your life ever again. I should like to thank you for your tenderness, but I am inclined to suspect that mayhap it was just a dream after all." Tossing her head, Jessica began to march away, only to be brought up sharply as she heard him murmur her name with the same yearning he'd begged her to stay two nights previously.

She froze, vacillating over whether to face him or leave, unsure she would be able to handle what she expected to see in his eyes. A crunch of gravel and a hand gripped her shoulder, swivelling her around. Duncan's eyes bored into hers, blue as cornflowers and Jessica heard a soft whimper.

Was that her, or the puppy? Dear lord, it was her! Honestly, she was hopeless.

"I cannot…" was all he managed then hauled her to him, his mouth crushing hers as he kissed her with a desperation that threatened to undermine her completely. Jessica's legs already rather wobbly from running, refused to hold her upright and she felt herself crumpling, but Duncan simply wrapped her tightly against him, his lips sending shockwaves of pleasure up and down her body. She had no idea how long they kissed but, by the time Duncan lifted his head, Jessica felt like the spinning top she had played with as a child. He stepped away and suddenly she felt cold.

"Oh God," he gasped, his tones anguished, "Jessica, please forgive my boldness, but all I can think about when you are close is how perfect you feel in my arms and the last thing I would ever wish to do is hurt you. You must see this cannot continue. Your life is in London, mine is here. I am too old for you and am not the man you think me to be. Believe me when I say I will cherish, for the rest of my life, the moments we have spent together, but you deserve someone younger, someone who can give you all *you* deserve — a life of happiness and joy. I am a cripple in both body and mind with nothing to offer one as beautiful as you." As he spoke, Duncan watched the colour drain from Jessica's face, the desolation in her eyes almost too much to bear.

The puppy, sensing all was not right in her little world, started pawing at Jessica and whining. Picking up the wriggling creature, Jessica buried her face in the warm fur trying to maintain her poise. Taking a steadying breath and holding his gaze, her eyes cooling to grey, she replied,

"Dun...*Mr* Barrington, while your sentiments are utterly ridiculous, I suppose I should respect your honesty. If *I* may be so bold — I think we are on the cusp of something special, something not many people are lucky enough to be granted and, had you been willing, I could think of nothing I would rather do than to let it take shape. I suspect it would turn out to be as exquisite as your carvings. However, you have made your position clear and I refuse to beg."

Dropping a deep curtsy, Jessica hurried away, a sob rising in her throat as tears cascaded down her face. How had this happened? How was it possible to fall in love in less than two days? Why did he kiss her not once, but several times? Why did he make her feel as though he cared for her only to rip out her heart? How could she have been so stupid? As she fled back to the main house, Jessica decided no man would ever get that close to her again.

Duncan watched her go, his own heart torn to shreds. Even accepting that falling in love at first sight, well, all right in his case probably second or third sight, was inconceivable, he knew without a shadow of a doubt it was so. Jessica Drummond had stolen his heart and it would be hers forever. Sentimental it may be, but no less true. He trudged along the road into the village, feeling like a complete cad, her stricken face taunting him. Arriving at Briar Cottage, his rambling, yet comfortable, home, he stuck his head into the kitchen, calling a hello to whoever was within. Maggie, his cook, used to her master's strange hours, replied that a hot meal would be ready forthwith. An hour later after a very tasty dinner and even though it was still only late afternoon he was in bed. Despite his exhaustion, however, sleep was a long time coming. Jessica's distress gnawing at him, and when eventually he fell into a fitful sleep, she haunted his dreams.

Back at Whiteoaks, Jessica, puppy in tow, disappeared into her bedchamber where she remained for the rest of the day, refusing to join the others for dinner or entertainment. The next morning, Billie worried for her guest, persuaded Jessica to help her in the herb room. Looking less than presentable — although Billie did not remark on it — Jessica, the puppy curled up at her feet, was soon absorbed in the world of balms and ointments, effectively distracting her for a time.

"Would you like to talk about it, Jessica?" Billie ventured while they mixed up a batch of aromatic oils. Jessica shook her head.

"I doubt you would wish to hear it, my lady. 'Tis rather a pathetic tale and I don't come out of it awfully well."

"Sometimes sharing your woes with a sympathetic ear helps mitigate the upset." Billie countered softly, not looking at Jessica, apparently engrossed in grinding a mix of herbs that smelt like Christmas. A smothered sob reached her and as she glanced across, she noticed her friend scrubbing a trail of tears from her cheek. "Come Jessica, please let me help."

"You can't help, my lady. No one can." Jessica squared her shoulders and as Billie watched, a hardness descended over the younger woman's features. *Oh Duncan*, thought the countess, *what have you done?*

Chapter Six

The last two days of her holiday were interminable to Jessica; all she wanted to do was return home, away from everything that reminded her of Duncan. The one bright spot was when she finally decided on a name for the puppy. She had been trying to teach it to sit and stay, but the puppy — as they are wont to do — ignored all instructions, continuing to frolic about like a spring lamb. For the first time since Duncan had issued his decree, she smiled, informing the puppy she was quite the trickiest little tyke. In that moment, it came to her — 'Trixie' and a more perfect name for such a scamp she could not imagine. Everyone pronounced themselves in agreement, so Trixie she became.

The evening before they were to set off back to London, Billie came to Jessica's bedchamber, and sat for a moment on the edge of the bed, watching Jessica and Sally as they were trying to best each other over who was the more proficient packer. The Drummonds did have staff, but Jessica was quite independently minded and enjoyed the challenge of seeing whether she could fold everything into her luggage in a neat and orderly fashion.

Jessica was laughing as Billie entered, but the countess noticed her pale features and was reminded that over the past couple of days she had seemed listless.

"Sally, might you give us a moment?" Billie smiled at the maid who grinned, curtsied and hurried along the hall to assist any of the other ladies whose packing had not yet been completed. "Jessica, come and sit by me." Billie patted the bed invitingly. Jessica did as she was asked, but said nothing twiddling her fingers on her lap, a sure sign of tension. "Jessica, I think perhaps you had better tell me what happened between you and Mr Barrington. Mayhap I can help." Jessica's eyes flew to Billie's and if possible her face went whiter still, but pressing her lips together, the younger woman shook her head.

"There is nothing to tell, my lady. Merely a mistake on my part." Harshly spoken, in stark contrast to her normal warm tones.

"Jessica," Billie chided. "I know you have developed feelings for Duncan as he has for you. Perhaps I should disclose a little of his life before you judge him so severely."

Jessica's jaw dropped. "H-how do you k-know I'm judging him?" her voice wobbled.

"Because I know how young women think. I am not much older than you and when I met Giles, we had our fair share of hiccups before we settled on the same page. There is usually much to learn about the person you lose your heart to."

Jessica stared at the floor, "I know something of Duncan's history. I am aware he lost his hand in battle and his injury caused him to be discharged from the army. That didn't give him the right to…" She stopped, unwilling to share so intimate an affair with Billie. In truth, she barely knew her hostess, and the hurt was too deep.

"I suspect the pair of you shared a kiss or three and you believe yourself in love with him," guessed Billie not altogether shrewdly.

"How could you possibly know that?" inadvertently giving herself away.

"I wasn't absolutely certain but you just confirmed it for me." Billie sighed and took Jessica's hand. "Let me tell you a bit more about Duncan Barrington." Billie went on to describe the full extent of Duncan's injuries and how badly the experience had affected him. Quietly and, without giving away a confidence, she explained about his black moods and why he had been tempted to end his life, until Theo Elliott had stepped in to teach the ex-soldier how to heal himself. Adding that Duncan still suffered from dark days and the reason he often worked through the night was because his rest was usually disturbed by nightmares. Jessica blushed at Billie's words, the countess correctly reading more into her guest's expression than Jessica realised.

"So, you see, even if Duncan was to fall in love with you, which — if his behaviour is anything to go by, I imagine he already has — he would never inflict his demons onto someone he cared about. He fears they may yet be his undoing and should he become close enough with another that a life together was possible, he worries he may harm them during one of his dark phases."

"I don't believe he would ever hurt another soul," Jessica whispered. "He is innately kind and respectful. Even if he was in the throes of terror or fear I believe he would recognise…" about to say 'me,' Jessica changed her mind at the last minute, choosing instead "…those who love him." She drew a tremulous breath. "Impossible as it seems, I do love him, my lady, but he has made it clear he considers himself too old and too broken, which is preposterous. What am I supposed to do? I leave for London tomorrow, likely never to see him again," a tear rolled down her cheek. "I told him I believed we shared something very special, but he doesn't think he can make me happy, which means he doesn't know me at all. Besides, it's too late because now he doesn't care to."

Three more tears followed the first one and without warning the dam broke as Jessica started sobbing uncontrollably. Sliding closer on the bed, Billie hugged the girl, rocking her as she would the child she was due to bear in about two months, letting her cry it out, but it took some time for the storm to abate.

Jessica had been holding herself on a tight leash, knowing the slightest softening would set off a bout of weeping such as this. By the time it was over she looked wrung out and complained of a headache. Billie suggested one of her drafts, which Jessica willingly accepted. Within minutes of sipping the strange tasting brew, Jessica was fast sleep and, after wiping the girl's tear-stained face, Billie left the room, asking the maid to check on her before she went to bed, just to make sure Jessica's rest remained undisturbed.

"She has been very upset, the poor dear," Billie confided to Sally, who nodded wisely.

"We are rather worried about her, she was so happy and bubbly and then the next minute, it was as though she had lost everything important to her."

"I rather think that is exactly how she feels Sally. I may have to interfere before this mess rights itself."

Sally chuckled, "As long as you remember to get proper rest while you're interfering, my lady. I don't want his Lordship getting all in a tizzy because you are exhausting yourself, you know how he worries." Billie laughed and agreed, going to find her husband, who was busy entertaining the rest of their guests and was very thankful to see his wife who always seemed to know exactly what the best games were.

The following day the remainder of the wedding guests left and Jessica found herself in a carriage with Sybil and Archie Miller; their company proving most congenial.

Mrs Drummond, aware Jessica was not her usual self, tried to talk to her daughter, but she refused to be drawn, merely commenting that she missed the city. Mrs Drummond knew there was more to it, but also knew the harder she pushed the more withdrawn her daughter would become.

Since Archie and Sybil were not related to Jessica and therefore would be unlikely to have any interest in what had happened, she felt much more comfortable and the three spent most of the journey back chatting about the shipyard and the women's refuge where Sybil worked — an effective distraction.

Before departing, Jessica — after thanking Billie and Giles for their gracious hospitality and friendship — had handed Billie two letters, one addressed to Theo Elliott, the other to Duncan, asking whether her hostess would be so kind as to pass them on once she was well on her way. Billie had smilingly agreed and hugged the girl to her, whispering that sometimes life had a funny way of working out; you just had to be patient.

Although Theo Elliott received his letter the same day the wedding guests left, responding immediately to the many questions therein, it was some time before Billie had the opportunity to deliver Jessica's letter to Duncan, as other matters took him away from the estate temporarily. Eventually, three days after Jessica departed and late in the afternoon, Billie strolled over to the workshops. The rhythmic sound of sawing and hammering was soothing and she paused for a moment at the entrance, watching the four men inside wholly absorbed in their respective tasks. She spotted a new carving on Duncan's bench, a far more whimsical piece than the furniture he normally worked on and, in that moment, knew she was doing the right thing. Her approach was perceived when her shadow fell across the floor.

Duncan turned, "Good afternoon, Lady Winchester," he greeted her, bowing, "I hope you are well. Is there something I can help you with?"

Billie grinned. "I am quite well, thank you, Duncan. Might I beg a word with you?" Duncan nodded and, wiping his hands on a convenient cloth, followed the diminutive countess into the courtyard.

"Walk with me?" she invited.

Happy to take a break, Duncan agreed and offered Billie his arm as they sauntered around to the main gardens. The thick snow was melting, and here and there, green patches were appearing in the stark whiteness, evidence of a slight easing in the wintry weather. It wouldn't last but was pleasant all the same. Billie and Duncan didn't converse as they made their way along the quiet pathways, each lost in contemplation. As they reached the fence separating the formal gardens from the Great Park, Billie stopped and, untucking her arm, leaned against the cold wood, gazing out over the undulating landscape at a view, which never failed to take her breath away.

After a moment, she faced her companion. "I realise 'tis impertinent of me to ask, Duncan, but would you be prepared to share something of what happened between you and Jessica?" Billie enquired, in compassionate tones.

Duncan glanced down seeing her concern and much as he didn't think it was any of her business, knew he would end up telling her. Billie had a way of extracting information without people realising she had done so. In fact, Duncan believed she would have made a very good spy, an occupation of which her family had some experience. He did, however try to deflect her.

"Lady Winchester, 'twas nothing need worry you. You have quite enough to contend with, first the wedding and soon the babe. You know Giles hates it when you overdo things. Miss Drummond and I enjoyed a brief acquaintance. Now she has returned home and my life will continue as always."

Billie chuckled, "Ah, but that is where you are wrong my friend. Your life has been irrevocably changed, it can never go back to the way it was before you met Miss Drummond. You have fallen under Jessica's spell and she yours." Duncan started to speak but she waved him into silence. "I know you think you are not worthy of her and that, because of your experiences you are unable to offer her a place in your life, but that is a bleak path and I do not, for one second, suppose you wish to follow it."

She paused to collect her thoughts. Billie knew she was treading a fine line between solicitude and meddling, but she truly believed both parties to this debacle just needed a gentle push in the right direction.

"You have wounded her heart, Duncan and perhaps you should try and undo the hurt, for I believe that in winning her back, you will also heal your soul." She squeezed his arm in entreaty, her unwavering expression demanding he heed her.

Duncan stared at the countess. Her words, more poetry than logic, struck a chord. From the moment she had walked away — in fact from the moment they had met — Jessica was always in his thoughts, no matter what he did, how hard he worked, how tired he became, she refused to relinquish her hold. Even though this made him feel wretched, he embraced it — penance for the pain he had inflicted on the only woman he would ever love.

"I fear I cannot undo it. I saw her face when last we spoke; she was devastated. Even if I did try to make amends, I doubt she would agree to meet me, never mind give me the chance to explain."

"Oh, I think you might find when happiness is at stake, resolutions have a tendency to fall by the wayside. You just need to choose the right words to help her understand. Yes, she may refuse to speak to you, she may declare she cannot bear the sight of you and never wants to see you again..."

Duncan winced at Billie's words, the gesture saying more than he could ever articulate,

"...but if she loves you, she will hear and when we listen with our hearts, the words are clearer. All who know you know of your burdens. You did not choose to be blown up on a battlefield, or lose your arm, or have to deal with the traumatic aftermath. That was not self-inflicted, but this is. You chose to walk away from Jessica without giving her a chance. She is not some weak-kneed flibbertigibbet. She is a clever, strong and loyal woman, who accepted you for who you are and understands more than you realise. Just think about it." Billie paused again, dithering over whether to continue, aware it is never easy for a man to have his actions questioned by a woman.

"Duncan, you are not alone, you have never been alone. 'Tis no weakness to ask for help, in fact it shows a deeper courage than those who refuse to accept what is freely offered. Now, I have said my piece, 'tis your life and unless you wish to revisit this topic, I shall never mention it again. However..." reaching inside her cloak, Billie pulled out the letter and handed it to Duncan. "...Jessica asked me to give this to you. Mayhap it will help with your decision."

Chapter Seven

Duncan took the folded sheet, turning it over and over in his hands. Even his name in her neat handwriting set his heart thudding. Slotting it into his pocket, he leaned his arms on the fence and, like Billie, gazed out over Winchester lands but he couldn't see the view, all he could see was Jessica's face. His head was crowded with thoughts and feelings and emotions; he needed space and peace and quiet, he needed time to sort through the noise, to come up with a plan. London was two days by carriage; he had no other reason to visit the capital except to see Jessica. Yes, that was enough but he couldn't just show up on her doorstep. Wouldn't it be better to contrive a meeting somehow? A surprise encounter, perhaps? That way she would not feel duty bound to talk to him.

"My lady, how does one go about such things?" he asked diffidently. "I do not understand the nuances and rules of Society. I am plain spoken and although I believe I have the ability to court a lady, I do not wish to upset her family, by acting contrarily to some higher expectations."

Billie chortled with laughter, "Duncan Barrington, you charmed Jessica in less than two days, you do not need to worry about your behaviour. Moreover, sometimes plain speaking is best, as it leaves no room for confusion. I think you will do fine. If you need an excuse, I am sure Giles has some business interest or other that you would be able to check on. I know he hates the city in winter, so should he hear you were planning to travel there, he would likely find a whole list of things to which you might attend."

Her cheerful response had the desired effect and Duncan began to feel less despondent. He knew it would not be easy; his behaviour had been reprehensible, even though his motives were laudable, but he also knew, if he didn't try he would regret it for the rest of his life.

At the end of the day, when the other men had left and before he set off home, Duncan sat on the bench just outside the workshop and, with some trepidation it must be admitted, opened Jessica's letter.

Dear ~~Mr Ba~~ Duncan,

By the time you read this, I will have left Whiteoaks. I am not brave enough to hand it to you personally as I presume you would not accept it, so I asked Billie to do the honours.

Duncan's heart contracted.

I find it hard to believe I have known you less than five days, yet it seems a lifetime. When first we met you were angry and cold and I thought this was solely my fault. Now, however, I know there are other factors, which affect your mood, factors I failed to recognise or comprehend, but wish I had.

When I came upon you in the workshop you told me your anger was your head's way of protecting your heart. I do not imagine you give your heart easily, and I never expected to fall in love, but I think you did and I have, and to be held by you, to be kissed by you was quite the most remarkable experience of my life. You made me feel more cherished than I ever dreamed possible, but then you pushed me away and while I cannot profess to be happy about it, I think perhaps I am beginning to understand.

What you need to understand though, is that you still have my heart and you will have it forever. Please keep it safe.

Jessica

Duncan felt tears slide down his cheeks and even though appalled by the fact he, a grown man, had been reduced to weeping by a mere slip of a woman, he was powerless to stop them. He didn't think his heart could ache any more, this letter proved him so very wrong. He read and re-read her words, hearing her voice, seeing her beautiful face and expressive eyes. Whatever it took, however long he had to fight, he would win her back.

Meanwhile, many miles away in a chilly office on the edge of the Thames, Jessica was seemingly immersed in trying to sort out all the paperwork and reports, which had piled up on Hugh's desk in their absence. Hugh himself was not due home until the morrow, he and Helena opting to remain at Whiteoaks a little longer. To be fair, they were newlyweds and needed some time to themselves, especially after what had happened two months previously. Still, Jessica missed her brother. For all he was six years her senior, he had always been there for her, as brother and then — following the sudden death, seven years previously, of their father — as guardian, and never had she needed his guidance more.

In the Drummond household, it was not unusual for the siblings to talk with each other about their lives, their concerns, their hopes and their dreams, and even though Hugh was now married, Jessica didn't think this aspect of their lives would change dramatically. She sat back in the chair, contemplating the desk with its scattering of documents and, as she had every day since her return, mused over how she might persuade that block-headed Duncan Barrington, she was quite possibly the best thing that ever happened to him. She would appreciate Hugh's perspective, after all, he had fought the idea of marriage for years until Helena appeared and shattered his convictions.

Nick was no use; he was completely focussed on the business and had no time for feminine nonsense, as he was wont to call it. He was learning all he could from Mr Holland, the master shipwright; in the hope Hugh might let him take responsibility for day-to-day construction and/or repair of any ships and all sea trials. Moreover, he was very much like Hugh had been — uninterested in matters of the heart.

Sighing and realising this was not getting her work done, Jessica pushed everything to do with Duncan to the back of her mind and concentrated on filing. By the end of the afternoon, she was finished, the office was back to its normal tidy state and she was pleased with her efforts. Dousing all the candles and making sure everything was locked and secure, she walked down to the main gates to wait for Nick.

Upon arriving home, Jessica was informed by Mr Rogers, their butler, that she had received a letter. Eagerly she plucked it from the plate and ran upstairs to read it in the privacy of her room, calling to her mother that she was just changing and would be down shortly. Breaking the seal, one she did not recognise, Jessica unfolded the sheets and began to scan the scrawled lines. It was from Theo Elliott and, while disappointed it was not from Duncan, was still keen to read his response.

Before she left Whiteoaks and despite her intentions, Jessica had written to the doctor asking him to tell her everything he could about battle injuries and trauma and whether there were any hospitals in London still caring for returned soldiers suffering from these afflictions explaining, in a very roundabout way, her interest.

Theo, who had discussed the matter at length with his wife — a lady with some experience of residual shock — provided ample information along with the names of two hospitals where she might find doctors specialising in such injuries. He added that she was welcome to use his name and had included a letter of introduction should one be required. Jessica hugged herself when she finished reading. Theo's letter gave her hope that maybe, just maybe, if she learned everything she could about the type of physical and mental challenges Duncan dealt with, she would understand why he felt undeserving of her. Then all she had to do was persuade him that she would be there to love and support him whatever he faced — in her opinion, a minor hurdle.

Two days before Christmas, Jessica managed to organise a free day to approach one of the two hospitals Theo had recommended. She opted for St Bart's; in the main because Theo trained there, but also Helena had mentioned that when she was much younger, it was one of the establishments her father had taken her, to visit with injured soldiers, and therefore might know some of the staff. Hugh and Helena's return, was both a delight and relief for Jessica and, despite

Hugh's doubts as to the sense in visiting a military ward, Helena must have talked him around for they offered to accompany her. As the carriage rumbled through the streets, Jessica recalled Helena's advice of the night before.

"You must remember these men do not need voyeurs. All have suffered severely or would not be in hospital. This is not something you do for fun. If you undertake to visit regularly, to offer any help the doctors may see fit to suggest, you will see any amount of distressing things, but you cannot let the men know how it affects you. You will need a strong stomach, for their wounds are not restricted to the mind. Many are so badly wounded, both mentally and physically, they can never look after themselves again and have nowhere else to go."

"Why these hospitals and not Bethlem?" Jessica had enquired, referring to the facility for the management and treatment of the mentally and criminally unfit, recently rebuilt at St George's Fields and, which housed many similarly impaired patients.

"Some have been relocated to Bethlem, but the doctors who deal in battle trauma prefer to keep as many veterans as possible under their care. Bethlem is not the most conducive place for a soldier or sailor to recover, more likely it will tip a fragile mind over the edge into madness. The men need succour and patience, not locking up and ignoring." Helena's comment reminding Jessica of the parliamentary inquiry into conditions at asylums all across the country, during which, those in charge had had their humanity questioned. Helena had not been able to suppress a shudder, prompting Hugh to draw her close and kiss her forehead, a comforting gesture, which made Jessica feel quite alone, wishing she had someone, well, all right wishing she had Duncan, to soothe her in much the same way.

Refusing to entertain that thought, Jessica forced her mind back to the present and it wasn't long before they came to a halt outside St Bart's. She was nervous now. This was important, she did not want to ruin her chance to understand what plagued Duncan. As they entered the building, an orderly appeared and asked their business. Hugh explained in authoritative tones why they were there. The young man nodded, motioned them to a wooden bench and disappeared back the way he had come.

Shortly thereafter a harried looking man came along the corridor, introduced himself as Doctor Napier and ushered them into a small office. Hugh, once again, clarified the reason for their visit, while Jessica stepped forward, showing the doctor Theo's letter. Frowning, he scrutinised it carefully, but when he noticed who the sender was, a huge smile wreathed his face.

"Theo Elliott! Well I never. How is he? Haven't seen him for, oh at least two years. I know he was in the city recently, but we missed each other." Helena, the one who knew Theo best, brought Dr Napier up to date on the Elliott family after which, she judged it acceptable to leave Jessica to discuss the matter in private, saying they would wait in the lofty entrance hall. As Helena and Hugh closed the door behind them, the doctor glanced once more at the letter. "So, you wish to learn about battle trauma and how it can affect the mind?" he asked Jessica, his eyes boring into her.

Jessica straightened her back. "I would like that very much, sir," she affirmed. "I have a fr...I know someone who suffers and he thinks I...errr...well that is immaterial. I should like to be able to understand what triggers his dark moods and whether there is a way of mitigating them, or better still averting them altogether. I accept they may haunt him for the rest of his life but I do not believe they should prevent him from enjoying that life to its fullest."

At the doctor's invitation, she explained how Duncan had come by his injuries as well as the length of time he had lain amongst his fallen comrades before he had been found and treated.

Dr Napier studied her impassively as she spoke, making Jessica worry he thought her on a frivolous mission, so she was in no way prepared for his next words.

"I am astounded by your perception, young lady. Not many women would go to such lengths to help a veteran. Even those with similar experiences are not always equipped to handle the terrors these men face every day." He tapped his chin. "Were I to allow you to visit, you must prepare yourself; this hospital is not for the faint hearted. You will see and hear things most ladies will never see, nor should they, for it is unlikely they could cope, and if you think you are going to have a fit of the vapours, you must leave the ward until you regain your composure. These men do not need to see pity or fear; they need a kind face, a gentle hand and someone with the patience of a saint. Do you think yourself capable?"

In the strongest voice she could muster Jessica said, "I do sir. Thank you for the opportunity, you will not regret your decision."

"I hope not. How often would you be able to help? Stability is vital, you cannot come and go as you please, they have schedules and routines that must not be upset."

"I work at Trentams Shipyard on Mondays, Tuesdays and Thursdays, but I am available on the other two days and would happily come on a Saturday and Sunday, should it be required."

"The weekends won't be necessary, that is usually when any family these men have, visit, but if you could be here by…" he ran his mind over the forthcoming calendar, aware Christmas was imminent, "…ten in the morning next Wednesday, I should be pleased." Jessica agreed and dropped a curtsy as the Doctor, his mind already back on his patients nodded absently, saying he looked forward to seeing her a week hence. Her mind whirling with anticipation, Jessica walked slowly along the corridor to where Hugh and Helena waited, and flopping down on the long bench seat next to them, told them all that had transpired.

"Goodness, I did not expect so favourable a meeting. I hope I don't embarrass you," she concluded, looking at her brother who grinned and patted her shoulder.

"I think you will surprise yourself, Jessica. I expect you will prove quite adept at the tasks they will have you doing, but pray tell, why is this so important to you?" He asked curiously, as they took their leave. Jessica didn't reply until they were in the carriage. Neither Hugh nor Helena knew of her *tendre* for

Duncan and she didn't want her brother to lose his temper over her behaviour.

"While at Whiteoaks, I chanced to meet someone for whom I developed an affection and I think he returned my feelings but occasionally he is troubled by melancholia and, because of this, believes himself unworthy of me."

Hugh raised an eyebrow at his spirited sister knowing there was more to this tale than met the eye, but accepted Helena would be the one more likely to wheedle it out of her. The rest needed no explanation; Jessica wouldn't be here at this hospital if her affection was not sincere.

"You care for this man?"

"I do, very much, but we parted on less than friendly terms and I believe he deliberately pushed me away because of some misguided notion that he is saving me from himself. Anyway, I hope by coming here, I might better understand him and mayhap there is a chance for us. If not, I am still helping those in need…" Jessica's voice faltered, the thought of never seeing Duncan again produced an ache so deep she didn't think it would ever ease.

Helena — recognition as to who Jessica referred, teasing at the edge of her consciousness but refusing to be pinned down — nudged Hugh and the pair coaxed Jessica into a brighter topic of conversation, which kept them occupied until they arrived home.

Chapter Eight

The next week flew by; Jessica was busy at Trentams during the day and spent any free hours preparing for her days at St Bart's. Trixie also took up much of her time; the puppy was growing quickly and Jessica ensured the creature had plenty of exercise, taking her for long walks through one of the many parks. She was endlessly amused that, on some days, if they had managed a couple of walks already, the poor dog refused to leave the warmth of the hearth, gazing at her with sad eyes and pretending to be part of the thick rug.

Jessica found these hours in the freezing air a balm. Just as she had at Whiteoaks, she would walk for miles, the dog by her side, carrying on a conversation with Trixie as though the animal understood and could offer advice. It did occur to her that anyone who overheard such discussions would consider her deranged, but found she didn't care.

Trixie was proving easy to train, she could sit and stay and, should Jessica occasionally remove the leash to allow the dog some freedom, would come to heel when called, remaining glued to her mistress' side until given the signal to run off again. Jessica was proud of the creature but never slackened in her training or relaxed her vigilance when they were out. The parks were full of dangers to small animals, such as horses and carriages, and Jessica didn't want the dog to run under hooves or get caught between wheels, so whenever either were close, kept Trixie on her leash. Around people, the puppy was very loving and could usually be found either asleep on someone's foot, or if she could sneak into the kitchens, sitting as close to cook as she could manage, hoping a scrap or two of food might inadvertently fall her way.

In between all this, Christmas came and went, but Jessica scarcely noticed it — her family, as usual, celebrating in an understated manner. They decorated their home, went to the Christmas service and enjoyed a sumptuous meal, swapping one or two small tokens — Trixie receiving the bulk of any gifts, which delighted Jessica no end. Hugh and Helena spent the day with them, before departing for an evening at Winchester House. Following tradition, St Stephen's Day saw them boxing up all manner of unwanted items, which Helena would take to Sanctuary House, the refuge where she worked. A pantomime in the evening attended by both the Drummond and Winchester families, wrapped up their seasonal festivities and the consensus was it had been most convivial.

Soon, they returned to their daily routine and Jessica's days were full, for which she was thankful as it left her no time to think. The weather was bitterly cold and there had been reports of heavy snow in the countryside, blocking many of the postal routes. Having received nothing from Duncan, Jessica had half persuaded herself this was the reason why, but it accorded only a modicum of comfort.

Thus, the Wednesday morning on which she would commence at St Bart's came around in the blink of an eye. Jessica, presenting herself at the doctor's office on the dot of 10am, was given a comprehensive tour of the wards she would be assisting on. Before they started, Dr Napier gave her a detailed description of every man including name, rank and injuries, how long each had been a patient and whether there was a likelihood any would ever leave the hospital. After which, he suggested she accompany him on his rounds so he could introduce her to the patients while carrying out his daily examinations.

The wards were a revelation. Jessica had expected they would be simply rows of beds, but the two rooms were more a cross between a bedroom and a study. They were long and airy with high ceilings and plenty of windows, all currently open allowing fresh air to circulate, under each of which stood a bed. Next to every bed, a small cupboard to store any personal items — maybe a book or letters, a hairbrush and perhaps one or two luxuries such as bar soap — and on top, a candle, neatly trimmed. At the other end, opposite the door, a space had been created to offer a homely feel. A collection of comfortable chairs and sofas were grouped around a roaring fire, which was flanked by two enormous bookcases full to bursting with books. Several tables, their chairs tucked neatly underneath, were scattered with broadsheets, and to complete the scene, a few smaller cupboards.

Some of the men were sitting at that end of the room, chatting amongst themselves. Had Jessica not known better, she might have presumed she had entered a gentleman's club — not that she had any experience of what went on inside them, but this was how she pictured they might appear — so relaxed did they seem, if one ignored the bandages, the canes and the vacant stares.

Bringing her attention back to Dr Napier, Jessica listened carefully and, used to retaining important information, committed everything the doctor said to memory. As she followed him through the wards, she greeted each soldier or sailor by name, keeping her voice low and her movements unhurried and was gratified when she received a response, even if it was just a smile. At the end of rounds, Dr Napier recommended, because it was her first day, that it might be best if she simply got to know the patients. To spend a little time with each man, making sure they had everything they needed. He also informed her that, during the day, the bed linens would be changed and, if she could assist the orderly with that task, it would be much appreciated. Jessica was more than happy to agree and the doctor, pleased this refined young lady hadn't run away screaming, nodded and left her to it.

A chair had been placed alongside each bed for the use of visitors or, in Jessica's case, herself. Beginning at one end of the first ward, she sat with each veteran chatting quietly, getting to know them while providing them with anything they might require such as water or a book, or an extra blanket before moving onto the next man.

Jessica did not rush and, should a patient seem disposed to talk for longer, she stayed with them. Many had been badly disfigured but she schooled herself not to react and spoke with the men as though she had known them forever. Some refused to speak — some, she came to discover, hadn't spoken since their arrival — turning away and ignoring her presence, but she still talked to them, telling them about herself and her work at the shipyard and her dog; either holding their hand or resting her fingers on an arm or leg, believing that often, touch says more than words ever can.

Helping the orderly, whose name was Isaac, in whatever capacity necessary, Jessica changed the sheets and was taught how to bathe any soldier who still struggled to leave his bed. She also asked whether she might observe how, for those soldiers still requiring wound care for whatever reason, their injuries should be cleaned, treated and dressed, surprising herself by not fainting or vomiting when she came face to face with the terrible damage inflicted.

It was clear there was much to do during the day and Isaac assured her they were grateful for any assistance, especially since the sights, sounds and smells of the wards didn't seem to upset her.

"We've had ladies coming in thinking to help, but bless 'em, as soon as they see one of our boys they come over all of a dither. No point even trying if you ain't got the stomach for it."

Jessica accepted this for the compliment she assumed it was. "In truth, I worried I might embarrass myself when you were demonstrating how to dress a wound, but I just told myself the Major..." she nodded towards the soldier to whom she was referring, "...has suffered far more than I could ever imagine and, over four years later, is still suffering. What I might feel while helping bind a wound is inconsequential." She shrugged. "That and gritting my teeth seemed to work." She grinned at Isaac who grinned back; impressed with Jessica's honesty, glad Dr Napier had taken on a woman who appeared eminently sensible.

They carried on, chatting quietly with each other or the men they were working with and the day was over almost before Jessica had chance to realise it had begun. Around four in the afternoon, Dr Napier came to see how she had fared and listened to a glowing report from Isaac.

"You have won Isaac over, Miss Drummond, no easy feat. That said, I know 'tis hard work. Are you willing to assist on a regular basis?"

"Oh, Dr Napier, I should be so pleased to help, if you think me suitable. To take even a little of the workload off your shoulders would gladden my heart," beaming a bright smile and dipping a curtsy as she spoke, making the doctor smile wryly.

"You have no need to curtsy to me, Miss Drummond. I imagine we are equals and as we will be seeing a lot of each other, too much bowing and curtseying could become tedious, if not downright farcical." He winked, taking the formality out of his words and making Jessica chuckle as she agreed wholeheartedly with his sentiments. Sometimes all the rules did get rather tiresome. They talked a little longer until another orderly appeared and informed Jessica her carriage awaited at the front of the hospital. Thanking Dr Napier and Isaac, and confirming she would return two days hence, Jessica fled down the stairs and through the maze of corridors, tumbling out of the building into the waning light, to see Nick waiting with the Drummond coach.

As Tom, their driver, assisted Jessica up, Nick listened to her enthusiastic monologue with a kind of resigned amusement, his sister was the most outgoing of the Drummond siblings, her zest for life well known. Both Hugh and he were quite solemn, a characteristic they had inherited from their father, probably a result of so many lonely hours at sea.

Jessica was like their mother. She had a lively and cheerful disposition, or at least she used to have; of late she was much quieter and even Nick, not the most perceptive of souls, knew their mother was concerned. This was the first time he had seen Jessica back to her usual bubbly self since…wait, how long had it been since she'd smiled…it had to have been just after Hugh's wedding. Now that was odd…Nick rolled it around in his head, but unable to piece it together filed it away for another day glad, for once, Jessica seemed happy. He asked a few pertinent questions, and she prattled on garrulously until they arrived home.

Jessica's days fell quickly into an absorbing routine, she was always busy at the shipyard and now twice a week she assisted at St Bart's. Slowly she came to know each veteran and their respective histories. She quickly recognised who could be teased and encouraged along and who responded better to quiet persuasion; who could manage their ablutions and who needed assistance. Those who strove for some level of independence as opposed to those who had virtually lost the will to live, mere shells of who they had once been. In no time, all became very dear to her and it seemed her presence lifted their spirits.

She spent time talking with them, listening to their woes and irritations, without offering trite advice. She wrote letters for any who required it and read to those who found concentrating on books too arduous. She was always smiling, even the grouchy patients failed to dampen her cheerful demeanour. Neither did she ever seem in a hurry to leave and often stayed longer than her scheduled time, simply because she didn't wish to walk out in the middle of a conversation.

Undertaking as much routine wound care as she was able, Jessica freed up Isaac and the other orderly, Charlie, to concentrate on more difficult cases, gratified they trusted her with such delicate tasks. Every evening, often too tired to eat a proper meal, she fell into bed, exhausted yet with a feeling of accomplishment. To the untrained eye, Jessica appeared content with her life, but — when not at the hospital — careful scrutiny would have revealed a hidden tension, a jaw not as relaxed as one might expect, a smile that did not reach her eyes and a disinterest in doing anything other than working or spending time with Trixie.

Eventually, Helena decided enough was enough and suggested to Hugh they invite Jessica along to one or two of the winter balls they were due to attend. Hugh was agreeable and one evening, a little over a month after her sojourn at Whiteoaks, Jessica found herself primped and fluffed and in a carriage with her brother and his wife on their way to a party celebrating the birthday of Lady Louisa Daubery, sister of Helena's best friend Tabitha.

"Remind me again, why I have to come to this party?" Jessica asked her sister-in-law, resignedly.

"Because I believe you need to enjoy something entirely unconnected to shipping and hospitals. While I am delighted you have found something worthwhile to fill your days, it should not be to the detriment of all else. You need balance in your life, something light-hearted and yes, a tad frivolous, for if not you will forget how to have fun." Jessica wriggled uncomfortably, but Helena wasn't finished with her. "You no longer visit with your friends or go for carriage rides or any of those pastimes I know you love. You confine your spare time to Trixie who, although very sweet, is not quite able to indulge in meaningful conversation as say Clare or Meredith..." referring to Jessica's two great friends, "...who are probably wondering where you have been lately. Jessica, if you are not careful you will shrivel up inside and I should be very distressed were that to happen. You are normally so wonderfully vivacious; you can light up a room simply by entering it, please do not lose that part of yourself." She paused and seemed about to say more but thought better of it, content to leave it for now.

Jessica's head shot up, her gaze colliding with Helena's who was watching her carefully.

"I am fine, Helena. Thank you for your concern, but you worry needlessly. I have not felt very sociable lately, 'tis all." She tried to smile artlessly but Helena didn't look remotely convinced, she did however turn the conversation to the evening's entertainment, letting the matter drop for the time being.

Moments later they arrived at Bridgewater House — city residence of the Daubery family — and were soon swallowed up into a ballroom full of light and music. Elegant ladies wafting about, their dresses swishing and shimmering like rainbows, gentlemen standing about in small groups discussing whatever men discussed at such gatherings. Hugh, other than to seek out drinks or food, never left Helena's side — not only were they newlyweds, but also neither had any wish to spend their evening apart. Helena introduced Jessica to several young ladies and it was not long before she was whisked away to dance with one of the many eligible young bucks, the night passing in a haze of colourful merriment.

Chapter Nine

One young man seemed especially enamoured of Jessica and managed to persuade her to dance with him twice throughout the evening. He introduced himself as Lord Piers Marchmont, the second son of the Marquis of Berkhampstead. He was a personable young man, but all Jessica could think of when she was dancing with him, was Duncan and how it would feel to be swirled around the dance floor in his arms. Nevertheless, she was flattered by Piers' attention and agreed to, maybe possibly, allowing him to escort her to some ball or other the following weekend. She did spend some time talking with him as part of a larger group and he was quite charming, so to extend their acquaintance would be no great hardship.

Later in the evening she made her way to where her brother and Helena were sitting and plumped down in the chair with little regard for grace.

"Ooof, I'm tired, my feet are hurting like the dickens and I don't think I have the energy to walk to the carriage." She informed them with a grin.

"You seem to have enjoyed yourself, who is that nice young man?" Helena waved her fan in Piers' direction.

"Lord Piers Marchmont. He seems quite affable. He's asked whether he might accompany me to the Grantley's ball next weekend." She didn't sound overly enthusiastic at the prospect, but at least she hadn't dismissed it out of hand.

Helen studied her carefully, Jessica's reticence at odds with her normal flamboyance.

"Jessica, I know what you said earlier this evening, but I think you and I should have a proper chat soon, if you would grant me that." Helena reached out and took Jessica's hand as she spoke, her lovely smoky violet eyes reading in her sister-in-law's face more than she realised. Her kindness made Jessica want to weep, but she hung onto her composure by stiffening her shoulders and forcing a smile to her lips.

"I would be glad of your counsel, Helena. Mayhap if you have some time on the morrow?" Strain clear in her voice, Jessica knew she had to talk to someone. Someone who might comprehend her confusion and Helena, barely a year older than she, would likely understand her better than most.

Helena frowned; this was more serious than she presumed. Contemplating Jessica's rigid posture, shadowed eyes and inexplicable restlessness, Helena recalled battling similar agitation when…goodness it was when she realised she was in love with Hugh! She bit down on a muffled exclamation drawing an astonished glance from her husband. She shook her head, her expression, indicating she would tell him later. Who? How? The when was obvious, it can only have been at Whiteoaks, 'twas then Jessica began to withdraw into herself. Who else knew? Did Billie know? If so, why hadn't she mentioned anything?

Helena ran her mind back over everything that had happened before and after her wedding. It couldn't possibly have occurred before, she would have noticed, but after their marriage, she and Hugh had barely come into contact with anyone else while they stayed at Whiteoaks, enjoying the privacy of one of the manor houses on the estate. Moreover, there were no young men remaining, it had only been family. The only other people Jessica might have met were estate workers, or those from the village. Helena knew everyone who lived and worked around Whiteoaks; some she dismissed easily, but as she pondered, several things nudging at the edge of her mind, coalesced; specifically the reason Jessica wanted to work at St Bart's and in a flash all became clear. Jessica was in love with Duncan Barrington.

Helena had known him all her life; he was a good man and a loyal friend to Giles. Duncan and the other youngsters from the village had never treated her or Charlotte, her older sister, any differently when they were children, playing together without a care for rank or status. Then the young men had gone off to war, most came back, but they were no longer the same carefree boys. War changed them — buried some, wounded others and Duncan suffered more than most from their small community. She knew something of his trauma, but not all, although since she met Hugh, she understood a lot more, her own husband had not escaped the conflict unscathed. Many bore scars hidden so deeply they would never be revealed. Helena had heard whispers that Duncan, not long after his return from the Peninsula, had considered taking his life, but after months of almost daily consultations with Theo Elliott — who was not only their local doctor, but also a specialist in the field of battle trauma — and other war veterans, he had turned his desperation into something positive.

Now it seemed Jessica had developed an affection for the man. What Helena didn't know was whether those feelings were reciprocated. Bringing her attention back to Jessica, who was waiting for her to answer, Helena simply smiled and nodded suggesting the early afternoon, weather permitting.

"A stroll through the park is always invigorating, especially at the moment when the weather traps us in our homes and we would be early enough to avoid nosey gossips and other distractions. Also, we could take Trixie, I'm sure she would appreciate an extra walk."

Jessica relaxed a fraction, "Thank you Helena, I am grateful. Now, as it is after midnight, please may we go home?" she beseeched, "I do not understand Society's fondness for keeping such late hours. I am falling asleep where I sit." The other two laughed and agreed, finding their hosts to thank them for a lovely evening. They were about to leave when Lord Piers sauntered over and caught Jessica's arm, a somewhat arrogant gesture and one Jessica didn't care for. Striving for politeness, she schooled her features, into a more amicable expression.

He greeted Hugh and Helena in the proper manner and then addressed Jessica. "Have you yet decided whether I may accompany you next week?" he asked a cheeky grin on his face. Jessica stared at him, he was quite good looking she supposed. His hair was a bit too perfect and his attire rather too fashionable for her liking but, despite his cockiness, he was friendly and cheerful and she didn't think an evening with him would be too arduous.

"I am still deliberating, Lord Piers..." She paused and his face fell, "...but I do believe I am inclined to accept." She smiled gently and Piers made a small whoop, grinning with unabashed delight.

"I am so pleased. I believe it will be a most enjoyable affair. I shall call for you at eight." He bowed over her hand, kissing it as she dropped a deep curtsy. "Until then Miss Drummond." He released her hand slowly, letting his fingers linger on hers a little longer than they ought. Jessica was nonplussed, this seemed rather forward, but as her only experience of such things was with Duncan, she couldn't really be sure. It did concern her, however, that she wanted to snatch her hand away from under his touch, which she presumed wasn't the expected reaction. Maybe she was just nervous. Jessica decided to ignore it and said her goodbyes, following Helena and Hugh through the door and out into the freezing air.

"Brrrr, this weather is enough to make us all hibernate. Come, hopefully we can beg a hot chocolate before we retire," said Hugh, hurrying the two women into the carriage and before long they were home.

The next afternoon, after Helena had returned from her duties at Sanctuary House and, once they had searched out Trixie, who was under the kitchen table willing tasty scraps to drop as though by magic into her mouth, the three set off. It was still very cold, but no more snow had fallen and the paths were clear. They walked for quite a while chatting about life in general until they found themselves near a wrought-iron bench. Wrapped snugly in heavy winter coats — hoods up — scarves and gloves, both women were warmed from their brisk promenade.

Jessica undid Trixie's leash and the pup bounded about nearby, expending some of her everlasting energy. Keeping a close eye on the creature, Jessica sat back and breathed in the fresh air, admiring the stark beauty of the scenery; leafless trees stood tall and black against the white backdrop, their branches creating tormented shadows across the frosted ground. All noise was muted and, for a brief moment, Jessica was reminded of the day she met Duncan, the irony of that, not lost on her. Unwilling to be the one to broach the subject, Jessica let the quiet wash over her, the tranquillity of the afternoon completely at odds with the tumult in her head.

"Shall I ask the question or will you just tell me?" Helena queried, her soft voice full of tenderness. Jessica stared straight ahead, took a deep breath and told her sister-in-law everything that transpired between Duncan and her, from their first meeting to that disastrous afternoon. She even confessed to leaving the letter for him. It took some telling, for Jessica found some parts difficult and others a little embarrassing; moreover, she was determined not to cry, so there were several pauses and silences, while she gathered herself, but finally it was all out.

Funnily enough, once she had finished, Jessica felt less bleak, but now she also knew without any doubt, her feelings for Duncan had not changed — not even distance and time could alter how much she loved him.

"Now I work at St Bart's hoping if I spend time with men suffering similar — be they probably more acute — symptoms, I at least can prove I am able to empathise with what he is going through even if I cannot ever truly understand it. Dr Napier was explaining about some of the advances in prosthetics and I am curious as to whether Duncan ever considered such a thing. It makes no difference to me whether he has one arm or no arms, I would love him regardless, but it would be such a help to him with his woodwork. Just the extra balance or grip when he's working with the smaller carvings would prove beneficial. Anyway, 'tis moot, for I don't expect we shall meet again." Jessica drew a rough breath, trying to control her emotions. That she would never again feel his lips touch hers made her unutterably sad.

Helena watched Jessica while she talked, impressed by her perception at the same time contemplating whether, as a respectable married lady, she could get away with banging Duncan's head against a brick wall. She knew him to be an honourable man who would never compromise a young woman. The mere fact his entanglement with Jessica had become rather intimate, indicated to Helena — who also knew he had never been one to wear his heart on his sleeve — that the man was as in love with Jessica as she with him. Helena tapped her lips, deciding how she might interfere without it appearing obvious. First, she would write to Billie, surely between them they could come up with something, her sister-in-law had shown a fondness for Jessica during their stay

"What of Lord Piers?" Helena pressed after they had exhausted the topic of Duncan Barrington.

Jessica shrugged, "He seems a very personable young man but my instinct tells me, should I agree to his courtship, he would want to rule me. He is somewhat condescending and I refuse to bow to any man. If I ever marry — and I will only marry for love — I wish my husband to be my partner not my master and I will not be dictated to. He does seem quite entertaining though."

Helena grinned as Jessica divulged this, remembering how she had said much the same thing to Hugh. Helena was unusually independent, something Hugh valued rather than decried.

"Be careful, then, don't let him think there is more to your acquaintance." Helena warned. "It would be impolite to leave him dangling."

"I do not imagine Lord Piers is overly interested in me, there are far too many diamonds floating about. I am probably more a convenient diversion until something better comes along." Helena frowned, Jessica might not be considered as dazzlingly glamorous as some of the current incomparables, but she was still a beautiful young lady. Elegant and refined, her sunny nature and warm demeanour, along with her quick-wit made Jessica far more attractive than she realised.

"You are perfectly lovely both inside and out. Please do not belittle yourself 'tis unbecoming." Helena's admonishment made Jessica flush and she bit down on a sharp retort. It was all right for Helena; she didn't even have to try, with her flawless complexion, arresting eyes and raven hair. Jessica knew her limitations and always believed her looks to be mediocre.

"Trust me, my Lady," she growled, reverting to formality in her ire. "I am not begging to be complimented. I am under no illusions about my appearance, so please do not insult my intelligence by pretending otherwise." She stood and began to stomp off to where Trixie was chasing a random feather, knowing she was behaving badly, yet unable to stop herself. It was easier to be angry than let her guard down and weep.

"Jessica! Please come back. I apologise and I wasn't clear enough. Trust me, not all beauty is natural; many use all manner of embellishments to enhance their attractiveness, which is hard to maintain and fades in time. You, however, have an ageless quality, a quiet allure, which is far more enticing. Plus you are so bright and cheerful, well normally, mayhap not quite so much at the moment. A person with such inner happiness glows with a beauty none can imitate." Helena's voice rang with conviction. Jessica turned and regarded Helena steadily; her sister-in-law walked over to where she waited and grasped her hands.

"He told me I was beautiful," Jessica muttered as Helena reached her, tears coursing down her cold cheeks. "He told me I was beautiful, then he pushed me away. I would rather be ugly and ignored than ever feel that pain again."

In quiet understanding, Helena drew her into a warm hug. "Jessica, my dear, I expect Duncan still believes you beautiful. We just need to work out how to get him to believe he can't live without you."

Chapter Ten

Jessica allowed herself a moment to indulge in the comfort of Helena's embrace, before moving away and drawing a deep breath, determined not to give in to yet another bout of sobs.

"I refuse to weep any more over this ridiculous scenario," she stated emphatically, as though deciding the matter dealt with. "I am no simpering female. If Duncan wants me, he knows where I am and I will not prostrate myself for anyone, let alone a man. We shall see what comes of Lord Piers' attentions. In the meantime, I shall continue my days as before. Come, let us walk down to the lake, Trixie looks as though she might be chasing the poor ducks." Jessica changed the subject before Helena could say anything else.

Helena accepted Jessica would discuss it no further, and made a mental note to talk to Hugh later about any man who might approach him for Jessica's hand who wasn't Duncan Barrington. She needed time to sort through this debacle — Lord Piers or no Lord Piers. For the rest of the walk, they concentrated on Trixie. Jessica was teaching the dog to fetch; Trixie was very happy to run after whatever was thrown, but generally preferred to lie down and chew it rather than bring it back to her owner. The creature's antics reduced the two women to helpless laughter, effectively distracting them from their more serious discussion.

That evening, Helena shared with Hugh all she had learned from Jessica, finishing up by exhorting him to refuse any suit. Hugh, while mildly perturbed at the idea that the sister he still thought of as a child — despite her working at Trentams — was old enough to be kissing a man, gladly agreed. After all, she was over one and twenty; she could make her own decisions. Now, knowing a little of Duncan's history, Hugh had nothing but respect for his fellow veteran and would not be displeased with the match.

Jessica, meanwhile, took a long hard look at herself, acknowledging what Helena said was correct. She *had* been ignoring her friends — not deliberately, more by omission — and it wasn't fair to them. They had been friends a long time and she knew her neglectful behaviour would likely have hurt them. She had to get over, or at least shove out of the way, her feelings for Duncan and concentrate on what she could control. Pleased with her decisions, Jessica applied herself to her work with her customary enthusiasm and in her few free hours visited with Meredith and Clare the three resuming their uproarious gossip sessions as though they had never been apart.

The ball she attended with Lord Piers was pleasant. He was too brash for Jessica's taste but he did make her laugh for which she could forgive him many faults. She even accepted his invitation to yet another party, without giving any encouragement she wanted more than a mild flirtation.

January became February, the months slipping by almost too quickly to notice. The days, although still cold had an air of promise, a lessening of the harshness that had gripped the country for so long. Here and there snowdrops appeared and with them a hope spring might creep in and break winter's frigid grasp.

Late one afternoon, Jessica was walking through the park with Trixie; they had been out for well over an hour and the pair were tiring, but to give the dog the chance at a few more minutes exercise and as no one else was abroad, Trixie had not yet been clipped onto her leash. They were not far from the gate when Jessica spotted a figure striding towards her. Wearing a long greatcoat and a beaver hat, he was very tall and somewhat forbidding. For a moment she faltered, there was no one else around, but as she did, Trixie gave a high-pitched yip and shot off towards the stranger.

"Trixie! Trixie! Heel!" Jessica called, in what she hoped were commanding tones. The dog ignored her and soon reached the figure who stooped to ruffle her ears and Jessica froze. She recognised the gesture, she'd seen it before, two months previously and even so simple an action set her heart racing. Forcing herself to remain calm, she walked slowly to meet Duncan Barrington, who was still messing about with Trixie, the pup now upside down, legs waving in the air desperate for a tickle. As she approached, he straightened and watched her warily. She was not going to speak to him first. "Trixie! Come." This time the dog responded, moving to Jessica's heel and sitting pertly next to her mistress' ankle. Jessica clipped the leash to Trixie's collar and waited, her expression giving nothing away.

"Miss Drummond, forgive me for appearing unannounced. I called at your home and Lady Helena directed me this way. I hope I have not interrupted your constitutional." His voice, that rich deep voice, sent shivers up her spine.

"How kind of you Mr Barrington and no, Trixie and I were on our way home." Her voice was cooler than the air. "Is there something I can do for you?"

"*Yes!*" He wanted to shout, "*You can let me kiss you and hold you and love you until you scream my name,*" but all he said was, "I was wondering whether you might spare me a moment or two of your time. I received your letter and thought talking to you might be better than trying to write a response."

"Yet it has taken you two months, a letter would have reached me weeks ago and would have saved you a journey," Jessica observed, with marked disinterest.

"Please forgive my tardiness. I intended to visit just after Christmas but we have been snowed in since a week after you left. Neither letter nor person would have travelled for nigh on a month."

They stood feet apart and Jessica didn't know what to do or say, their last meeting still too raw. She stared at Duncan, realising she had forgotten nothing about him, his features so dearly familiar. His craggy face reflecting the ordeals of his past, his unruly hair the colour of ripe chestnuts, begging to be tamed, and his blue eyes — their depths dark today like the midnight sky, pierced her soul. Damn, why was he here and why did he have to be so bloody handsome?

The silence lengthened, and then she heard it.

"Jessica." A murmur so filled with desire she felt her body crackle in response. Unbidden, all the hurt and anger she had fought so hard to suppress came bubbling up to the surface and refused to be quieted.

"No, you can't do this to me again. You cannot toy with me. I am not a plaything you can toss aside when you tire of me or I become inconvenient or you panic. You said I bewitched you — well, here," she waved in his general direction, "I release you from my spell. Thank you for taking the time to visit with me, it was a kindness." Lifting her hands almost as though trying to push him away, her voice not quite steady.

It was enough to give Duncan hope. He took a step towards her, she took one back, shaking her head muttering, "no, not again."

"Jessica, your letter your words, did you mean them?" His question carried an earnest plea.

Jessica fidgeted a moment, debating with herself, before finally deciding to go with honesty.

"Of course. There would be no point writing them otherwise," raising her chin slightly, a hint of pride in the gesture.

"Then perhaps you would let me make amends. Allow me to court you, to prove I was asinine, that I should never have hurt you so badly or let you go and that you mean more to me than anyone else on earth." Laying his heart on the line, he held her gaze. "Might you give me a second chance?"

Jessica gaped at him; this was unexpected. He sounded uncertain. Was it worth the risk? She knew her love for him was irrevocable but was it better to halt this now, before she chanced him withdrawing from her again? The memory of his kisses flickered through her and her heart thudded. She wanted nothing more than to be in his embrace, but trust once lost is not easily recovered, so she hesitated, the pain of his rejection still as a knife to her breast.

Duncan recognised the apprehension in her face and he could feel his own despair rising like bile in his throat. She was going to say no, she was going to turn him away. He knew it was no more than he deserved, but he was determined to try. Well, if she *was* going to spurn him, he would not let her go without one last attempt to change her mind. He closed the gap between them, whipping his arm around her and, before Jessica could say anything, his lips were on hers. He kissed her with bruising intensity, softening to a caress, his lips moving over hers lazily and with a most sublime tenderness.

Jessica stopped arguing with herself that this was insanity, stopped caring that they were standing where anyone might come upon them, stopped worrying about how this was upsetting her nicely organised thoughts, in fact she stopped thinking about everything, her mind emptied and all sense faded into the background as his lips wove their magic. Duncan kissed her until she forgot to breathe, not releasing her lips until Jessica thought she was floating somewhere high above the snowy park.

Eventually, he broke their kiss, but did not relinquish his hold. "I love you, Jessica Drummond and whether you like it or not, I am determined to win you back." His eyes bored into hers and she was riveted by the emotion in their inky depths.

"Well, i-if you s-say so," she stammered, still trying to catch her breath, knowing she was powerless when it came to Duncan.

"I do say so and if you are agreeable, I should like to do this properly. Escort you to the social events you choose to attend, invite you to join me for a carriage ride or visit the museum or an art gallery, even just to walk Trixie here," leaning down to pat the dog who, miraculously, was lying patiently at their feet. Trixie woofed, but whether in agreement or boredom, they couldn't tell. Jessica pondered his words, letting the time spin out, not wanting to seem eager. The minutes ticked by slowly, slowly and part of her relished seeing him wait — after everything he had put her through — it seemed fitting.

Duncan held his breath.

Finally, she relented, "I am persuaded to consent to your suggestion. I feel it only fair, however, to point out that another has begun to ply his suit." Jessica tilted her head so she could see how this affected Duncan. She noticed him flinch, perversely pleased at his reaction.

"Another has asked for your hand?" he asked, hoarsely.

"No, he has simply shown interest and has escorted me to the occasional ball and will do so again in three days. For politeness' sake, I will not now decline his invitation." Duncan looked as though she had punched him in the stomach. "It is not my intent to hurt you, Duncan, but what did you expect? You made it very clear you did not want me in your life. Lord Piers, is affable and 'tis not quite as…" she didn't want to say heartbreaking, it seemed overly dramatic, "…sentimental."

Duncan, listening carefully, heard more from what she didn't say than what she did, but a tiny devil inside of him wanted her to make that last point less ambiguous.

"So, will he steal your heart? Will you be able to forget what we shared, what I believe — should you dare to trust — you wish to recapture? Will you tremble when he kisses you?" he whispered in her ear, lips skimming her soft skin "Will you moan for him?"

Jessica shuddered, heat coiling through her, his words enough to set her treacherous body on fire. She sucked in a steadying breath. "Well, we'll just have to see, won't we?"

Her answer gave Duncan some encouragement, but he could see she wasn't ready to forgive him. He couldn't blame her, and he wasn't going to force the issue, but neither was he about to give up.

"Thank you, Miss Drummond. I have enjoyed our conversation and it is wonderful to see you. I apologise for intruding on your walk, but might I call on you again before I return to Oak Stanton?" He released her, stepping away, his boots crunching on the icy pathway. Jessica felt chilled without his arms around her but she still wasn't ready to fall back into them — blithely ignoring the fact that she'd done exactly that, scarce moments ago.

"Should you feel so inclined, I would not rebuff your overtures." She replied cloaking herself in formality. "I bid you good day, Mr Barrington. I-I…" Jessica couldn't bring herself to finish and quickly covered her hesitation by gathering Trixie's lead, which she had managed to drop during that mind-blowing kiss, thankful the scatty creature had been disposed to stay put. She all but ran along through the path and out through the gates, glancing back once to see Duncan, motionless, staring after her, but she was too far away to read his expression.

Duncan watched her leave; he knew this would be hard, but to learn another had already begun to worm his way into Jessica's affections had come as a shock. Jessica was correct in her assertion, however, it was his own fault. God what a mess! Slowly he followed her footsteps a little way, but rather than continue their path, turned left at the entrance to the park, making his way back to Winchester House — his home while in London, generously offered by Giles — where he was greeted with a fine whisky and pleasant conversation as the evening slipped quietly away.

Chapter Eleven

Jessica told no one the details of her encounter in the park. She liked that it was her secret. Helena eyed her questioningly when she returned from her walk but Jessica shook her head, hoping her sister-in-law understood some things were not for sharing. Helena had worked out all she needed to anyway. Jessica's sparkling eyes told their own tale.

For reasons she could not explain, Jessica was compelled to take extra care with her preparations for the upcoming ball hosted by the Marquis and Marchioness of Hereford. She spent considerable time digging through her wardrobe for her most beautiful dress, making sure the matching shoes were presentable and that she had a suitable piece of jewellery to complete the ensemble. Eventually Jessica was satisfied she was as prepared as she could be, and carried on with her busy life. Wednesday at the hospital was uneventful, but after a day with Hugh at Trentams, during which he plied her with not so subtle questions about her well-being — no doubt primed by Helena — Jessica was glad when Friday came around and she was due back at St Bart's.

She arrived early, as was her practise, soon absorbed in her tasks. The veterans were now so used to her presence it seemed to them she'd always been there. Her unpretentious attitude and unfailing cheer brightened their lives and she, in turn, was grateful for their acceptance, still learning everything she could about how their symptoms manifested and the best way to treat or avert them.

Jessica was busy tidying up their lunch platters when a rumble ran through the building. She paused and cocked her head listening. It came again, thunder! The last couple of days had been unseasonably mild and the weather-wise had predicted this turn. Lightning flickered beyond the many windows as blue sky morphed into a sickly green, darkening with a rapidity suggestive of a wild storm. Jessica sighed with frustration, hoping it would pass quickly, the thought of going out to a ball in such weather most unappealing.

Despite her misgiving's about the evening's plans, Jessica loved storms; the power of nature both awed and terrified her, its untameable ferocity never failing to enthral her. So, not one to be alarmed, she simply continued with what she was doing, once she had closed the windows to keep out the lashing hail. On her way back to the ward about twenty minutes later, after returning the platters to the kitchens, Jessica was startled to hear an unearthly wail. She shoved open the door to see Major Vaughan, Patrick, in the throes of a flash back. The major had lost his left leg and the sight in both eyes during one of the battles and, with his family unable to care for him, had remained at St Bart's. He was usually a placid soul, but Jessica had perused Dr Napier's notes thoroughly and knew he suffered from severe trauma. She rightly guessed the thunder had reminded him of canon fire.

Without hesitation, Jessica walked over to where the major was sitting on the floor, his face twisted in horror as he screamed for stretcher-bearers to come and rescue his soldiers. There was no doubt through his sightless eyes he could see the battlefield as clearly as she could see him.

"Major Vaughan," she said raising her voice enough that it was audible over the cacophony raging overhead, but without shouting. "Patrick, I'm here, you are safe, 'tis only thunder. You are not in France. Listen to my voice." She sat on the floor next to him and rested her hand on his arm, crooning to him, trying to call him back from the terror consuming him. Patrick couldn't or wouldn't respond. His vision turned inwards, the blood and the cries of his men drowning out everything else, but Jessica persisted.

The door opened to admit Isaac, come to inform Jessica she had a visitor and was not unduly surprised to see her on the floor in the middle of the ward, trying to soothe one of their patients.

"She's there sir," pointing her out to the tall man who had walked in behind him, and whose identity remained shielded by the gloom.

Duncan Barrington gawked at the scene, yet somehow, it sat well with him. Helena had informed him of Jessica's whereabouts, with the caveat he be mindful she probably didn't want him to know, so discretion would be wise. Duncan stayed in the shadows, not wanting to draw attention to his arrival, content just to observe.

"Please do not tell her I'm here, the patient's need is far greater than mine."

Isaac appraised the man, noting his folded sleeve and soldierly bearing and nodded his understanding. "She brings a brightness into their grim world and no mistake," he said. "Nothing is too much or too hard for her and she stays far longer than she ought. Don't think I know many women like her who'd spend their days caring for men most have given up on. She's a clever 'un too, reading anything and everything the Doc can give her on battle trauma. Allus asking questions about how to recognise symptoms. She's a treasure and I won't have anyone say different." Isaac frowned at Duncan; unsure why this austere looking man was here, hoping it wasn't to interfere.

Duncan raised his hand; "I am not here to take Miss Drummond from the ward. We are acquainted and I am interested in her work here. Please, I'll stay out of the way."

A gruff acknowledgement and Isaac moved into the ward, going along and checking on the other men, in case any were similarly afflicted by the rumbling noise and the major's wails.

Duncan understood the patient's terror. His own horror came to him in nightmares and although it was years since he had suffered an attack such as that affecting the major, he empathised wholeheartedly, the weeks after his injury rearing up in his memory. Unobtrusively, he slipped right into the ward and sat under one of the windows, out of Jessica's line of sight and just watched.

Jessica was fighting a losing battle of her own. The torment stalking Patrick held him too tightly and she didn't even know whether he could hear her through the tempest above them and the tumult in his mind.

"Patrick please, hear my voice. 'Tis me, Jessica. Your men are rescued, you have saved them and now you need to come with me, where there is a warm bed and dry clothes and a hot meal. Hold my hand and I will bring you home." The man moaned, long tremors rippling through his body and he tried to fight her off. He was a strong man and Duncan, fearing for her safety, was poised to yank her out of harm's way should it prove necessary.

Unfazed, Jessica caught Patrick's flailing arms and, trusting her instincts, simply drew him against her. She tucked his head into her neck and, rocking him as though a babe, began to sing.

It was a lullaby, the lilting melody swirling around her, quietly at first but as she sang, one by one the men stopped what they were doing, mesmerised by the pure, chorister-like quality of her voice, which reached every corner despite the clamour from the storm. All were transfixed and Duncan noticed that finally, her efforts were beginning to calm Major Vaughan. Patrick stopped moaning and, although his body was still wracked by tremors, he was no longer screaming for help.

As the notes died away, Duncan realised several veterans had tears in their eyes and one soldier seemed particularly spellbound but the moment passed so quickly Duncan thought he had imagined it.

Instinctively, Jessica had done what so many women before her knew to do when their children, regardless of age, need comfort. A simple lullaby had achieved more than all the new-fangled therapies put together. While Duncan watched, Patrick drifted off, exhausted from the bout. Isaac called for Charlie and the two orderlies lifted the stricken man onto his bed, covered him with blankets and left him to sleep it off.

Stiff from sitting on the floor for so long, Jessica was stretching her aching legs and back and contemplating whether anyone would mind if she stayed where she was for the rest of the afternoon, when a large hand hooked itself around her elbow, lifting her effortlessly to her feet. Twisting around, she swallowed a squawk when she came face to face, well more like face to chest, with Duncan.

"What are you doing here?" she hissed, in undertones.

"And a very good afternoon to you too, Miss Drummond. How lovely to see you."

Jessica glowered at him, but he just winked at her.

"Who told you I work here?" she demanded, fiercely. Then, "Oh, 'twas Helena I suppose; you Whiteoaks folk do stick together. Not enough she kn..." Jessica stopped abruptly. To tell Duncan, Helena knew about their tryst was tantamount to admitting she cared enough to talk about him and that wouldn't do.

Duncan grinned unrepentantly. "She did warn me you would be unhappy about my knowing, but 'tis nothing to hide. I am astonished at what you do here and if you permit me to say so, rather honoured."

Jessica frowned in puzzlement. "Honoured? Explain yourself, Sir."

"Had we not met, I doubt you would have cause to consider the long term wounded and traumatised. 'Tis unlikely they would come to your attention. Thus, mayhap our...errr...encounter was not wholly wasted. Anyone who helps these men has my undying admiration. I know what they suffer. We are not an easy group to help."

Unable to help herself, Jessica leaned forward and touched his bad arm, stroking slender fingers over his sleeve.

"Nothing we shared was wasted, but yes, if not for you, I would have remained blind to this. For that I am truly grateful. I have learned so much. Moreover, these men have fascinating tales to tell and I am thinking of noting them down, maybe I could put together a small book, like a journal. If it sells, perhaps we could allocate the proceeds to their care, provide a few luxuries. I have no idea exactly what that would entail but I'm sure Dr Napier would have some suggestions."

Duncan stared at Jessica, her affection for these men shining from eyes that glowed like sunlight in the dim room. It was all he could do not to gather her into his arms and kiss her right here in front of all her charges. As it was he simply nodded and said it was time he left her to her day.

"I hope to see you this evening though," he murmured as she walked with him to the stairs.

Jessica spun to face him. "This evening?" she queried, puzzled.

"At the Hereford's ball," Duncan replied with studied nonchalance.

"What...wait...how did you manage that?" unable to curb the startled tone in her voice, for Duncan was not a member of or known to the *ton*. She was secretly impressed not only had he an invitation to a Society ball, but also, he was going to attend.

"I am escorting Lady Winchester, in lieu of Giles," he clarified rather absently, leaving Jessica to ruminate over how many people conspired to make the invitation seem uncontrived. Making no comment however, she merely smiled her understanding and, throwing caution to the winds, Duncan bent and crushed her lips with his. "Don't forget I love you, Miss Drummond," he added and disappeared down the great staircase.

Jessica, trying to control the chaos in her head his kiss had elicited, watched him until he reached the bottom stair, whereupon he looked up and gave her a brief wave. She raised her hand, a small smile teasing at her mouth as she strolled back to the ward.

Once there, she was immediately immersed in making sure all the patients were settled after the storm, which still rumbled, although seemed to have moved down river. She tried to focus on the tasks at hand, so that everything else went out of her head until it was time to leave. She knew she should hurry home, but she was tired; drained after trying to assuage Patrick's distress. It was the first time she had witnessed such an acute reaction and now she thought back on it, it was unnerving, causing her to ponder whether Duncan was right in encouraging her to forget him? Then she remembered his most recent declaration, his smile and his kiss and his arms and everything else faded into insignificance. It didn't matter, even if he did have an episode like that, she wasn't frightened of him.

She trusted he would never hurt her, even when trapped in nightmares.

Jessica arrived home, thankful to discover Emily had drawn her a bath. She indulged in a long soak while Emily brushed her hair; the rhythmic strokes so soothing she almost fell asleep. Eventually she dried herself off and let the young maid assist her into the beautiful dress, a vision in dark bronze silk, the perfect complement to her eyes and creamy skin. Emily separated and plaited Jessica's locks before twisting them into a heavy chignon the elaborate weave of the plaits giving the style an exotic appearance — a few strands left loose to curl around her face. As she checked her appearance in the mirror she recalled the voice inside her head prompting her to make every effort for this particular evening and was very glad she'd listened.

Sliding her tired feet into matching leather slippers, Jessica found her mantle and she was ready.

Much later, Jessica was being danced off her feet at the ball, Lord Marchmont had been most attentive, but she managed to restrict him to two sets with a nice gap between each one. Currently she was dancing with a young man called Roger Ferrers — youngest son of Viscount Grantley, whom she had met a few weeks previously. An affable young man, neither had any romantic interest in the other, but a pleasant friendship had developed and it was rather nice to have at least one gentleman at these functions on whom you could rely, simply to chat or dance, with no ulterior motive.

While apparently engrossed in the complicated steps of the dance, Mr Ferrers was amusing Jessica with his cheeky comments about some of those attending.

"I hope you are not including me in your scandalous observations," she giggled, tapping his chest with her fan in feigned exasperation.

"Never, Miss Drummond," her assured, laughing at her expression, then he sobered, studying her for a moment, "but if you permit me, may I offer you a word of advice?" His tone was so serious, Jessica faltered almost tripping over her feet.

"Assuredly you may, Mr Ferrers. What is so important that we lose our place?" She grinned impishly as he looked around, realising they had somehow detached themselves from the set. He smiled sheepishly and drew her to one side.

"Lord Piers is a bit of a bounder. He likes to sweep young women off their feet, dazzle them with his attention and then drop them as soon as he's done with his flirtation. I do not wish you to be caught in his games."

Jessica turned to look at Piers who was dancing with the daughter of a duke. He seemed slightly bored, his smile not quite natural and she wondered whether he'd looked like that when dancing with her.

"Thank you, but you have no need to concern yourself, Mr Ferrers. I am not enamoured of Lord Marchmont, he is simply a pleasant companion with whom to attend this party."

Something in her voice made Roger glance down at her, Jessica was gazing off into space, her eyes unfocused and he realised she was seeing a completely different scene.

"Ahhh, say no more Miss Drummond, I think I understand." More astute than most young men of the ton, Roger Ferrers had two older sisters and he recognised Jessica's expression. Changing the subject, they chatted desultorily for a few moments, then Jessica heard footsteps behind her and a deep voice spoke close to her ear making her squeak with surprise.

Chapter Twelve

"Are you taken for this next set, Miss Drummond?"

"I…err…Mr Fer…should…maybe…" Jessica stammered.

Roger chuckled and pushed her forward. "Go, Miss Drummond. I do believe I am in dire need of a drink."

Jessica was swept into Duncan's arms and they began to glide across the ballroom.

"I am very gratified to hear young Lord Piers is merely a pleasant companion. Do I dare trust you are saving yourself for another?" His question hung between them as they drifted around the dance floor. Jessica bit her lip as she stared up at him.

"Perhaps" she allowed.

A glimmer of a smile crossed Duncan's face. "May I say how beautiful you look tonight, Miss Drummond? You fair take my breath away."

Jessica blushed at the compliment, and her heart hiccuped. Dear lord, how she loved him. He looked incredibly handsome this evening, dressed in beige trousers, a tailcoat of the darkest green hugging his broad shoulders. A cream waistcoat, white shirt, and cravat the same shade as his coat completed the outfit. His hair was as unruly as ever and Jessica itched to run her fingers through it.

"Would you be so kind as to join me for a ride in the park on Sunday?" he asked while they danced.

She nodded shyly. "Thank you, Mr Barrington, I should like that." They concentrated on the dance, but as the music faded, Duncan very casually, ushered her off the floor and into one of the shadowy alcoves surrounding the ballroom. "W-what are you doing? If we are caught…" She never finished her sentence.

Duncan gently backed her against the wall, his mouth claiming hers and she was lost. One arm held her close while his hand trailed over her throat and neck, followed by his lips,

100

teasing her soft skin. Jessica's breathing became irregular and it was all she could do not to cry out her longing under his expert touch.

"D-Duncan," she whispered frantically, when she managed to catch her breath, "P-please, not here."

He heard the panic in her voice and lifted his head. "Fine, Miss Drummond. Where do you suggest?" he growled, as she hung onto her sanity by a thread.

"I d-don't care, just not here." Realising what she was agreeing to, Jessica couldn't have stopped this madness had she wanted to, which she didn't, but she certainly did not want to be caught in so compromising a position at the home of a marquis. Duncan pulled away; straightening his jacket while Jessica smoothed her hair and seconds later they strolled along the halls looking perfectly innocent.

Jessica sought out both Mr Ferrers and Lord Piers, explaining a friend of the family would be escorting her home, thanking them for their attentions during the evening.

"Might you still accompany me to the museum as we discussed? Or will you be busy entertaining your family's friend?" Piers asked snarkily, scowling at Duncan, who grinned back, not in the slightest perturbed.

Jessica tapped the young man on his arm, "Behave, Lord Piers, petulance is unbecoming." She smiled sweetly at him and he had the grace to blush. "Of course I shall accompany you. I am very excited to see the exhibits and am looking forward to it immensely, but if you would rather take another..." she paused and glanced over at the stunningly beautiful lady he had been dancing with earlier. "... I would certainly understand." Piers followed her eyes and chuckled softly.

"She doesn't care for museums, says they are cold and boring. I too am looking forward to it."

Jessica inclined her head, and out of Pier's line of sight, dropped a slow wink at Roger, who turned his sudden bark of laughter into a cough. Agreeing on a time with Lord Piers, she and Duncan said their goodbyes.

"What of Lady Winchester?" worried Jessica, as they sought their hosts. "She will think you have stolen her coach."

"I will return for her ladyship after I have escorted you safely home. She is aware of my reason for being in town and seems more than happy to aid my cause."

Jessica was dumfounded, pondering once more the collusion amongst her enterprising family and friends, but had no time to question it further. After thanking their hosts and collecting Emily — who had been chatting with another maid in the retiring room — the couple stepped out into the cool night.

The Trevallier coach stood waiting and Duncan helped Jessica inside, Emily indicating she preferred to sit with Owen, the Trevallier's driver. Handing Emily a blanket, Duncan provided Owen with the Drummond's address, before climbing in and sitting opposite Jessica. As the coach rolled forward, Jessica noticed him watching her, an odd glint in his eyes.

"What?" she demanded.

"You would still visit the museum with him? After what just happened?" Duncan's sounded nettled.

"I cannot withdraw from an invitation, Duncan! It would be the height of rudeness. What sort of person do you think I am?" she retorted. "Last week, Lord Piers invited me to view the Greek exhibit and I agreed. What's the harm? I am not some naïve debutante, unable to see behind the glitter and the titles. You and Mr Ferrers can stop worrying, I know what his game is and I am not taken in. I will accompany Lord Piers to the museum, because politeness dictates I do." Irritation chilled her voice; annoyed she had to justify her actions. "Please do not presume just because you kissed me, you can tell me what to do, who to see and how to behave. I am no one's property." Her temper was bubbling and she made a determined effort to steady herself. Why did they always end up in an argument? She rubbed her hand over her forehead; already wearied from the long day, now she had to negotiate this emotional maze. All at once, everything was too hard and she bowed her head. "I can't keep fighting you," she whispered, frustrated at the useless tears pricking behind her eyelids.

Duncan stared at Jessica. Her face was etched with fatigue and sadness and, in the dim glow thrown by the carriage lantern he spied a hint of dampness beneath her closed eyes. His heart lurched, she was slipping away again.

"Jessica, I do not wish to rule you or dictate to you. Please accept my apologies for being so crass. 'Tis just the idea of you spending time with another man, one who can offer you far more than I, rends my soul. I know someone like Lord Piers would be a most suitable match and I know I should step aside and allow you to take that opportunity, but I find I am unable to let you go."

Jessica's head jerked up and as she met his gaze, gulped at the intensity in Duncan's eyes, feeling heat scorch through her.

"I-if you say s-so," she stuttered, amazed at his astounding ability to reduce her to a gibbering wreck.

"I do say so," he growled, reaching for her, whisking her into his arms and kissing her as though he would never stop. His hand roved over her slim body, the rustle of silk as sensuous as his kiss. After long moments when Jessica was quite certain the lightning storm had returned, he drew back, but did not let her go, cradling her against him, his cheek pillowed on her head.

"Jessica my darling, you drive me to distraction, I cannot think straight when you are near. My desire to make love to you right here in this carriage is only marginally outweighed by my desire to wait until we can make love for as long as we choose without worrying about who might come upon us, or your brother calling me out." Jessica chuckled, and snuggled against him, revelling in being wrapped in his arms. Never had she felt so safe. She felt his chest rise and fall with a deep breath, then a gentle hand cupped her chin, lifting her head so he could look into her eyes.

"We have known each other only a short while and though it was chance caused our paths to cross, I am eternally grateful they did. I know I am not perfect. I am much older than you and war scarred me, leaving me with a darkness I struggle to overcome. I am a simple carpenter who cannot offer you riches or estates or fine living, but I can offer you my heart and my soul. They are already yours; I think they have been since you presented me with a bedraggled puppy in the middle of a snowy field, terrified your skirmish with the briars had been in vain."

"I was starting to wonder whether you were trying to persuade or discourage me." Jessica murmured and, doing what she'd been wanting to do since they danced, ran her fingers through his hair, bringing his head down so she could kiss him. Twisting on his lap until they faced each other, she continued kissing him, her hands stroking across his muscular frame, feeling the heat from his skin through the fine material of his shirt. Duncan shuddered under the magic of her fingers; his heart rate tripled and he knew it would be easy to lose control.

He broke their kiss, sucking air into his lungs. "Not here, not yet," he croaked hoarsely, "Jessica, I am determined to do this right, to let the world see how much you mean to me. I know this isn't the best time and this carriage is absolutely the wrong place and I realise, after what I did to you, this is far too soon, but I find I cannot wait for either time or place to be perfect. Every day we are apart is a day wasted and I do not wish to squander a single moment more. I love you with every fibre of my being, might you consider putting me out of my misery and do me the honour of becoming my wife?"

Jessica, who had been peering at him in the dimness, got such a shock, she nearly fell off his knee. He grabbed her at the last minute and settled her back against him. She nuzzled his neck, her lips drifting to the curve of his ear, mulling over his declaration. Yes, she loved him, and yes she wanted to marry him, but what of her life here? What of her work with the soldiers? She would have to give it up to move to Oak Stanton. For the first time in her life she was irresolute.

"Before I answer, may I ask you something?" she implored.

"Of course," a little bewildered.

"First of all, I confess I love you too, more than life itself, but what of my work at St Bart's? Although I am only a volunteer, I believe I am helping those soldiers and to abandon them so soon seems callous. My job at Trentams is not a concern. Hugh will easily find someone to replace me; Helena knows many women as capable, if not more so, than I. Duncan, I cannot think of anything more wonderful than sharing my life with you, but how do we make it so both of us are happy? I do not expect you to give up your job at Whiteoaks, neither do I want to resign from the hospital...perhaps this is too hard..." she trailed off, desolation roiling through her, everything she ever wanted was here within her grasp and still she couldn't reach it.

The tears Jessica had managed to hold at bay began trickling down her cheeks and, blinking to keep them back, she moved to get off Duncan's knee, to put a distance between them. Duncan was having none of it and pulled her close, kissing her forehead and stroking his hand over her back.

"We will make it work my love," he murmured. "We may not have the most conventional of marriages, but I cannot let you go, not again. I know I have just proposed, but I still wish to do this properly, so even if you say yes, I don't mind if you prefer not to announce it immediately, although I would be very pleased if we could tell your family sometime soon. While I am here, let us enjoy getting to know each other without the pressures I believe are associated with wedding preparations. I cannot stay in the city too long I have obligations to fulfil, but I will come back as often as my calendar allows. Between us, I am sure we will be able to work something out, something, which suits us both, even if that means there may be occasions when we are apart. It is our life, our marriage and our decision. What do you think?"

She hiccuped, swallowing the sobs that had risen in her throat at the thought of having him walk out of her life a second time and tried to smile. Her lips trembled and her breathing was a bit shaky but it was a smile all the same.

"Yes."

At that, Duncan tightened his embrace and kissed away her tears before recapturing her lips in the most passionately satisfying kiss yet, and Jessica didn't think he could possibly better his previous attempts.

Moments later the carriage rolled to a halt outside the Drummond residence.

"I don't want to say goodnight," Jessica said, absently fingering Duncan's cravat.

"Neither do I, but we can meet on the morrow. As I am not in the city for many more days, please allow me the privilege of spending them with you."

She nodded shyly, then had a sudden thought.

"Oh, what about the museum?"

"Attend with Lord Piers. I will happen upon you during the afternoon and we shall see whether he can be persuaded to cede his suit." Duncan grinned, kissing her nose. Hopping out of the coach, he helped Jessica down, squeezing her hand as he bowed over it before kissing her palm. "Until tomorrow, my love." He murmured.

Jessica dropped a neat curtsy. "I am counting the hours." She ran up the steps to the front door, opened by Mr Rogers as she reached the top. She turned and smiled, the wonderfully spontaneous smile that seemed just for him and Duncan contemplated whether the moon had exploded, for night seemed to become day. He grinned back and watched her disappear into the lighted hallway. The door closed and she was gone. Climbing back into the coach, he sat back and let the rocking of the vehicle lull his chaotic thoughts. It would be complicated, but they would come up with a plan. The most important thing was that she had said yes — hopefully the rest would fall into place.

Chapter Thirteen

The next afternoon, while strolling through the cool hallways of the museum, Jessica was trying to work out why Piers had invited her in the first place. For the most part, he had been sullen and, when she did manage to drag a comment from him, he was peevish in his responses. She was flummoxed; the Elgin Collection was an extraordinary display and Jessica always found the other exhibits splendid, so she was at a loss to understand her companion's behaviour.

It wasn't Jessica's first visit to the museum; it was somewhere she would occasionally while away an afternoon, but she hadn't yet seen the Parthenon marbles even though they had been on display for over a year. According to the literature, Lord Elgin had stored the marbles at his own home, allowing invited guests to view them, until he was forced to sell them to the British government for less than half of what he paid to procure them. Subsequently they were transferred to the British museum and this special exhibition had been created. Jessica was entranced and had spent nearly two hours reading every piece of information about how they had been collected and transported, where each piece had been in relation to other pieces and from what part of the Parthenon they had been acquired. She was also fascinated by the impact these sculptures had already made on current ideas about art, style and fashion.

Jessica wasn't entirely convinced their removal was in the best interest of the Greek people but, as they were under the rule of the Ottomans, she supposed they didn't have much say in the matter. She was about to comment on this to Piers when she noticed his lowering expression.

"Lord Piers, what is wrong today? You seem in high dudgeon. If you did not wish to come here, why did you bother asking me?"

"I did not expect you to be so interested in a few damn carvings. I hoped we might breeze through the museum and then chance a walk along the riverside. That maybe I would have you to myself for a while."

Jessica pinned him with an exasperated gaze. "Are you telling me this was a ruse to get me alone?"

Piers flushed, "Well it was rather."

"Why?" Jessica was curious more than annoyed. He shifted uncomfortably, yanking at his cravat. "Lord Piers?"

"I was wondering whether you might be willing to…errr…that is…possibly…you would let me…umm…kiss you." The last few words tumbled out so fast Jessica had to run them through her head twice before she understood what he was gabbling about. Instead of being upset, the sheer audacity of the man caused her to burst out laughing, drawing outraged frowns from the throng of museum goers wandering the quiet halls. She covered her mouth with her hand, rocking with mirth.

"Oh, my Lord, you are too funny. You don't really want to kiss me and you have no desire to take this flirtation any further. I thought we were simply enjoying each other's company until your next conquest came along, in fact I presumed you were using me as a way to attract them."

Now it was Piers' turn to gawk. "How on earth did you work that out?"

"Lord Piers, I am not of the *ton*. I have no title and, although my family's company is wealthy, I am not in line to inherit. I am of no use to you in your quest for a wife, other than as a method of attracting those whom you do think suitable. A handsome man who has a dalliance with an unknown female is a sure way to set the rumour mill grinding. In an instant, you become most intriguing to all those mamas looking to marry off their daughters and *voila*, your platter is full of delightful young ladies."

He stared at her open mouthed. "I do beg your pardon Miss Drummond, it was never my intent to hurt you and I really would like to steal a kiss." He added cheekily.

"Of course, you didn't, you silly man and I am not hurt, not even a little bit. I have enjoyed our acquaintance," amusement still warming her tones, "Now, if you turn slightly to your left, there is a young lady trying not to look as though she's watching you. No, don't make it obvious," as Piers pivoted on his heel. "I think it might be Lady Esther, Lord Hereford's daughter, with whom I recall you danced twice last evening. You must agree, she is quite astonishingly beautiful and I believe just turned nineteen, the perfect age." She grinned at Piers, whose dazzled expression confirmed just how taken he was with Lady Esther. Jessica tapped him on the chest with her finger, "Go, talk to her but remember, my Lord, do not toy with her emotions. To do so needlessly, ill becomes you. And just to help you along..." she leaned close and grazed his cheek with her lips. "Now off with you and be a gentleman." Piers stared at Jessica, maybe realising that he was about to lose a jewel far more valuable than all the diamonds of the *ton* put together, but too late, she was walking away.

Jessica strolled casually across the room, glancing over her shoulder to see Piers approach Lady Esther. A smile lit the young lady's face and, somehow, Jessica knew they would be fine. As she turned back she walked straight into a tall, solid object. Mortified, she thought she must have blundered into one of the sculptures, but as she backed off, to her relief and embarrassment, she heard a low chuckle.

"That was prudently handled, my love," a voice muttered in her ear, sparking shivers down her spine. Trying to keep her dignity intact, she stepped away and continued along the corridor to the next room. He caught her easily; silently offering her his arm, which she accepted and he relished the way her fingers curled around his sleeve. They meandered through the exhibition halls, chatting quietly about what was on display before eventually coming out into the waning afternoon.

"Would you...that is if you're not..." *Goodness*, groaned Jessica to herself, *I cannot do this courting thing.* "Let me try again. Would you be interested in joining me for dinner this evening? There may be several members of my family there, but I cannot see another way of us being able to share a meal." She paused, "Oh, unless that is not appropriate."

Duncan grinned at her. "That would be most agreeable, but if you would like to spend an evening just the two of us, the Trevallier residence is empty. Lady Winchester has left today for Whiteoaks to be with Billie; the babe is due any day." His brow creased. "Unless I am the one behaving improperly," he ruminated.

Jessica giggled. "We are quite the pair aren't we...?" her tones full of mirth, "...and, while I do believe an evening at Winchester House would be quite delightful, I suspect we should bow to propriety and eat at my home. Mama might take on if she thinks I'm breaking the rules." Duncan smiled in agreement and, after seeking out Emily who was waiting patiently near the entrance, found a hackney directing it to Drummond House where they were set down less than twenty minutes later.

A very excited Trixie greeted them at the door, fawning all over Duncan, as Jessica advised Mr Rogers there would be one extra for dinner that evening. Relieving both of their outerwear, Mr Rogers confirmed Mrs Drummond was in the parlour and there were no other callers.

"Come on," Jessica urged. "Let's get this over with. I must warn you, Mama will doubtless interrogate you in a manner reminiscent of a government operative investigating a foreign agent. Allow her this pleasure, I am her only daughter." Her puckish expression, making Duncan chuckle.

"I will do my best to answer her questions with the loquaciousness of a spy about to spill all his secrets," he assured her, as Jessica pushed open the door into the parlour. To her surprise, Helena was there also; she and Hugh had taken to spending their Saturdays looking at possible townhouses and thus were rarely home during the afternoon. Helena beamed when she saw Duncan.

"Good afternoon, Duncan, how lovely to see you. I hope you are enjoying your time in the city?" she welcomed him. "May I present Mrs Drummond, Jessica's mother? Mama, do you remember Mr Barrington from Whiteoaks? He is the gentleman who, with Mr Montgomery, went to look for Jessica the morning she found Trixie."

Mrs Drummond, trying not to appear surprised at this unexpected guest, pinned Duncan with an inscrutable stare, recalling he was a close friend of Giles and she had seen him with Jessica once or twice during their last few days at Whiteoaks.

Duncan bowed over her hand, "It is a pleasure to see you again, Mrs Drummond," he smiled winningly and Dorothea Drummond felt herself relax under his courteous gaze.

"What brings you to London, Mr Barrington?" she enquired, nodding for him to sit in one of the comfortable wingback chairs fanned out around the roaring fire. Duncan made himself comfortable and explained his business in the capital. That Giles entrusted this man with estate matters impressed Mrs Drummond and the two soon fell into animated conversation regarding the attractions of London in the winter versus those of the country. Out of their eye line, Helena raised an eyebrow at Jessica, who grinned and shook her head indicating, without words, she would tell her sister-in-law everything later.

The evening passed quickly, the whole family warming to Duncan, their lively and inclusive chatter making him feel as though he had known them for years and it was with reluctance he took his leave as midnight approached.

Jessica walked him to the door, "Will I see you tomorrow?" she whispered as they paused on the threshold.

"Of course, what time would be suitable? Might I be so bold as to invite you to accompany me for that carriage ride I mentioned yesterday and, weather permitting, a short walk, following which, perhaps luncheon?" maintaining an air of cool politeness, aware that Mr Rogers hovered.

"What a lovely idea, Mr Barrington, that sounds most agreeable. I am looking forward to it already." She pondered a moment, stretching out their farewell. "If you were to call around 11, I will make sure I am ready." She smiled up at him and Duncan felt his heart thud, her eyes in the candlelight glowing like fine brandy. He bowed over her hand; squeezing her fingers for slightly longer than necessary, before dropping a light kiss on her palm.

"Until tomorrow," his voice dropped to a murmur, "my love." And he was gone, disappearing into the night. Jessica remained motionless, a pensiveness settling over her. By tacit consent neither had mentioned their plans to marry during the evening. Jessica deemed it too soon to spring the news on her mother and, more than that, she relished the secrecy. It was delicious this knowing, and although part of her wanted to shout their commitment to the four winds, to keep it between them for a little longer gave her a wicked thrill.

As Jessica drifted into the library, four pairs of eyes bore into her. She said nothing, merely smiled serenely at them. The others looked at each other and then back to Jessica; finally, Hugh spoke.

"Is there something you feel you would like to share with us Jessica?" he asked, his normally grave face alight with mischief.

Jessica glared at her brother, aware he knew more than he was letting on. "There is nothing to share. Mr Barrington is...errr...a...mmm...a friend." She couldn't come up with another description; acquaintance seemed too remote and anything else would give her away. "He was kind to me at Whiteoaks and thought to pay his respects while in the city. He has invited me to join him tomorrow and I have accepted, that is all," willing her family to let it go. Helena, sensitive to the delicacy of the situation adroitly change the topic of conversation and soon Duncan was all but forgotten.

Promptly at 11, for to delay was to waste precious time with Jessica, Duncan presented himself at the Drummond residence. Mr Rogers showed him into the parlour and shortly thereafter he heard the trip of footsteps and Jessica whirled into the room, dressed in a becoming gown, the shade of which seemed something between green and gold. Managing not to fling herself into his arms just in time, she slid to a rather precipitous halt right in front of him.

"Mr Barrington, how marvellous and we are lucky," Duncan raised a quizzical brow as she continued, "the sun shines as though spring was already here." Jessica's face shone with excitement. As Hugh was otherwise engaged, Helena had offered to act as chaperone and she appeared in the doorway, greeting Duncan in her usual friendly manner.

"Come on then you two, let us enjoy this break in the weather while we have the opportunity, it will close in again soon enough." She corralled the couple in front of her rather like a mother hen, to Duncan's amusement. Jessica paused to drag on her winter cloak, following the others down the steps to where the Winchester carriage awaited. Its top was down, but the two women assured Duncan it was fine, they were looking forward to some fresh air. He assisted both ladies up the steps and, while they tucked a large rug over their knees, climbed in to sit opposite them as the driver clicked the reins and the carriage lurched forward.

Morning was generally not the time to indulge in carriage rides, so the parks would be reasonably quiet, but a chaperone did not allow for much privacy. Unbeknownst to the pair, however, Helena had sent a missive to her friend Tabitha, suggesting they meet in the park, the wording of the note indicating to Tabitha that Helena had an ulterior motive. Thus, maybe twenty minutes later as they rolled to halt, Helena wasn't surprised to see her best friend riding towards them on Blaze, her favourite mare.

"Goodness, it's Tabitha! How fortuitous, I haven't seen her for a sennight." Helena waved enthusiastically at her friend who wheeled her mount around to trot alongside.

"Helena, what are you doing here? I thought you were visiting houses today with Hugh." Tabitha cried in apparent astonishment at Helena's presence.

Helena shook her head. "He and Nick have something to attend to at the yard, he will be home by luncheon. We have two houses to view this afternoon."

Tabitha was amused by her friend's insistence on inspecting prospective houses herself, most would send their man of business. Not so Helena, she was determined to have her say in her marital home, she and Hugh delighting in exploring all available residences. Tabitha dismounted and looped the reins through the handle on the side of the driver's footrest.

"Good morning, Owen," she beamed. "Please would you keep an eye on Blaze?"

Owen grinned his agreement, assisting Tabitha into the carriage, whereupon she shooed Jessica and Duncan out of their seats.

"Go on you two, take yourselves off for a stroll and let Helena and I have a proper gossip." She urged. Jessica was about to refuse when she caught her sister-in-law's eye. Jessica was astonished, was she being encouraged to spend time alone with Duncan? Was it possible? She stared at Helena who inclined her head very slightly and turned to Tabitha, the two ladies immediately catching up on their lives, completely ignoring the couple now standing rather awkwardly on the path.

Jessica glanced at Duncan, who was watching her a slight smile curving his lips. "Well, I did not expect that," she admitted, blushing a little as she walked over to where he waited.

"Lady Helena was always the least predictable of the Trevalliers," he revealed as she joined him, tucking her arm under his. "She got away with more too." He started laughing and went on to describe some of Helena's more madcap exploits, reducing Jessica to helpless laughter, but in no way surprising her. After what had happened the previous year, nothing anyone told her about Helena would surprise her. This led to stories about their respective childhoods and they were interested to discover they were not dissimilar. Both came from loving families who sought to offer them every opportunity. The only difference was Duncan had grown up in the country and Jessica in the city.

Engrossed in conversation, neither realised they had walked a fair distance and the carriage was no longer in sight. They were quite alone.

Chapter Fourteen

Following the path towards the lake, they came to a weeping willow, the weak sunlight through its trailing branches scattering convoluted patterns over the last vestiges of snow. Jessica paused, entranced by the shadows, watching them dance in the breeze. It was so peaceful. Without thinking, she leaned against Duncan sensing, rather than hearing, his breath catch.

"Oh, I beg your pardon," she fumbled, "that was…rather I…what I mean is…I shouldn't…" Jessica clammed up, hearing her garbled words. She started to pull away but Duncan, chuckling quietly, slipped his arm around her shoulders and let his fingers stroke over her cloak, the gesture causing all manner of interesting sensations to ripple along her body.

"Please don't move, Jessica, 'tis a wonderful feeling having you so close." His voice was warm and after a few moments, he turned to face her, his hand curving round the back of her head. Jessica felt her heart rate quicken and she knew he was going to kiss her. Even though there was no one in the vicinity, there was still a risk — one she found didn't worry her in the slightest. She held his gaze, willing him to not to pull away, to decide that discretion was the better part of valour. *Quite frankly*, she thought to herself, *discretion is highly overrated.*

Duncan's chuckle blossomed into outright mirth and she stared at him in confusion. "So, discretion is overrated is it?"

Jessica, startled from her reverie, gasped, "I said that out loud?" mortified he heard her. Duncan nodded, his eyes crinkling in amusement and he bent closer brushing his lips over hers, silencing her excuses. A tremor ran through her and she moved further into his embrace, clutching the lapels of his coat and fitting herself to his burly frame. He lifted his head and stared into her eyes, his own darkening to cobalt.

Jessica snuggled closer. "Don't stop now," she entreated, chaste tones at odds with her words, as she entangled gloved fingers through his tousled hair. "That was fine as an entrée, but I'd like to taste the main course." Aware her words were nothing short of shameless, but right at that moment, the need to feel his lips on hers was more important than all the rules in the world put together.

A laugh rumbled through Duncan's chest, as he obliged with intoxicating tenderness, making Jessica moan, desire pulsing through her. His kiss deepened as time seemed suspended, and when he eventually lifted his head, both were breathing hard.

"Jessica, my love, you will be the finish of me," Duncan choked out, rubbing his thumb over her bottom lip, before stealing another kiss. "I cannot get enough of you. Was our decision to wait misguided? Perhaps we should reconsider?" Jessica angled her head so she could see him properly, studying his face. He would be returning to Whiteoaks soon and to be apart from him would be harder than she could ever have imagined. It had been bad enough when she believed their burgeoning romance thwarted — then, she had been able to harden her heart and push all thoughts of him aside, now, it would be a hundred times worse. Yet, still something held her back.

"Duncan, while that does sound most enticing, I find myself hesitating." Duncan began to interrupt but she raised her hand placatingly. "Now, before you take on, 'tis not that I do not want to marry you, I do more than anything, but I don't want to rush. You are the first man who has cared enough to offer for me and I would like to savour our betrothal." She paused, then mused thoughtfully, "I am hoping it will be the only one I have."

Intent on trying to express herself clearly, Jessica didn't notice the twitch of Duncan's lips or the slight relaxing of his stance, at this aside. "To do all the things you mentioned; long walks, visiting art galleries or museums, reading by the fire in the library, talking like we have done this morning and yes, plenty of kissing, I do like that part," artlessly added.

Her hand smoothed over his cheek and along his jaw, while she collected her thoughts. "We should allow ourselves the pleasure of simply spending time together, courting. Yes, we might love each other but do we *like* each other? I do not think we have known each other long enough to be sure. If we are going to be married, 'tis for the rest of our lives and, as such, we must also be friends. I cannot countenance a life bound to a man who wants to bed me, yet has no desire to share the minutiae of his day — what he was working on, who he met with, his worries and his joys."

Jessica realised her words were a strange mix of bold and diffident, but there was no other way she could think of to get her point across. She rubbed her forehead distractedly, worrying he wouldn't understand, that he thought she was pushing him away.

"I know what we already have is special and I believe it will grow into something extraordinary, but I don't want passion, wonderful though it is, to cloud our senses. If we rush into marriage we have missed out on the journey and I think we will both discover the journey is as momentous as the destination."

She stopped abruptly, chewing on her lip, trembling a little from the wave of emotions washing over her. In reality, all she wanted was for Duncan to sweep her off her feet and carry her away, far away where it was just the two of them and they could forget the rest of the world. However, even though not a member of the elite, Jessica was still bound by many of the same rules, constraints and conventions. It was exhausting and, for once, she wished to flout every last one of them. Until her dream became a possibility, the couple were expected to honour those strictures and Jessica believed her argument gave them the best of both worlds. There was also some truth to her words.

Perhaps because of his own struggles, surprisingly, Duncan empathised with Jessica's remarks rather better than she anticipated. There was no doubt he wanted to marry her as quickly as humanly possible, allowing their ardour to follow its natural course, but he was astute enough to realise that in agreeing to this courtship, Jessica would know how much he honoured her worth and respected her wishes. Yes, of course they could learn about each other once wed, but Jessica *did* deserve to be courted, to experience the pleasure of being escorted to all manner of occasions by a man who wants nothing more than to relish her delight in them. To steal a kiss or grasp a hand when they believed no one was looking; to leave each other breathless and wanting more, revelling in the knowledge the moment their desire could be quenched drew tantalisingly closer.

"D-Duncan?" Jessica stammered, after he had been quiet for several minutes ruminating over her words. "Talk to me, don't shut me out, please."

Duncan gazed at her, her anxious expression making his chest constrict. "Sorry, love, I'm not shutting you out. I was just mulling over what you said and I agree. I want us to go on this journey together, let us see where our path leads for if your kisses are anything to go by, the destination will be well worth the wait." Jessica blushed bright red at his not so subtle implication and buried her head in his chest. Laughing, Duncan lifted her chin and dropped a kiss on her cold nose. "Now, I do not wish to bring Lady Helena's wrath down on my head for keeping you, so let us make our way back to the carriage and along the way, make some plans."

"Are you sure? You honestly don't mind us waiting a little longer?"

Duncan shook his head. "I honestly don't mind. Funnily enough, I am beginning to like the sound of it. I can think of so many things with which to tempt you." A wicked grin curving his lips.

Jessica smiled back, her heart in her eyes and the happiness shining from her face was so bright, Duncan would not have been in the slightest surprised had meadows of spring flowers popped into existence right in front of them. One last hug and they strolled slowly towards where the carriage was parked. Helena and Tabitha were still deep in conversation and barely noticed the arrival of the two who had been gone for well over an hour. While they waited for the women to conclude their conversation, Jessica and Duncan availed themselves of a nearby bench, chattering about what they might do in the few days before Duncan had to leave the city. They came up with several interesting ideas and, just as they had chosen what to do the following day, Helena acknowledged them.

Goodbyes were made and Tabitha rode off, Blaze kicking up showers of snow, as Helena directed Owen to her old home, where Jessica and Duncan were expected for lunch. As plenty of staff remained at the Winchester House, despite their mistress being at Whiteoaks, Helena considered it unnecessary to continue as chaperone, but did feel moved to comment they should be aware she was trusting them to act decorously.

"I will use this coach for our viewings this afternoon. Hugh and I will collect you later."

Jessica smiled gratefully. "Thank you, Helena. I...we...are grateful for your thoughtfulness."

Helena grinned and nodded to Owen, the carriage rumbling towards the Drummond residence, not too far away.

Jessica and Duncan took full advantage of their snatched hours of relative privacy and, if by chance, they indulged more in kissing than talking, neither was complaining.

The next few days flew by and, before long, it was time for Duncan to return to Oak Stanton. Even though he was leaving for home, Jessica remained determined to keep Duncan's proposal a secret for a little longer; despite it being obvious to any who saw them together this courtship was no frivolous flirtation. The night before Duncan was due to depart the couple found themselves alone in the library at the Drummond's home. How Helena had orchestrated this, Jessica had no clue but she was eternally grateful.

"I know I will be busy when you're gone, but I will miss you so much." She murmured as Duncan held her close, kissing her nose, her cheeks and the tips of her ears.

"And I you. I will try to visit again in a month or so, and promise to write as often as time allows." Duncan assured her.

As they stood together, Jessica remembered something and fished about in her pocket. "I know 'tis rather girlish, but I would like you to have this," she said, handing him a small yet heavy object wrapped in a delicately embroidered handkerchief. Puzzled, Duncan peeled the material away to reveal a small pocket watch. Its design was quite plain but as he turned it over he noticed there was little clasp on the back. He opened it carefully to find a small lock of hair secreted within. He raised his eyes to Jessica who was watching him a little warily, uncertain whether he would think her moonstruck for offering him such a trinket.

"Jessica?" Astonished at her gift, Duncan was almost overwhelmed by the depth of emotion receiving it engendered. Fob watches were not inexpensive, and the significance of being given so personal an heirloom was not lost on him. It could not have been easy for her to part with it.

"It was my father's. Hugh gave it to me a year or so ago, apparently at Papa's request. My brothers each have their own, and I think Papa wanted me to have something, which had been important to him. He loved it and used to keep a lock of Mama's hair in it; perhaps it warmed him to have even so small a piece of her with him while he was away at sea. I thought perhaps, as we are going to be apart, you might like...that is...a piece...I wasn't sure...errr..." Jessica ground to an uncomfortable halt, twiddling with the fringe on her shawl, which for some unknown reason lay over the back of the chair. Was she being presumptuous to think Duncan might want a lock of her hair in an old pocket watch? It seemed so romantic when she came up with the idea.

"My love, this is the most thoughtful gift anyone has given me." Duncan said, drawing her against him, moulding her to his large body, kissing her as though they had a lifetime not a few moments. Jessica responded, the now familiar heat coiling through her, licking along her veins. She kissed him back with everything in her, knowing this was the last time she would feel his lips on hers for many weeks.

As they lost themselves in each other, Duncan let his hand trace her shape, as though he needed to memorise her. He teased up her back, over her shoulder and along her neck, coming to rest for a moment in the hollow at the base of her throat. Underneath his fingers, he could feel Jessica's pulse fluttering wildly, at the same time as he became aware of her hands searching under his waistcoat, then under his shirt, stroking over his warm skin tracing his muscles, sending his heart rate through the ceiling and sparking a blaze within him, hotter than the flames crackling in the huge grate.

Eventually Duncan broke their embrace, it would be easy to forget where they were, aware of the possibility that any of the Drummond family might decide to check on the two in the library.

"Jessica, I must go, otherwise I will never leave," he took a breath, his reason for this visit never far from his mind. "Thank you for your generosity of spirit when I did not deserve it, thank you for your unselfish heart and your loving soul, thank you for welcoming me back into your life when 'twas I who slammed the door. As you walked away, I felt as though my world had been ripped apart; you never left my thoughts and your beautiful face haunted my every move. The greatest mistake of my life was letting you go and, even though you had every right to spurn me, I had to try; I had to find out whether you would forgive me. Jessica Drummond, I love you more than words can say and I am already counting the days until we can meet again."

Jessica stared at him, the warmth in his blue eyes, mesmerised her, holding her captive. She knew she needed to set him straight. Of all the things they had discussed, their unceremonious parting at Whiteoaks had not been addressed in a satisfactory manner. She opened her mouth, closed and opened it again, knowing she must look like a fish, left behind by the tide, lips flapping for air.

Swallowing hard, Jessica made a determined effort to reply. "Duncan, when you insisted we could not be together, that you had nothing to offer me, I recall informing you your sentiments were ridiculous. Nothing since has changed my opinion. Yes, your behaviour was deplorable; your assumption I am incapable of understanding your trauma, that I am some feeble flower who would crumple in the face of adversity, hurt me deeply and says little for your judgement. Moreover, I do not believe you would ever harm me, even in the throes of trauma and the reason for my volunteering at St Bart's was, is, to learn how to recognise and help overcome what troubles you." Not wanting to upset him, she hurried on as Duncan's expression changed, indicating he feared where she was heading. "That said, I *never* lost the belief we share something so special it was worth fighting for and all you needed was for me to disabuse you of your addlebrained notions. Duncan, you have my heart; you had it then, you have it still, it will always be yours. Until we are one, guard it well."

Jessica reached up on tiptoe and kissed him gently, taking his hand and entwining their fingers together. Her voice dropped to a whisper.

"Travel safe, my love. I cannot bring myself to say goodbye so, until we meet again..." she couldn't continue, and squeezing his fingers one last time, fled the room before the tears pricking under her eyelids began to fall. Passing Helena in the hall, Jessica muttered something about Duncan leaving and was upstairs and in her bedchamber before the young woman could fathom her sister-in-law's garbled words.

Duncan came out of the library, his expression pensive. Glancing up he saw Helena, "It is time I took my leave, Lady Helena. Thank you for your hospitality, after all that has transpired, it has been a blessing I did not expect. Please thank the Drummond family for welcoming me into their home. I hope to see you again soon."

Helena acknowledged his thanks, walking with him to the front door, as Mr Rogers appeared with Duncan's coat. The air was chill and Duncan hoped any snow would hold off, travel at this time of year being arduous enough. Bowing over Helena's hand he turned and headed down the steps to where the Winchester carriage waited, his plea coming back to her on the still air —

"Look after her." And he was gone.

Helena watched as the carriage rumbled away, then climbed the stairs to Jessica's room. About to knock, she hesitated as she heard the sound of muffled sobs and decided to leave the girl alone. Time enough on the morrow.

She entered her own bedchamber, finding Hugh sitting by the fire. He smiled and stood to help her out of her gown

"Barrington gone?" he queried, kissing her shoulders as the silky material slithered down her arms.

"Yes. Jessica will need our compassion over the next few days 'til she adjusts to Duncan's absence. She will miss him more than she will ever admit. We must make sure she doesn't overdo things at either of her jobs as a way of compensating."

Hugh nodded, distracted by his wife's ivory skin, his fingers seducing her.

"Might we discuss it tomorrow, my love," he groaned. Helena chuckled and twisted in his embrace giving into his insistent lips as their ever-simmering passion pushed other cares aside.

The house darkened and soon all were asleep.

Not far away, in another bedchamber, Duncan Barrington finished packing his meagre luggage and sat on the bed contemplating Jessica's words. Turning the fob watch over and over in his hand, he could not help but open the clasp and touch the ringlet of hair. Aware he was behaving like a lovesick calf, he carefully removed the curly tress and pressed it to his lips.

"Until we meet again my love." He murmured, echoing Jessica's farewell, before tucking the strand safely back and closing the clasp. Sleep was a long time coming, but towards dawn he fell into a fitful slumber, dreaming of a beautiful young woman whose breathtaking smile completed his world.

Chapter Fifteen

The days after Duncan left would have been miserable if not for a life so busy there was no time for Jessica to mope. She threw herself into both of her jobs, helping Hugh in whatever capacity he needed, then disappeared into the rarefied atmosphere of St Bart's for her allocated two days. Recently discovering some of the veterans had no family to visit them over the weekend, Jessica took it upon herself to pop in for couple of hours on either day if she was free. She was careful not to overdo it, but it was better to be at St Bart's than sitting by herself at home where she was likely to dwell on the fact that the man she loved was miles away. Jessica also made sure she spent time with Meredith and Clare too, the three young women delighting in cosy afternoons by the fire sipping tea and gossiping about all manner of interesting things.

As February blew into March, they received the glad news that Billie Trevallier had given birth to a son, and both mother and child were doing well. The christening was to be held at Whiteoaks at the end of the month; a celebration Helena and Hugh planned to attend, an intuitive Billie including Jessica in the invitation. To that end, Jessica had written to Duncan advising him of the possibility. It was something to look forward to and would save Duncan a journey to the city.

So, all in all, life was pleasant if Jessica was able to ignore the constant tug on her heartstrings. She was learning more and more at the hospital and had broached the subject of capturing the stories of those soldiers willing to share their experiences. Dr Napier was amenable simply saying it was up to her to organise everything, the rest of his staff did not have time to assist. Jessica was excited at the prospect, believing the untold stories of these men important, not only as a record of how individuals were scarred by their time in battle, but also as a way of bringing their plight to the attention of society at large, as war, once over is quickly forgotten by those untouched.

Thus, over the course of several visits, after completing her regular chores, Jessica, talked with all the veterans, explaining what she hoped to do and asking whether they would be prepared to make public their stories. Some still refused to speak at all, others found the memories too painful but there was a solid core of men who considered her idea worthy of their attention and she began to compile detailed notes about the reality of war.

Major Vaughan was one such soldier who, although sceptical at first — accusing Jessica of trying to exploit them — soon realised the serious nature of her endeavours, and it was he who persuaded many of those who were hesitant, to share as much as they felt able. Some were reluctant to have their families brought to the attention of a judgemental public simply by association, but Jessica assured any who preferred not to be named, that their identities would remain undisclosed.

She thoroughly enjoyed it. Even though the men's stories were harrowing in the extreme, she was gratified they trusted her. In the short time she had been working at St Bart's, Jessica had come to care for them all, even those whose only communication with her had been a blank stare. Now, her evenings were spent writing up her notes and soon a large pile of papers, covered with neat handwriting, began to form on her escritoire.

One afternoon, while tidying up the reading area, Jessica was approached by one of the more taciturn soldiers. A lieutenant by the name of Toby Langdon, who while physically uninjured, suffered a mental anguish no amount of treatment seemed able to alleviate. According to Dr Napier, no one had any idea what he had witnessed but it was catastrophic enough that he rarely spoke. Lieutenant Langdon simply sat on his bed or in one of the chairs by the fire, his gaze turned inward, presumably reliving the trauma that refused to relinquish its grip.

Occasionally, he would be prostrated by a bout of raging temper, which came out of the blue, but so far none had been able to detect its trigger. One of Dr Napier's colleagues had been working with the veteran for a couple of years and they believed a breakthrough was close but were aware, once revealed, the truth could cause greater problems.

Jessica often sat with those who still struggled to communicate, chatting away about her work at Trentams, or what Trixie had been up to, or the latest Society scandal, if for no other reason than they came to trust her presence. She was therefore, gratified when the lieutenant asked whether she might spare him a moment.

"Of course, Lieutenant, what is it you require?" Jessica smiled at the veteran, her expression one of gentle encouragement.

"I wondered whether you might be interested in my story," he replied, diffidently.

"Why, Lieutenant Langdon, I can think of no one else's story I would rather listen to," she said warmly, secretly delighted he felt comfortable raising the topic. Would you like to start now, or wait until I come again on Friday?"

"May we start now?"

Jessica nodded. "Of course, let me find my papers." She shot off to the other end of the room, where her work was tucked tidily away in a nook near the door, grabbing a few blank sheets, a quill and a pot of ink, hurrying back to the table. The veteran had taken a seat and was leaning on his elbows, his rigid posture and the slight flush to his cheeks the only indications he wasn't entirely relaxed.

"Now, all I want you to do is talk. I don't want you to try to explain any of it, just tell me what you recall and if at any time it becomes too hard, we can stop. If, in the future, you decide you would rather I didn't include it, I promise I will take it out. Does that seem fair?"

Toby smiled, just a little. It wasn't much, but as this was the first time Jessica had seen anything more than the faintest flicker of emotion, she was satisfied with his response.

Jessica settled herself so she was facing the lieutenant while she wrote, this way Toby would see what she was doing. She found this beneficial; to catch the expressions of those who were speaking made their discourse more than just words, she could record their emotions too. Moreover, she found her subjects felt less uneasy about the process when they could see what she was writing. Toby began to talk, at first his recollections were disjointed and most did not relate to any battles, more they pertained to where he was billeted, the food he had eaten and the people he had met.

Lieutenant Langdon had been injured during the Battle of Toulouse, one of the last engagements of the war and a battle, had communications been more expeditious, that should never have been fought, for Napoleon had already abdicated — the first of two. Even though the event occurred nearly five years previously, as Toby talked, it was obvious, that to him it was still happening. He described the offensive in the present tense and in such detail, Jessica could smell the fear and the gunpowder and the blood. It was all she could do not to stop him, her interest in recording his agony only marginally outweighing her horror.

Halfway through explaining how his regiment, the 18th Hussars, had seized the bridge at Croix d'Orade he came to an abrupt halt.

"Lieutenant..." Jessica prompted. "...Toby, do you want to stop for today?" he didn't respond, his mind far away. Wanting to reassure him he was safe, Jessica started talking about anything but the war, trying to bring him back to the airy room, where two people were sitting at a table near a cosy fire. Blinking rapidly, he stared and reached towards her.

"Jessamine, sing to me," quietly pleading.

Startled Jessica took the soldier's hand. "Toby, 'tis Jessica. Who is Jessamine?"

Toby shook his head as though trying to clear it and slowly his eyes re-focussed on his current surroundings. He snatched his hand away and wariness replaced entreaty.

"Never mind, 'tis of no matter," his tones brooked no further questions. "Tomorrow, we can talk again, tomorrow."

He shoved back his chair, stalked along the room and out through the door which slammed behind him. Jessica watched him go, perplexed, but not unduly surprised. She had seen similar reactions with some of the other men. To re-live their worst nightmares could not be easy and she knew they needed time to regain their equanimity. She just hoped Toby would be willing to finish his tale.

The next day, while she was busy at Trentams, Jessica mulled over what Toby had said. Who was this Jessamine and how did she fit in? As far as she was aware, Toby had no family here in London. His elderly parents lived near the Scottish border and could only visit occasionally. He was not married and the only friends he had were those at St Bart's. It was a bit of a conundrum and Jessica was intrigued enough to want to unravel it.

Friday saw her back at the hospital; she didn't say anything to Toby other than to offer him the same greeting she gave all the veterans. She bustled about doing this and that, cleaning and bandaging wounds, changing beds and topping up glasses of water, tidying the room. In the early afternoon, Jessica was stacking the clean towels and blankets in the storeroom at the end of the corridor when she was disturbed by the feeling of a hand stroking her hair. She jumped, swallowing a shriek as she spun on her heel finding Lieutenant Langdon behind her, a curiously dreamy look on his face.

"T-Toby, you scared me," she admonished, trying to steady her tones. Her heart was thumping and his vacant stare unnerved her. It wasn't that she hadn't seen such expressions before, it was more here, away from everyone else, it was unexpected. Toby didn't answer, so she took his arm, guiding him back to the ward. "Come on, sir, let me get you where it's warm. Won't do you any good standing here in the chilly corridor," she coaxed, gently. He went with her meekly, and didn't protest when she escorted him to one of the big wingback chairs near the fire. She watched him for a few minutes wondering what was going on in his head, but he did no more than rest his head against the worn leather and shut his eyes.

"Isaac?" Making her way to where the orderly was chatting with one of the other patients, "I apologise for interrupting, but when you're free might I beg a word?"

Isaac nodded, concluding his conversation moments later, joining Jessica at the desk near the door.

"Isaac, who is Jessamine? Did she used to visit Toby?" Jessica spoke in undertones, her disquiet obvious.

Isaac looked confused. "Jessamine? I don't know of any Jessamine. Why?"

"Lieutenant Langdon has taken to calling me Jessamine and I presumed he was confusing me with another volunteer. The other day, he was describing the preparations for the Battle of Toulouse, when he asked me to sing, but he referred to me as Jessamine. He approached me," she hastened to add, before Isaac could question it. "Do you think there's the slightest possibility what he told me triggered a buried memory?"

Jessica went on to explain what had just happened outside the ward, leaving Isaac somewhat perturbed, but with no answers, affirming he would mention it to Dr Napier.

"Lieutenant Langdon has barely spoken since he were admitted to St Bart's and that's nigh on five years past. He never offered any details about his military service and no one has any idea how he were wounded. You are the first person he's spoken more than a few words to and I confess I am surprised."

Isaac paused, wondering how much he could comfortably share with this young woman who coped so admirably with the peculiarities of this ward. He came to a decision; he wasn't divulging anything she could not discover herself should she feel moved to review the patient files.

"According to the scant records we have, he were found wandering near Toulouse, several days after the battle, covered in blood but with no visible injuries. He were transported to a field hospital, but never told anyone how he got to where they found him or what happened to his fellow soldiers — although we know more about the latter now. Because he weren't wounded, the lieutenant re-joined his regiment, but his state of mind was too unstable and his commanding officer deduced it wise to discharge him honourably. The doctors call it a state of catalepsy — like a waking stupor," he clarified at Jessica's uncomprehending look. "Who this Jessamine is, however, I have no idea and as far as I am aware, we've never had anyone working here with that name. Mebbe it was someone from France?"

They discussed it a little longer, but couldn't come up with any answers, so filed it away for the time being, both confirming they would keep an eye on Toby in case any other information was forthcoming, or unusual symptoms manifested.

The days continued and for Jessica, it was as though this curious incident had never happened. Lieutenant Langdon seemed to have withdrawn into himself and refused to talk about the war any more. Jessica left him alone, knowing to press him would send the soldier further into his shell. Isaac informed her there had been a couple of instances when a night orderly had been forced to summon the doctor owing to Toby trying to climb out of the window in his sleep. When stopped, he had turned on the orderly, in an attempt to fight him off, before collapsing in a quivering heap, words spewing from him in an unintelligible stream.

Jessica was most concerned the origin of Toby's attacks stemmed from the day he had spoken to her, but Isaac reassured her this was often the natural progression of trauma, especially when sufferers were finally facing up to the root cause. Persuaded, Jessica carried on as though nothing had changed, hoping Toby would eventually feel disposed to confide in her again.

Chapter Sixteen

The brief holiday — if one could refer to the ten days away, of which four were dedicated to travel, as a holiday — to Whiteoaks for the christening was a great success. The Drummond contingent arrived late one Tuesday afternoon to an ecstatic welcome from Billie and Giles. The former refusing to be coddled by the rest of her family and the latter desperately worried she was tiring herself out — it only being a month since the birth of Maximilian Trevallier. Billie pooh-poohed all attempts at wrapping her in cotton wool, and Giles had long known Billie did not like to be 'managed' as she called it. Truth be told, the young countess was the picture of health, relishing her new role as a mother.

Whiteoaks was full to bursting with guests and Jessica barely had a moment to herself. All manner of entertainment had been organised, not to mention the preparations for the christening, affording scant opportunity to sneak away during the first day. Moreover, even though Jessica trusted Duncan's affection for her, she found herself unaccountably nervous and did not feel comfortable seeking him out, rather hoping he would find her instead.

The only window of time she did have to herself was first thing in the morning. Elated to be back at the estate where she could explore the countryside to her heart's content, Jessica resumed her habit of disappearing into the Great Park every day before breakfast, quite alone save for Trixie, her loyal shadow — the pair walking for miles.

On the second morning after her arrival, she was nearing the rise of a low rolling hill, from the top of which she would see Whiteoaks in all its glory. The sun had not long risen and the world, painted in shades of pink and gold, was breathtaking. Trixie was gambolling about, chasing goodness knows what and having a marvellous time doing so, while Jessica enjoyed the serenity of being the only one abroad.

Just as she set foot on the top of the slope, she heard the thunder of hooves and paused, her heart aware of who was approaching, long before she saw the rider.

The huge stallion slowed to a gentle trot and, only a few feet away from Jessica, the rider slid off, striding towards her, a wide smile on his face.

"My dear, Miss Drummond! What an unexpected surprise," he declared, his roughish tone indicating the complete opposite. Reaching her, he grasped her hand, bowing over it and, after hesitating for a second, kissed the inside of her wrist, sending a delicious frisson up her arm.

"Why, Mr Barrington, how lovely to see you again. 'Tis a fine morning for a ride, is it not? I have just been partaking of a constitutional and admit to feeling most invigorated." Jessica sketched a curtsy, her eyes brimming with amusement. Formalities addressed, the two simply stared, finding it hard to believe they were standing so close after what seemed like an eternity apart.

"My love, I have missed you," The rich timbre of Duncan's voice dropping, as he fought the urge to haul her against him. "I hoped you might visit the workshop last afternoon, but realised it would seem an odd pastime for one such as you."

Jessica cocked her head, "One such as me? What's that supposed to mean? Do you think me somehow too impor—" starting to splutter her indignation, which was effectively hushed by Duncan giving into said urge and kissing her soundly. "Oh…" she murmured and sank into his embrace, forgetting they were likely in full view of anyone glancing out of any of the many windows at Whiteoaks, although, thankfully from this distance, their identity would be inconclusive.

"Did I mention I missed you?" Duncan repeated softly, when, eventually, he released her lips.

"Hmmm, you may have done. In truth, however, I am not convinced you were terribly clear on that point." Jessica winked impishly.

"Something I feel I should rectify this instant," proceeding to do so, most eloquently.

"I believe I am persuaded," Jessica gasped minutes later, as the world came back into focus, her breathing coming in short bursts. "Good morning to you too." She felt laughter rumble through his chest as he held her close.

"I love you, Jessica Drummond," he said, kissing her forehead.

"I love you too, Duncan Barrington. Now, much as this is simply the most marvellous way to start the day, I have been walking for quite some time and suppose I should head home. No doubt they'll send out a search party — again, if I'm not at breakfast. Come Trixie!"

The dog bounded up to the couple, launching herself at Duncan before turning upside down and presenting her furry belly for the appropriate greeting. Duncan obliged, then patted the creature on her rump and she scooted off on her next adventure.

"She's growing so fast," he chuckled. "I can't believe this great lolloping lump was once the tiny scrap you found not far from where we stand."

Jessica turned on her heel surveying the landscape, quite different today, no longer blanketed in snow. "Just there," she indicated the riot of briar, now rather less vicious looking than it had been in mid-winter. Green shoots beginning to cover the barbs that tore at her hair and clothes. Duncan rolled up one of Jessica's sleeves; a smattering of thin, pale, jagged lines all that remained of the many scratches inflicted. He stroked his finger over them

"I was such a brute to you that day," he sighed, "demanding you get on a horse; uncaring you were obviously fearful of doing so, not to mention tired and overwrought. In fact, when I look back on those few days, sometimes I struggle to understand why you ever agreed to speak to me again. I did nothing but make your time here a misery." He took a breath, "I am truly sorry, Jessica. I hope one day you might forgive me for my crass behaviour."

"Oh, I think you have apologised enough and I forgave you long ago." Jessica grasped his hand. "Now, when I look back, I recall a certain evening in your workshop being far more memorable than your lapse in manners," she twinkled up at him, a saucy grin on her face.

Duncan felt his breath catch as he stared into her eyes, the early sunlight making their tawny depths sparkle like fire.

"Well, I find myself working late quite often these days," he mused, "it takes my mind off someone I met — the most enchanting young lady, but she lives so far away..." he left the sentence dangling, unwilling to place Jessica in an untenable position, debating whether it would be unfair of him to beg her to spare him brief moments, when the rest of the house was quiet. He, as always, reckoned without Jessica.

"I do occasionally find that sleep eludes me and, as you are aware, a short stroll in the night air, usually settles my mind." She replied guilelessly.

As they were talking, Duncan had grabbed Orion's reins and, having offered Jessica his arm, the pair enjoyed a brisk walk back through the Park. It wasn't long before they reached the fence delineating the park from the formal gardens.

"I must leave you here, love. I cannot in all conscience lead Orion through Samuel's beautifully tended garden, he would never forgive me. I hope to see you later." He bent over her hand, his thumb rubbing over her palm.

"I hope so too," she whispered and, before she could change her mind, hurried through the maze of pathways surrounding newly turned flowerbeds already sprouting new growth, glancing back once before she disappeared into the house. Duncan waited until she was out of sight, then using the fence to mount Orion, nudged the great horse into a brisk gallop around to the stables.

The week of festivities continued, and, to her chagrin, Jessica found the hours between dawn and dusk filled, leaving little chance to escape unnoticed, for any length of time. Without drawing attention to themselves, however, the couple did manage to spend a small part of each day together. Busy in his workshops, Duncan was unable to get away as much as he would have liked, but Jessica was quite content simply to watch him work. His clever fingers creating beautiful pieces, from his growing collection of carvings, to delicate furniture to solid fence posts. Jessica was in awe of his dexterity, the loss of his left hand no impediment to his talent.

He had finished the dog she requested he make for her and it was as though he had used Trixie as a model. It was perfect and Jessica found she could not stop touching it, expecting the fur to ripple under her fingers and the ears to flop in the same way as did her beloved pet's.

During these snatched hours they talked, sharing their day-to-day lives, planning their future, a future, so far, known only to them, Jessica continuing to revel in the secrecy. Late every evening, when all was quiet, she would slip out of the main house to join Duncan in the warmth of his workshop. Even though it had been his idea, he did suggest her nightly visits were perhaps a tad reckless but Jessica didn't care, declaring that if they were caught he would simply have to marry her.

Tonight, she arrived in a whisper of satin and silk, her attire entirely unsuitable for the time of year, but she was beset by an irrational desire to appear elegant yet seductive; little realising that she could have worn a burlap sack and Duncan would have found her alluring. Duncan set down the piece he was whittling and swept her into his arms, kissing her until the room spun.

"And a very good evening to you too," she murmured, smiling against his mouth, her breathing rather unsteady.

"I missed you today," he replied, nuzzling her neck and entwining his fingers through her hair, which fell in riotous curls down her back.

"Well, Helena wished to give me a tour of the village and we were invited to tea with Lady Elliot. I enjoyed both so much. Oh, Duncan, Lady Elliott is lovely, perhaps rather subdued, but such a fascinating person. We had a wonderful afternoon talking on all manner of topics. She knows something of trauma, she didn't say how, but I believe it to be personal. Anyway, she was most interested in my work at St Bart's and offered some suggestions that I hope to implement on my return to the city." Jessica chattered on artlessly, Duncan happy to listen, her lyrical voice soothing. He still struggled to sleep through the night hence, as Billie had previously explained, his hours spent in the workshops, but listening to Jessica, all the noise that nagged and tormented his mind, fell away and he heard only her.

Tucked on his knee, her head resting in the crook of his neck, Jessica became aware Duncan was no longer answering her. Twisting carefully, she saw he had fallen fast asleep. Studying his face in the dying light from the fire, she noticed weariness etched in the lines around his mouth and eyes and it was all she could do not smooth them away. His dark chestnut hair, with a sprinkling of grey here and there — and, as ever, an unruly mop — begged for fingers to be run through it; his shirt, open at the collar, revealed a tanned v of skin and a hint of chest hair. His long burly physique, muscles flexing as he breathed slow and deep, seemed carved out just for her.

Her heart swelled; she loved him beyond reason or explanation and, whatever happened, that would never be doused, despite his demons or the miles parting them or the difference in their years. She knew many of her friends would think her addled, considering marriage to a man nearly a decade her senior, but she was barely aware of it, all she knew was their meeting, their coming together, their falling in love was absolutely as it should be. After all, it hadn't been the most auspicious start, yet here she was, curled up on his knee as though she had been doing so for a lifetime. Unable to help herself, Jessica slid her hand under his shirt, stroking his skin. She nestled back against his shoulder, the beat of his heart along with the warmth of the room soporific, and without warning, joined him in slumber.

Hours later, the fire merely smouldering ash in the grate, Duncan jolted awake, disorientated and stiff from sleeping in the chair. It was still dark and he experienced a moment of panic, as it seemed he had lost the ability to move his damaged arm. As he came fully awake, he realised it was Jessica, fast asleep snuggled into him, her legs drawn up under her skirts, her head pillowed on his shoulder and her arm draped over his waist, slender fingers resting on the skin under his shirt. Without waking her, he shifted slightly so he could study her in repose, not something most men ever had the chance to do until wed. Her face was a little pale, her hair — in complete disarray — tumbled in rivulets across her shoulders and over his arm, reminding him of golden barley undulating in a summer's breeze. He was lost, completely and irrevocably lost. She was his and he wanted nothing more than to have her curl up on his knee every night for the rest of his life. Unfortunately, common sense dictated right now, she needed to return to her bedchamber before they were discovered.

"Jessica," he cupped her face stroking along her cheek, trying to wake her without causing fright. She stirred, but only pushed herself closer. "Jessica," a little louder now. "Sweetheart, you need to return to your chamber. The house will be waking soon and however much I love you, I cannot let you risk your reputation."

She opened drowsy eyes, blinking in the unfamiliar room, then stifled a squawk realising where she was, sleep banished in an instant.

"Duncan?" she gasped, "Oh, I am so sorry, I didn't intend to fall asleep, but you were so comfortable and I felt so safe and I—" he cut her off by kissing her soundly.

"Not your fault," he murmured, somewhat throatily, several minutes later, "but might I suggest you leave now? Please Jessica, we can meet again later."

"You were so tired and slept so deeply," she whispered, turning in his arms to stare into his weary face. "I just thought to let you rest undisturbed for a while." He smiled at her concern, rubbing his thumb gently over her bottom lip.

"Thank you, my love. You should know, I slept better with you in my arms and in this chair than I have for many a long night in my own bed, and for once, without dreams. Seems you have a calming effect on my mind."

Jessica chuckled. "I think that was more likely a lucky coincidence," she contended. Stretching and carefully getting off Duncan's lap, Jessica brushed down her skirts and made sure her cloak was securely fastened. If anyone happened upon her so early, she could claim insomnia.

Duncan went over to the fire and stoked it back to life, dropping two logs onto it and watching until he was sure the dying embers caught hold. Walking back to where Jessica waited, he wrapped her close and kissed the top of her head.

"Go, sleep out the night in your far more suitable bedchamber. Dawn is not far away; there is little point me going home. Sarah will give me breakfast and I can usually wash up in the scullery. They are used to me." Duncan guided her towards the door and, after checking to make sure no one was about, stood aside to let her pass. At the last minute he grasped her hand, pulling her against him for a hard and very passionate kiss.

"Oh my," Jessica groaned as he released her. "How am I supposed to sleep now?" She felt a laugh rumble through him as he gently pushed her towards the house

"Hopefully very well, my love." And he retreated into the workshop, the door clicking shut behind him before she could persuade him to change his mind and continue that heart-stopping kiss.

Jessica ran quietly across the courtyard and into the house, managing to get to her chamber unseen. She undressed, and dragging her nightrail over her head, fell into bed; sleep claimed her immediately, her dreams proving most satisfactory.

Chapter Seventeen

The next morning, Jessica awoke a little later than usual, but nobody at the breakfast table questioned her tardiness. It was her last day at Whiteoaks and she was aware of a strange ache growing in her heart. She would have to say goodbye to Duncan again and, much as she didn't want to give up her work at St Bart's, she knew this parting would be a wrench, neither having any idea how long it would be until they would meet again. Maybe she was a fool not to agree to marry sooner rather than later. At least that way they could... she stopped that thought before it went any further. Her cheeks flushed hot as images formed in her head.

"Jessica, you are a wanton hussy!" admonishing herself in the mirror, as she readied herself for her morning walk. "Honestly, what would Mama think?" Eternally grateful her mother was a two-day carriage ride away.

"What would your Mama think of what?" Helena asked, amusement in her tones, as she knocked on the door, which stood ajar, coming into the room as Jessica's voice trailed off in shock.

"Helena! What did ... I didn't expect ... why I'm..." she bit her lip and tried again. "Was there something you wanted?"

Helena chucked, "I was wondering whether I might join you for your constitutional? 'Tis a beautiful morning and Giles has dragged Hugh into some estate meeting with his stewards. I was going to go on my own then I remembered you enjoy a walk and I do not believe you have been yet today." A silent question hovered in her words, but Jessica just smiled and agreed, pulling on her sturdy boots and shrugging into her cloak.

"I would love it above all things," she assured her sister-in-law. "Come, we should make the most of it, for the next two days will see us confined to a dusty carriage. I do not intend to wear my wretched bonnet, so don't think to ask me." As

Helena hated them too she was of no mind to argue, and moments later the two women were strolling across the vast hall, when a bright voice gave them pause.

"May I accompany you?" Billie sailed down the stairs with a rapidity indicating little regard for gentility, not to mention tripping on her skirts, her face wreathed in smiles.

"Of course." Helena grinned as the diminutive countess skidded to a halt next to them.

"I need fresh air, Giles is with the stewards this morning, so he is not around to prevent me. I believe I will go mad if I don't feel the breeze on my skin. It seems as though I've been shut indoors for ever."

The other two giggled at her frustrated expression and waited as Thomas brought her cloak and outdoor shoes.

"Thank you, Thomas," Billie beamed at her butler, who grinned back, quite used to his mistress's irrepressible nature by now.

"There'll be hot coffee on your return," was all he said. Billie thanked him again and the three women swept along the corridor, out through the back door and into the sunlight.

"Oh, this is bliss," breathed Billie as they came around the side of the main house. The sun sparkled on the remnants of dew still clinging to the grass and new growth blanketed the trees in vivid green shawls of the finest gossamer. Hardy witch hazel shrubs planted along the farthest pathways, still bore the last of their cheerful yellow blossoms, slowly making way for daffodils, interspersed with bright blue scillas, both of which were flowering in great profusion as far as the eye could see. Samuel and his gardeners never removed them; they were left to their own random devices, the Winchesters of the belief that some things didn't need to be structured. Although snow still clung to sheltered corners, the last few days had been mild, encouraging this spurt of blooms — a colourful carpet after the endless winter whiteness.

The three women gossiped about nothing particularly deep and meaningful, just enjoying each other's company. Billie would miss these two when they left. Already sharing a close friendship with Helena, Billie found Jessica to be just as congenial. During this visit the three had indulged in lively debates on a variety of subjects, that never included the latest fashions, sewing, or who the *ton* was currently shunning. All three were spirited, independently minded ladies who refused to allow Society's constraints to prevent them obtaining their desires, something which had brought two of them closer to peril than they ought to have been. Thankfully disaster had been averted, Helena and Billie both surviving their ordeals, and perhaps becoming a little less impulsive in the process, to the relief of their respective spouses.

Jessica listened as Billie and Helena fell into a heated discussion about houses and how to determine what was suitable, both agreeing with the other but sounding as though they were arguing, it was quite comical. Their voices washed over her and her mind wandered, recalling the previous night. Duncan's face swam over her vision and she experienced a sharp jab of … was it pain?… she couldn't decide, it seemed to stab and twist. She sat down abruptly on a convenient tree stump, her thoughts swirling. She couldn't go on like this. They had to come to some kind of decision. Did she leave London or did he leave Oak Stanton? Neither option was tenable, for one would lose so much, but the idea of being apart for months at a time was intolerable. What were they going to do?

She became aware it had fallen quiet and brought her attention back to the other two, who were staring at her, wearing matching expressions of amusement.

"Come on, Jessica Drummond, 'tis time you told us what's going on in that head of yours. You have been far too quiet of late and I am beginning to feel uneasy."

"Helena! I have not, you do exaggerate," chided Jessica, grinning at her brother's wife.

Helena turned to Billie, "I believe my sister-in-law to be struggling with a conundrum." She tapped her chin contemplatively. "I think it involves Mr Barrington…" Jessica felt her cheeks growing pink, "…and if I'm not mistaken, I feel sure it is to do with marriage." At this last Jessica gaped. How could Helena possibly know that? She, Jessica, had never uttered a word and they had been so careful about revealing their feelings and intentions whenever anyone else was present.

"H-how could...did y...I mean...because...only..." for the second time that day Helena had reduced her to a gibbering idiot. Jessica shook her head trying to force some sense into it. Helena and Billie just smiled knowingly.

"Jess, how long have we been friends?" Helena asked. Jessica mumbled something unintelligible. "Nearly a year and my friendship with Duncan extends back to my childhood. I know you are in love with Duncan and he with you; it doesn't take a wild stretch of imagination to presume he has asked for your hand. Why haven't you told me?"

Jessica sighed and looked at the two women in front of her, the impulse to confide in them almost overwhelming. It was all well and good keeping things secret and there was no doubt she had enjoyed the deliciousness of it to date, but she needed a fresh perspective, someone who could guide her through this mire. Someone who might help her work out what to do. Taking a deep breath, she started to speak and it all came tumbling out, perhaps rather more quickly than she intended but eventually, after asking many questions, Billie and Helena knew everything.

"'Tis just, I was the one who said I wanted to wait, I don't want to give up my work at St Bart's, I believe I am helping. Neither do I want to be apart from Duncan. He thinks we can make it work, and mayhap we can, but I don't think I want it to...I mean I don't think I want to be apart from him for months at a time." She sniffed, feeling tears threatening, "I know that makes me pathetic, but what is the point of being married and not being together? We might as well not bother." Her shoulders slumped forlornly prompting Billie to draw her into a warm hug.

"Oh, my dear let us see whether we three can come up with a better plan. One where you may need to be apart for a little while, but works toward you being together in one place. You just have to decide where that is. Do you wish to be here in the countryside, or would you prefer to remain in London?"

"I couldn't take Duncan from here. He loves this place, it soothes him and I know it has helped him adjust. But what would I do? I cannot sit idle, I would go mad."

While Jessica was talking, Billie and Helena were ruminating over the problem; suddenly Helena whooped, causing the other two to stare at her askance.

"Sorry, I just had an idea. Why don't we ask whether you might assist Theo? He is a busy doctor; the village is growing and 'tis only him. Oh, I know you can't dispense medicine, or diagnose illnesses..." she waved her hand, as Jessica tried to interrupt, "...but you could treat wounds, do home visits — you know to check on those who are sick or injured and abed — a sort of district assistant. Billie used to help, but now there's Max, and you still intend to teach, don't you?" She enquired of the young countess who nodded vigorously.

"Why, Helena, how clever, that is a wonderful idea! What do you think Jessica? I know Theo has been struggling lately; to have someone lift his burden would be most satisfactory." Billie urged Jessica, who let the idea roll around her head. The more she thought about it the more perfect it sounded. Would Duncan be happy? She should ask him before she approached Theo.

"Do you think we might seek out Dr Elliott before I leave on the morrow, I would like something to look forward to. The thought of saying goodbye is..." she trailed off unable to articulate her sadness for fear those pesky tears would brim over.

Billie made a decision, "Let us return to the house. You can talk to Duncan, and then we three will visit with the Elliotts this afternoon," Jessica started to say something, Billie waved her hand, "do not fret, they are quite used to me turning up at all hours.

"I was going to say, what about Max?" Jessica remarked.

Billie clapped her hand to her mouth, wailing — "Oh my goodness, I forgot about my own son! What kind of a mother am I? He's only a month old and already I've forgotten about him..."

Helena and Jessica fell about laughing at Billie's horrified expression.

"Stop panicking Billie," giggled Helena, "'twas only a lapse. I'm sure as soon as he wants feeding, you'd have remembered. Come on we have work to do." As they strolled back toward Whiteoaks, Jessica asked whether they would mind if she spoke to Duncan straight away.

"I want to make sure he realises I'm doing this of my own accord and, although we want to be together, I don't him to feel as though his life and work here has forced my hand. I'm not sure quite how I'll persuade him of this, but I believe 'tis important we talk it through."

The other two nodded sagely, understanding Jessica completely. They continued to chat about their plan as they walked, reaching the house shortly thereafter and making their way around to the workshops.

The door was wide open, the sounds of hammering and sawing wafted across the courtyard.

"Allow me," said Billie, striding in purposefully. The noise stopped abruptly and a muffled conversation could be heard, then Billie and Duncan appeared in the doorway.

"Luncheon will be served in an hour, Jessica, that will give us plenty of time for this afternoon's visit." Billie grabbed Helena's arm and dragged her to the back door, ignoring that young woman's protest about the couple needing a chaperone.

"I think they're well beyond needing a chaperone, Helena." Came back to them on the breeze, amusement clear in Billie's voice.

Jessica and Duncan looked at each other. Jessica shifted awkwardly from one foot to the other and Duncan felt rather baffled at this unexpected interruption to his day.

"Billie said you have something you wish to discuss with me," he queried quietly, after several moments of silence neither seemed able to break.

"I do. Might you be so kind as to walk with me for a few moments?" He could see Jessica was dithering and his heart hitched.

144

"Is everything all right, love?" he asked in low tones, reaching for her hand, the warmth of his grip steadied her nerves and he was pleased to feel an answering squeeze through her gloved fingers. He tucked her hand through his arm as they walked around the side of the workshops, following the long driveway towards the huge wrought iron gates.

"I told Billie and Helena this morning," Jessica confessed, her voice wavering a little.

Duncan glanced down at her.

"We...ll," drawing out the word, "actually Helena guessed and then it sort of...it's just...I felt I...it was such a relief."

"What is it that worries you then?" he asked gently, slowing to a halt and turning her to face him, keeping hold of her hand.

"I'm not worried, it's just they, well Helena, made a suggestion, one I think admirable, but I did not want to pursue it until I discussed it with you." She gazed up at him, seeing only tender encouragement in his expression.

"I am intrigued. What is it?"

"Before I go on, please don't think I'm doing this for you, well I am, but it's also for me, I want this nearly as much as I want you," she gulped, recognising the boldness of her words, "s-sorry, I didn't mean...that is...oh the devil with it, why can't I ever just speak like an intelligent adult?" She entreated.

Duncan chuckled, kissing her forehead, "Just tell me, love."

So, she did, trying to explain in a manner she hoped would convince him it was her choice and she had come to this decision independent of how they had begun to plan their lives together.

"Wait, let me get this straight. Are you saying, if Dr Elliott agrees to this idea, you would move to Oak Stanton and we would live together all the time? We wouldn't be apart?" Duncan clarified. She nodded, biting her lip, her stomach tying itself in knots as she tried to gauge reaction, his face revealing nothing. "And you were worried I might think your decision was swayed by my life here?" Jessica nodded again, not trusting herself to speak. This was a pivotal moment and she knew it could go either way. Duncan was still something of a closed book to her and, although the story was becoming clearer, the ending was still cloaked in mystery.

He was quiet for long moments.

"D-Duncan, please talk to me. Have I done the wrong thing? D-did you prefer that we live apart? I didn't think, perhaps you n-need your own s-space?" Stumbling over her words, panic coiling through her. Oh no, had she misunderstood everything? Maybe he didn't want them to live together. What was wrong with her? She was too impetuous, jumping in without weighing the consequences. Yes, he said he wanted to marry her, but maybe that was only because before she broached this idea, it was likely they would only meet occasionally. Perhaps he was so used to living alone, that to have a wife there, in his home or close to his work, all the time would be too much. He still hadn't spoken, and she felt sobs building. No not again, she couldn't do this again!

Chapter Eighteen

Heart cracking, she turned, fingers slipping from Duncan's large hand, and abruptly Jessica felt a chasm begin to form, the distance between them a tangible thing. She hadn't taken a single step, however, when his arm snaked around her dragging her against his hard body.

"And just where do you think you are going?" he growled, his deep voice sending shivers coursing through her

"I th-thought you … I can't … please. Don't s-say it, I can't bear it. Just let me leave. I'm s-sorry, I n-never really…" As the garbled words fell from her lips, Jessica tried to make her normally practical and sensible brain stop behaving in so capricious a fashion, conceding this whole being in love thing made one act quite irrationally. Honestly it turned intelligent women into simpering watering pots.

"Jessica Drummond, what on God's green earth makes you think I would want to spend any more of my wretched life *without* you? I would marry you today if we could. I want you by my side every day and in my bed every night. You are all I think about and, if I am ever lucky enough to snatch a few hours' sleep, you haunt my dreams, chasing away my nightmares. I am simply staggered you care enough for me to consider leaving your world, your life and your passion in the city to tie yourself to a quiet village in the middle of nowhere with a very questionable husband, and it was taking my head a little while to process it."

Jessica sucked in a shuddering breath, blinking away bothersome tears still lurking, relief flooding through her. Standing on tiptoe and cupping his face, she murmured

"Duncan Barrington, when will you accept 'tis you who are my world, my life and my passion. I came to this decision quite deliberately and I am not tying myself to you, we are binding ourselves together. Moreover, while you might consider yourself, erroneously I might add, questionable, I believe you will find, I am your answer."

An inarticulate sound was wrested from Duncan's core and, uncaring that they were in the middle of the driveway, that anyone might come upon them either on foot or by carriage, that it was only minutes away from the hour when all manner of people made their way to the big house for luncheon, he slanted his mouth over hers, his kiss so intense it threatened to undo her completely. One arm still around her, he used his hand to good effect, fingers threading through her lustrous hair, coming to rest on the back of her neck.

Jessica moaned, giving herself over to the bliss he was inducing. His lips, branding her as his, moved from her mouth down her throat to her neck, hovering over the pulse fluttering frantically. She pushed aside his waistcoat, tugging at his shirt, desperate to feel his skin under hers. As her inquisitive fingers stroked his muscles, Duncan quaked, her touch enough to fan those unquenchable embers, which always smouldered and fire scorched through him.

"Jess..." a ragged groan, his use of her diminutive, an endearment and a plea.

"D-Duncan, I love you, please..." she whispered not really sure what it was she needed, but knowing only he could grant it. Duncan needed no further bidding, the decorative wrought iron of the gate proving most convenient. His hand followed his lips, trailing from her cheek to her shoulders to the rise of her breast, dipping slightly to sweep under her décolletage. Jessica trembled, her body behaving in the most reckless fashion, yet she was powerless to stop it and had absolutely no intention of doing so.

As Duncan's fingers swept over her stomach, taunting and teasing, his lips recaptured hers. Jessica opened to him, tongues tangling and both lost themselves in the intoxicating sweetness. Still it wasn't enough, and needing more, she pushed closer, fitting herself to his strapping frame, her body begging for his.

Duncan fought for control, there was no way he was taking Jessica here in the middle of the driveway — although...no, **no** he absolutely could not — his body also crying out for hers, in

148

fact, he was quite amazed she couldn't hear it, it was almost deafening him.

Ignoring the voice of reason, which was suggesting, somewhat insistently, this was madness, Jessica's fingers began to fiddle with the fall of Duncan's trousers, following an instinct she didn't understand but trusted implicitly. She felt tremors running through him and his breathing sounded strangled.

"Jess. God! Urrgghhh..." He lost the ability to speak as the last button fell away and slender fingers encircled sensitive flesh. Unbridled passion slammed into him and his hand slid under her dress, gliding up a stocking clad leg to her thigh, seeking her centre. As his fingers brushed against her heat, Jessica's head fell back and her legs started to buckle. Refusing to let her fall, Duncan simply pressed her against the gate — the cold, unyielding iron doing nothing to cool their ardour — as he brought her to a peak she had no idea she could reach. His relentless fingers wove their sorcery until she shattered around him.

After what seemed like hours riding a crest, Jessica drifted back to reality, blood still pounding through her veins, breathing coming in jagged spurts. As the world reformed around her, she realised she was wrapped against Duncan and he was nuzzling behind her ear, quite the most exquisite torture.

"D-Duncan..." her mouth felt as though it was full of hair ribbon — maybe it was her own hair ribbon, it would not have surprised her in the slightest, everything seemed topsy-turvy.

"Yes, love," he murmured into her hair, warm breath tickling her skin.

"Please tell me you'll do that again," blushing at her shamelessness, yet desperate for him to assure her this was only the beginning, not the end.

"As often as you wish my darling," kissing her neck, "however I feel it only polite to warn you, the next time will take longer, will be far more blissful and be in considerably more comfortable surrounds."

She leaned away from him, her brows creasing in confusion.

"Explain yourself, sir."

He did, taking wicked delight in watching her cheeks, already pink, flush to bright red. Jessica wasn't entirely ignorant, but to have it spelled out sent her into a confusion of arousal mixed with self-consciousness. Watching all this flit across her vivid face, her hair mussed, her clothing in disarray and her eyes gazing at him with such faith, it was all Duncan could do, not to give in and follow through right there. It was only the knowledge she was an innocent and he yearned to be as gentlemanly as possible — well maybe not a complete gentleman — about stealing that innocence, which held him back. That and the fact he loved her so dearly, he was determined to do this properly.

"Jess? Wait, may I call you Jess?" he ventured, blithely ignoring the fact he had just done so — twice — the less formal version of her name creating another layer of intimacy between them.

"Of course," smiling up at him, her heart finally settling to a steadier beat. "I think I'll stick to Duncan for you though. Neither 'Dunc' nor 'Can' really sit well with me." Her tones flippant, drawing a low chuckle from the man holding her.

"So, Jess, may we please marry as soon as possible? I know you must return to London on the morrow and I already miss you, but perhaps we could arrange a date for about two months hence?" He tilted her chin, staring into her shining eyes, bewitched by their tawny depths.

"I do believe that would be quite suitable," she replied primly. "We should probably speak to Hugh. I know I am of age, but I think he would appreciate being approached. He is a good brother and guardian, I would like him to feel part of this."

"I have every intention of asking Hugh for your hand. I consider him a friend and have always accepted the importance of convention." He smiled gently, tucking an errant strand of hair off her face. "Do you think we should return to the house? Billie mentioned luncheon and I recall you are visiting the Elliotts this afternoon," he reminded her. Jessica quickly tried to make herself look presentable, re-plaiting her hair, before smoothing her skirts with fingers that still trembled.

"Will I pass muster?" she pleaded.

Duncan raked his eyes over her, eliciting yet another fiery blush.

"Stop, or I'll have no option but to insist you demonstrate what you so eloquently described moments ago." She swatted at him, eyes brimming with amusement.

Chuckling at her expression, Duncan assured her she looked utterly perfect, if not rather ravished, making her giggle. Offering her his arm, they strolled back to the house, falling into easy chatter until they parted at the workshop. Duncan risked another kiss and she whispered she would find him later, to tell him how the visit with Dr Elliott went, squeezing his fingers before vanishing into the house.

Billie and Helena were kind enough not to remark on her slightly tousled appearance, merely suggesting she think of tidying her hair before they set out. It was quite clear by their expressions; however, they knew exactly what she'd been up to.

"Am I to presume Mr Barrington was amenable to your suggestion, Jessica?" Helena enquired, a wry smile tugging on her lips. Jessica nodded shyly, faint colour staining her cheeks for what felt like the hundredth time that day.

"He admitted to being excessively pleased and would like to speak with Hugh before we leave tomorrow. That is assuming Dr Elliott agrees to our...my...proposal." She qualified.

Billie, with a very unladylike whoop of joy, beamed at her two friends. "Another wedding, how exciting. Oh, please marry here. I love hosting weddings."

Helena laughed recalling her own special day just over three months previously. "She really does Jess, think about it, I'm sure your Mama wouldn't mind."

"I'm not sure I should impose on your hospitality any more than I already have," Jessica demurred. "You have been so generous. I don't want anyone to think I am stepping beyond the bounds of my station."

Billie's jaw dropped, "Stepping beyond the bounds of your station? Good gracious Jessica! Whatever gave you the impression I care about anybody's station, other than to be sure they are safe, comfortable and properly fed?"

"I-it's just…I am not…only my family…oh…" she hesitated, not quite sure how to explain without offending Billie.

"I think she worries others will think her a parvenu — the Drummonds being merchant class." Helena clarified, taking pity on Jessica who was getting tongue-tied again.

"Fiddlesticks!" Billie refuted. "What utter nonsense. I would be honoured to host your wedding, Jessica. Duncan is like family to us and, as his mother lives with his sister up near Newcastle, there's no one here about to organise the celebration for him. Oh, unless of course you prefer to marry in London." She clapped her hand over her mouth as she realised she was rather dragooning Jessica into something she might not want.

"Wait, Billie," grinned Jessica, the countess' appalled expression making the whole thing seem very funny. "We h-haven't s-spoken to Hugh yet, or D-Dr Elliott. P-poor Duncan w-will be overwhelmed." She spluttered, going off into gales of laughter at the incongruity of the situation. Jessica had gone from thinking she would not be able to marry for months, to having it planned while she was eating lunch and, unexpectedly, found this hilarious. Her laughter was infectious and the other two joined in, their mirth continuing to bubble throughout luncheon, making for the most ridiculous conversation.

Much later when they had gathered their senses, enjoyed a light meal — and Jessica had tidied her hair — they were on their way to Oak Stanton to call upon Theo and Grace.

As the carriage rolled to a halt outside The Gables, Grace Elliott opened the door, calling to someone within before coming to meet them at the gate.

"I thought I heard a carriage," she cried gaily, receiving her guests with a bright smile. "What a lovely surprise. Come in come in, I'm sure Agnes baked fresh biscuits this morning, ginger snaps if the heavenly aroma was anything to go by." Grace ushered them through her elegant home into a cosy room at the back, known as the Snug; it was Grace's favourite room and, where they found Theo Elliott, trying to light his pipe, without much success. He stood when they entered, grinning as both Billie and Helena hugged him.

"Miss Drummond," he inclined his head as Jessica dropped a neat curtsy. "I hope my letter was of assistance to you."

"Dr Elliott, sir, it was so kind of you. I love working there. I think I am of help to Dr Napier, who asked me to pass on his regards and to make sure I mentioned the debacle regarding a collection of ligaments and tendons. He said you'd know what he meant." Jessica looked puzzled as she said this, remembering Dr Napier's expression.

Theo was quiet for a moment, then bit down on a bark of laughter, his shoulders shaking with mirth.

"Please tell Dr Napier...no wait, I will write to him myself. Ligaments and tendons indeed." Theo chuckled quietly, presumably reminiscing on his training. Grace raised an eyebrow at her husband, a grin on her face, and as Jessica watched, Theo merely inclined his head, but the glance that passed between them — their silent communion, was an echo of the way Duncan looked at her and it made her feel warm all over.

"I gather this is not just a social call?" Grace said after they had been served hot coffee, munched on the scrumptious ginger snaps and shared some local gossip.

Billie shook her head. "We have a plan, one where Jessica can live here but not give up working with the sick and injured," she said. "Would you like me to explain, dear?" she asked Jessica in a motherly fashion, to the amusement of the others.

Jessica nodded, a trickle of unease threading through her. It sounded like the answer to her prayers when they first discussed it, now it seemed rather presumptuous. Billie went on to tell Theo and Grace what they had been discussing, including that Jessica and Duncan wanted to marry. The latter came as a surprise to Theo who had no idea, but not to Grace in whom Billie had confided about the couple's growing love, long ago.

"And you didn't see fit to tell me, love?" Theo chided his wife gently.

"No, Theo, it was not my secret to tell." Grace smiled sweetly, not in slightest contrite at withholding such news. "I knew either Billie or Duncan would tell you when they were good and ready and I wasn't sure how many people were privy to it."

"To be honest, I did not know for sure until this morning, Jessica kept it very nicely to herself, but it has been brewing since, oh before Christmas, wouldn't you agree Jessica?" Throwing an arch grin at the focus of their conversation, who blushed — again! "Anyway, we wheedled it out of her and until today neither knew how they would manage. It seems as though theirs would be a marriage of distance and although I imagine when first discussed, it sounded feasible, I do believe spending months apart is no longer quite so attractive a proposition."

Jessica felt it appropriate to clarify further. "Dr Elliott, I don't want you to think I intend to abandon Dr Napier and the veterans. I will continue my work there until I have found someone who might replace me, even if that doesn't happen until after I am married. I know I am not indispensable, but I think my efforts have lifted some of the more mundane chores from the shoulders of those who care for the soldiers. It would be unconscionable of me to allow that burden to weigh them down again. Two dear friends, who have suffered me jabbering on about St Bart's, have already expressed an interest in assisting. Should Dr Napier be prepared to offer them a chance, they would gladly take over." She concluded, holding her breath hoping Theo might be amenable.

Chapter Nineteen

Theo listened carefully, Billie and Helena's scheme seemingly a gift from God. In truth, he *was* finding it difficult to manage his practice at the moment. Helena was correct, in that the population of the village and Whiteoaks estate had increased, and he did not always have the time to call in on his patients as often as he would like. There was also another reason. Grace had told her husband she was expecting their first baby and, despite his own expertise, Theo wasn't taking any chances. Thus, frequent visits to London to consult specialists were probable in the not too distant future. Although Theo had a locum who could be relied upon to treat injuries and illness, regular house calls and checks tended to be neglected.

"Your suggestion has merit and I do believe it will solve many of my current dilemmas." He tapped his chin thoughtfully. "With your permission, Jessica, I will write to Napier. For even though I am certain you are eminently capable, I would be grateful for his insight into how much responsibility I might give you. It also affords me the opportunity to extend my appreciation to him for allowing you to assist him, even for so short a period. Might I ask that you deliver a missive from me when next you are at St Bart's?"

"Thank you, Dr Elliott, and I would be glad to." Jessica dipped another neat curtsy and, as Theo went to the study to pen a letter to his friend, the four ladies chatted about dresses and shoes and all things wedding related. Another pleasant hour elapsed, then Billie declared it was time to leave the Elliott's to their afternoon, hustling Helena and Jessica into the carriage.

"For not only do I think it's high time we left you to it, I think my son might be getting hungry," Billie had eschewed the expected wet nurse, preferring to feed Max herself, and was becoming uncomfortably aware her baby son's feeding time

155

was imminent. "Would you believe, with all that drama, I all but forgot about him this morning?" She admitted, ruefully, her dismayed expression reducing the others to helpless giggles.

"Nothing you do ever surprises me, Billie Trevallier," chortled Theo, handing Jessica a sealed letter. "Thank you, Miss Drummond. I look forward to your return to Oak Stanton with interest."

Jessica smiled shyly, "As do I, and please call me Jessica. Miss Drummond sounds so formal." Theo acquiesced with a nod of his head as he and Grace waved them off, his arm around his wife, her head resting on his shoulder.

"I think this could be quite the most wonderful solution, Theo," commented Grace as the carriage trundled down the street.

"I agree, love. Sometimes I think Billie has the power of foresight, for she always seems to know precisely what is required, before we even realise it ourselves."

His wife chuckled and taking advantage of their solitude, kissed her husband soundly, causing his head to spin and all plans for the rest of the day to vanish in an instant.

Meanwhile, the carriage rolled through the country lanes and up the long drive to Whiteoaks, Jessica unable to prevent a flush blooming over her cheeks as they passed the great gates. At the sight of the red brick of the big house, mellow in the afternoon sunlight, welcoming them home, Helena sighed; she would never tire of this first glimpse of its ageing beauty — her childhood home, where memories of her father still whispered through the rooms. She loved Hugh and never wanted to live away from him, but she missed this place. Jessica noticed her wistful expression and pressed her hand.

"'Tis but a carriage ride away," she murmured softly. Helena smiled, squeezing Jessica's fingers gently, in acknowledgement of her perception.

As Jake, one of the grooms, assisted the women from the carriage, Giles and Hugh strode out of the steward's office where they had been ensconced for much of the day. Trixie bounded out with them, for she had spent the day with Oscar and Nip — Giles' hounds — wagging her way to Jessica for the requisite tickle, which was delivered with enthusiasm.

"Thomas informs me hot coffee is served ladies, shall we?" Giles grinned cheerfully, sweeping his wife into a warm hug, Hugh following suit with Helena.

"After our meetings today, I may have to include a shot of whisky. What say you, Drummond?" he added, as Hugh laughed an assent, the group falling into lively chatter about the day's business as they made their way to the beautifully apportioned library, a favourite of both Billie and Giles.

They had been sitting for a little while, when Jessica excused herself, tripping around to the workshops where Duncan was engrossed in repairing a huge old carved chest. As her shadow fell across the entrance he glanced up, his slow smile making her heart leap.

"Good afternoon, Miss Drummond," he greeted, wiping his hands on an old rag.

"Hello," she whispered the need to touch him only tempered by two of Duncan's staff engaged in fixing a carriage wheel at the other side of the workshop.

"What can I do for you?"

"Hugh is done for day and I wondered whether...that is, should you decide...perhaps now might be..." *Goodness Jessica,* she chided herself, *learn to form a sentence woman.* Taking a deep breath, she said

"Hugh is available and I thought this might be a good time to talk with him." Puffing out the last few words in a rush. Duncan chuckled and agreed.

"Give me five minutes and I'll freshen up," he said, striding into the scullery and removing as much dust and sawdust as possible without actually dunking himself full length in the large sink. Towelling off, he found a clean shirt in a tall cupboard in the workshop and after a few more minutes was ready.

"Presentable?" he arched an eyebrow questioningly. Jessica nodded

"You're *always* presentable to me," she confided, and he drew her close for a quick kiss, which ended up somewhat longer, the pair easily forgetting all else around them.

Reluctantly, Duncan broke their kiss. "Come, I want this to be official," he grinned and tucking her hand under his arm, led her into the house. As they arrived at the library door, Jessica felt nervous. What if Hugh said no. Then remembered she was of age and this was purely as a courtesy, but she didn't want him to say no. She didn't want him to disapprove. She hesitated, pulling back.

"Jess?" Duncan queried. "What troubles you? Am I pressuring you to marry too soon?"

She shook her head.

"What then?"

"I'm afraid he will say no," anxiously, wringing her hands.

"Well, we won't know until I ask, will we? Come on love, the longer you stand here the more agitated you will become." He leaned close to her ear "I love you," his voice reverberated right through her, his breath warm on her skin, soothing her. She nodded

"Right, I'm ready." Smoothing her skirts and patting her hair, which was still slightly ruffled after the carriage ride, she knocked.

"Enter," Jessica heard Giles invite and, upon opening the door, saw astonishment on the earl's face when he realised who it was.

"Jessica, you have no need to knock, you are as family here!" He expostulated.

"I beg your pardon, my Lord," his eyes went wider at this formality, "but, I hoped Hugh might spare me, us, a moment," she beseeched, gazing at her brother, who looked as startled as Giles at her request, but nodded anyway. Billie immediately diverted everyone else's attention by asking a nonsensical question about animal husbandry.

Hugh came into the hallway, his confusion mounting when he spotted Duncan waiting there too.

"Barrington." Hugh inclined his head at the man who had visited their home not so long ago, his brain still apparently not catching up. Duncan nodded a reply, but offered no explanation for his presence.

"What is it, Jess?" Hugh asked, nonplussed; although, later when talking it over with Helena, his wife did feel moved to comment he must be a simpleton not to have discerned what was going on.

"Walk with us?" Jessica asked. Completely baffled now, Hugh offered her his arm, the three making their way outside and around to the gardens

"What is it, Jess?" He reiterated, once they were well away from the house. Duncan, who hadn't uttered a word since Jessica had knocked on the library door, finally spoke.

"I wish to ask for your consent to marry Jessica." He said quietly, but resolutely. Hugh's jaw dropped and he stopped dead in his tracks, almost tripping Jessica up.

"Hugh!" she admonished.

"You wish to what?" Ignoring her reprove, Hugh stood firm, staring hard at Duncan, who repeated his request, adding —

"sir, please before you say it, I know I am not of the same status as your family…" Hugh made an odd sound. "…I am simply a retired soldier, but I work hard and earn enough to keep your sister in a very comfortable manner. I also have additional income from an inheritance and my army pension; my family home is quite sizeable and currently I reside there alone save my meagre staff. I accept I am unable to offer her an extravagant lifestyle, and I realise you probably hoped for a far better match, but I love your sister more than anything in this world and I promise to ensure her well-being and happiness is always my first priority." Duncan ground to a halt, unsure whether his entreaty was enough. Whilst he knew Jessica did not need her brother's permission, he did not want to cause disharmony, or upset her family.

Despite their courtship blossoming almost in front of him, not to mention Helena's plea not so very long ago, Hugh had not expected Duncan to approach him quite as soon. Thus, his request was the last thing Hugh anticipated, and his reaction less considered than it should have been.

"Jessica!" he barked, sounding quite fierce. Jessica gulped, her nerves threatening to bubble over.

"Y-yes," she stuttered, staring at her brother through eyes like saucers, biting her lip. Hugh suddenly registered she looked terrified. He paused, weighing up Duncan's words and the sincerity in his tone, simultaneously recalling Jessica's decision to assist at St Bart's and her happiness when in Duncan's company. This was her marriage proposal; a man, one presumably she loved in return, was offering for her and he was making it something to be fearful of instead of an occasion for joy. Hugh remembered the day he proposed to Helena, still one of the happiest of his life and cursed himself for being so insensitive. He drew a steadying breath.

"Jessica," his tones gentle now, "pray tell, do you wish to marry this man?" Jessica smiled at Duncan — a smile so full of love, Hugh felt his chest constrict — before looking her brother straight in the eye.

"More than anything I have ever wanted or will ever want in my life," she affirmed emphatically.

"As you are of age, I have no call to prevent you, however, I admit to being delighted you sought my approval. I am pleased to accept your suit, Mr Barrington and may I be the first to congratulate and wish you both every happiness?" Jessica whooped, flinging her arms around her brother, who gave into a chuckle and hugged her close. "Are you sure?" he whispered and felt her nod. It was enough. Releasing her, he shook hands with Duncan who was beaming from ear to ear.

There was a strange sort of clattering from the direction of the house, as abruptly, three people burst out of the large French windows in the library, sweeping over the lawns to envelop both Jessica and Duncan in either a warm embrace or a firm handshake. Everyone was talking and no one was listening, but, in the stillness of the late afternoon, their elation could be heard clear across the Great Park.

Allowing everyone their excitement for several minutes, Giles soon suggested they return to the library where, his wife informed him, celebratory drinks were being organised. Billie and Helena wise to what was unfolding, had spoken to Thomas

— that fine gentleman bustling away to arrange something befitting the impromptu festivities.

As they all strolled back towards the house, Jessica slowed her steps prompting Duncan to do the same. He grasped her hand, drawing her against him, uncaring whether or not it was proper.

"So, we are betrothed, a state of affairs to which I admit being rather partial." His formal words belied by the joy in his tones. "Jess, my only love, I believe I am the happiest man in England tonight." Jessica gazed into his eyes, the waning light darkening the brilliant blue to a deeper, softer shade.

"The feeling is mutual, sir…" she murmured, risking a kiss on his cheek. "…errr…although I'm a woman, so…" Duncan effectively prevented her tongue from tying itself into any more knots; his lips cool and firm lingering over hers, a promise and a caress.

"Do you think perchance you might be able to visit this evening?" he asked against her mouth. She nodded.

"I am not leaving without a proper goodbye," she replied, grinning mischievously at him. He smothered a laugh.

"Good, well, in that case, shall we join the others? They seem pleased for us. I wasn't sure with your brother for a while there, he seemed somewhat reticent."

"I think he was just surprised. I imagine anyone offering for me is a shock to him. My life, my work at both the hospital and the shipyard, are not environments which encourage suitors." She conceded wryly, as they entered the library through the French doors, the room's warm ambience a welcome contrast to the cooling afternoon.

The evening slipped away in a most convivial manner, Duncan having been persuaded to stay for the meal, despite declaring he was in no way dressed for such fine surroundings a sentiment Billie pooh-poohed immediately.

"You know we never stand on ceremony, Duncan Barrington and 'tis your betrothal, don't make me pull rank." Duncan raised his arms in surrender knowing Billie would have her way and she was likely to use the 'new mother' argument too if he didn't do as asked. Much later, after a lot of sumptuous food, more than one glass of wine and delightful conversation, the talk began to dwindle. A long day, topped off with an unexpected celebration was catching up with them all, thoughts of a good night's sleep too tempting to resist, especially as the three Drummonds had an early start on the morrow. Thanking Billie and Giles for a lovely evening, Duncan excused himself, Jessica walking with him to the back door.

"I will be there soon," she said quietly, holding his gaze, as he grasped her fingers, lifting her hand to kiss her palm.

"I am counting the minutes," he replied and disappeared into the darkness.

Jessica stood a moment, hugging herself; exulting quietly at the events of the day, a day now etched in her soul. Slowly she walked back to the library, to be drawn into cheerful chatter, allowing herself to bask in the joy of her family and friends for a few more minutes, as they sipped the last of their hot chocolate. She was a little sad her mother and Nick weren't there to share her news, but hopefully they would be just as pleased for her.

Chapter Twenty

As the moon spun its web of stars across the obsidian sky and when all was peaceful, Jessica appeared at the door of the workshop, anticipation making her tremble, memories of their earlier intimacy sending heat simmering through her. She paused on the threshold and drank him in. Duncan was standing by the fire, holding a carving, the one he had made for her. He was polishing it, but the care with which he did so seemed more than a mere wooden sculpture warranted.

As though attuned to her, he turned and, despite his face being in shadow, silhouetted by the firelight, she could still discern the flicker in his eyes. Her heart thudded and her breath caught. She would never tire of seeing his reaction to her presence, the strength of his love flowed from him, surrounding and embracing her, as palpable as his touch. It was as humbling as it was thrilling.

"Jess," he breathed. She flew over the flagged floor into his arms, mouths clashing and heat flaring as he kissed her into insensibility. It went on and on, until Jessica was sure they were spinning like sycamore keys in a gale. Hands roamed, fingers searched, lips teased and desire seethed.

After what seemed an eternity, Duncan lifted his head and, cupping her face in his large hand, his arm around her back holding her as close as he could, gazed into her eyes — glassy from the force of her emotions.

"How will I manage not seeing you every day?" he appealed, perhaps more to himself than Jessica, stroking his thumb along her jaw line and down the front of her neck.

Pensive now, Jessica sighed and stepped away, wandering around the workshop, picking up the odd carving, running her fingers over the aged wood of the furniture, her skirts rustling, the only sound save the hiss of the fire

"I never expected it to be as difficult as this," she acknowledged. "I know there will be much to do when I return to London, leaving little time to ponder our separation. A ridiculous amount of paperwork no doubt awaits me at Trentams and I admit to looking forward to going back to St Bart's, but it will seem only a half-life without being able to share my day with you. Even if we might only find time for a brief conversation or short evening constitutional, just to see you would be enough." She paused, staring into the hearth, hypnotised by the way the flames coiled around the wood, their dance mirroring the fire still flickering along her veins and spiralling around her centre.

"Jess…" Duncan's voice, a little hoarse, broke through her reverie and she turned to find him next to her, drawn as a moth to a candle. "Please, try not to be downhearted 'twill not be for long, and mayhap I can visit the city before we are wed. I know I cannot make this easier for you, but I am counting the days until we never need be apart again."

Jessica's throat clogged as her eyes filled with ridiculous tears. She blinked and tried to swallow; she was an adult and adults didn't cry — she absolutely refused to cry. This was not how she had planned their farewell, looking all miserable and pathetic. She wanted to smile and be cheerful, to let him see how much she loved him, but her heart ached and the effort to make her lips curve upwards seemed too great.

Raising her head, she studied his face, imprinting his features into her mind. "I'm sorry, I was determined this would not be a sad moment but I feel as though I am breaking," she whispered, wistful tones tearing at Duncan.

He groaned and enclosed her in his arms, scattering her face with kisses, butterfly soft. Halting, he pulled away, entranced by her tawny eyes, fathomless in the shadows and, in that instant, it seemed time was suspended. Neither moved; gazes locked, breath quickened and hearts drummed. Jessica swallowed again, opened her mouth and then closed it, words deserting her. Minutes ticked by, they remained motionless.

A log in the grate burst with a loud pop, sparks skittering over the cold flagstones and it was as though a spell had been lifted. They came together in an almost desperate frenzy and, had Duncan not been resolved to make love to Jessica in far more salubrious surroundings, as a respectable man should, he would have taken her there and then, stone floors be damned. As it was, it took every ounce of self-control he had to rein in his ardour, and both were shaken by the power of their emotions when he finally broke their kiss.

"Jessica Drummond, my beloved betrothed, even though we must say goodbye, you never truly leave me, for although distance separates us, I feel you in my heart. Here…" he pressed Jessica's hand against his waistcoat pocket where she felt the outline of something solid and round and realised it was the fob watch. "…this way, I always have you near…" he couldn't go on.

Jessica leaned away slightly to look up at him, before threading unsteady fingers through his unruly hair.

"Duncan Barrington, you know you hold my heart. It has been yours since first we met and you will always have it, I am only complete when I am with you. Keep it safe." She kissed him again, warmed by the heat from his body and the thud of his heart against her breast. "Until we meet again…" the phrase now a familiar tune, her voice trailed off and she fled without looking back.

Duncan stood for long moments; the chill he felt, nothing to do with the night air drifting in through the open door. Eventually, shaking his head, he closed the door quietly and shoved another log on the fire. Aware sleep would elude him, he began to work on a large armoire from one of the estate houses which required stripping and refinishing, hoping the mundane, yet comfortable routine would distract him long enough that his equilibrium might be restored.

Two days later, a carriage rolled to a halt on a darkening street on an early April evening. Three tired people and one sleepy dog tumbled out, stretching their bodies, relieved to be home after being confined in the coach for so long. Their departure from Whiteoaks had been more difficult than any had anticipated. Helena, who preferred the peace of the country to the city anyway, always found it hard to leave the home she had grown up in. Hugh, used to being at sea, was another who savoured the solace of quiet places and Jessica simply missed Duncan.

Still, they had busy lives to which they must attend and once on their journey, excitement at the prospect of reuniting with their families and returning to work, lifted low spirits. Jessica had not sought out Duncan the morning of their departure. She found she couldn't bear it, for to prolong their farewell merely exacerbated her sense of loss.

Tom, Hugh's driver, began to unload the luggage assisted by Ned, one of the grooms, stacking everything neatly on the step to be carried in, once Mr Rogers had ushered the weary travellers into the warmth of the house, and relieved them of their dusty cloaks. Both Dorothea Drummond and Nick were home and clamoured for the gossip about the christening, after which Jessica, far more diffidently than was her wont, explained what had transpired between Duncan and her, and that Hugh had approved his suit.

"Am I to surmise from this, you are now betrothed to Mr Barrington?" her mother observed, amused at Jessica's reserve, not in the slightest surprised at this development, astutely recalling her daughter's behaviour when in Duncan's company during his recent visit.

"Yes, Mama. I am sorry you were not there to share this with us, but it all rather snowballed because of me working for Dr Elliott." Forgetting her mother had no idea about this either. Helena noticing Mrs Drummond's befuddlement, clarified and, although saddened Jessica's choices would take her a reasonable distance from London, her mother pronounced herself excessively pleased. Even Nick congratulated his sister, although he was heard to mutter that all this love and nonsense was too sickeningly sweet for him. Laughing at his jaded outlook, the family began to discuss the wedding and the evening slipped by in a haze of laughter and good will.

The following day, Jessica accompanied Hugh to Trentams, their day disappearing under a mountain of paperwork requiring either filing, answering or destroying. Nick had been very efficient in his management of the yard in Hugh's absence but some documents required Hugh's attention or signature and Nick couldn't file to save his life. Thus, it was mid-evening before they left the docks and Jessica, knowing she needed to be up in good time to get to St Bart's on the morrow, went straight to bed forgoing her dinner.

Jessica settled back into her routine at the hospital seamlessly. She delivered Theo's letter to Dr Napier, who confessed he had missed her vivacity, and Isaac greeted her with a warm hug, which both surprised and delighted her. She was immediately engrossed in her regular chores and the day flew by. About to leave, she found the doctor, Isaac and Charlie in the office adjacent to the ward and, requesting a moment of their time, informed them of her impending marriage, adding that if they were amenable, her friends Clare and Meredith had pronounced themselves keen to assist in her stead, should Dr Napier consider them suitable, of course.

"Neither are prone to hysterics and are quite the most practical beings, far more so than I," she assured her listeners. "I will not leave until I am sure they and you are happy with the transition and if for any reason you are dissatisfied, I will continue until such times as an adequate replacement is found."

"Jessica Drummond, do you mean to tell me you would delay your wedding because of these two wards?" Dr Napier demanded peering at her over the rims of his spectacles. Jessica nodded. "You will do no such thing. We managed before your arrival and are quite capable of doing so again. I imagine your friends will prove wholly competent so this discussion is moot. Bring them around as soon as possible and we will see how they cope. I assume this letter from Dr Elliott..." tapping the still sealed missive atop a pile of reports, "...relates to your remove to Oak Stanton?" Jessica confirmed this was indeed the case. "I will attend to it shortly. Now off with you, you have more important things to be worrying about than this hospital."

His dismissal was more abrupt than he intended and Jessica flushed, sensing reproach in his tone. She hadn't intended to sound as though she was indispensable, rather she worried she was letting them down. Thanking them quietly, she turned to go, only to be stopped in her tracks seconds later as Dr Napier came around his desk and quite unexpectedly drew her into an avuncular hug, which amused and reassured her, the doctor being only a year or two older than Hugh.

"I beg your pardon, Jessica, I fear my surprise at your news got the better of me. Please do not think me angry or upset, and I...we all...wish you every happiness. 'Tis just we will miss you. You have brightened the lives of these men and your cheery presence will be difficult to replace."

Relieved, she grinned. "Oh, I think you will find my friends are just as irrepressible as I, Dr Napier. I am certain you will not be disappointed in their abilities." She smiled at the two orderlies and dipped a low curtsy. "I think today this is appropriate. I will see you all next week." She added, rushing out before they could say any more.

The following week, Jessica arranged for Meredith and Clare to accompany her to St Bart's. The two young ladies were, Dr Napier was pleased to note, as unflappable as Jessica, even when one of the soldiers took a bad turn during their initial visit. Rather than stand back and wait for one of the regular staff to take over, Clare calmly dealt with it, soothing the distressed man until his panic subsided. Meredith distracting the others with the most ludicrous tale about her brother's antics during the war, not only diffusing the tension but also allowing the soldiers to see her empathy was no pretence.

Thus, the days resumed their pattern. Jessica worked at St Bart's on Wednesdays with Meredith and Fridays with Clare and it wasn't long before Dr Napier deemed the newest recruits able to manage without Jessica's supervision. Meredith added Monday to her Wednesday shift, while Clare covered Tuesday and Thursday, and both would eventually work together on a Friday once Jessica had resigned. That, between them, the two women were happy to assist the entire week pleased both doctor and orderlies no end.

Regrettably for Jessica, who hoped he might reveal more of his story, Lieutenant Langdon remained withdrawn. According to Isaac, he had been this way the entire time Jessica was away, and had suffered through several nightmares. Jessica made sure to spend a little extra time with him every visit, talking about this and that, nothing of any consequence just general chitchat, but he refused to respond. She persevered, believing whatever haunted him needed an outlet or he would never recover.

All in all, Jessica was happy. She missed Duncan, his face was never far from her thoughts, but she knew their separation was finite, it would, hopefully, not be too long and they would be together, so she resolved to make the best of it, her naturally sunny personality coming to the fore, banishing her woes.

Chapter Twenty One

The happiness was not to last. One cold and grey Wednesday morning, perhaps three weeks after returning from Whiteoaks, trouble began to brew. Jessica had completed her chores and was chatting with Corporal Jamison over a hot coffee. Wounded at Waterloo, Jamison — formerly of the Scott's Greys — lost a leg and an eye to a slashing sabre after his horse had been killed by musket fire. He was one of the more pragmatic veterans usually quite cheerful with his lot, simply glad to be alive, home safe, and away from war. Jessica found his descriptions of the battles and their aftermath fascinating, if not rather gruesome and had already written several pages detailing his experiences.

They had only been talking for about half an hour when Lieutenant Langdon began screaming. He stalked up and down the ward, waving his fist, yelling at all and sundry, his words making little sense. Jessica was on her own, Meredith on an errand for Dr Napier and Isaac checking something on another floor. Refusing to let his behaviour alarm her, Jessica set aside her coffee and walked slowly along the ward to where the lieutenant was haranguing one of the other soldiers, accusing him of murder and mayhem, the poor man gawking in confusion.

"Lieutenant Langdon. Toby," she spoke clearly and deliberately, her tones unruffled. Toby ignored her. "Toby, look at me."

He turned and stared at her and at first it didn't seem as though he recognised her.

"Toby," she tried again, cajoling, "come, sit down by the fire, there is some hot coffee and the newspaper."

He continued to stare, his unblinking gaze unnerving, but as she watched, something shifted and his face lost some of its fury.

"Jessamine? Jessamine is that you?" his heartfelt plea in stark contrast to his anger.

"No, Toby, 'tis me Jessica. You are home, in London. This isn't France." He spun around, eyeing his fellow veterans, still gripped by some horror only he could see. "Toby, please come with me." She reached his side and taking his hand led him to the leather chairs surrounding the hearth. Guiding him to one of them, she waited until he sat down, and handed him one of the broadsheets. He glanced at it, but just when Jessica thought he was beginning to relax, he bunched up the paper and ripped it apart, hurling the shreds onto the floor. Bounding out of the chair, he roared something about Toulouse and Bayonne and idiocy and wasted lives, banging his fists on the table in front of him in his agitation.

Jessica tried again, never raising her voice, and suddenly remembered her lullaby and how it seemed to comfort Major Vaughan. Would it work for Toby? She could only try; nothing else was easing his rage. She began to croon, the sweet purity of her voice carrying to the far corners of the room. As they had the previous time, the men paused whatever they were doing to listen. Toby continued to stomp up and down, but she sensed his pace slowing. Jessica pretended to ignore him and wandered the room, as though busy with her tasks; folding blankets, filling cups with water, tidying the tables, picking up books, re-arranging the desks and tables, anything to keep her fingers occupied and Toby distracted.

Finishing the song, Jessica continued onto another and then another when, unbidden the French folk song *au clair de la lune* popped into her head. Her grandmother had sung it to her when a child, and even though Jessica realised this might make things worse — the French words perhaps triggering something in the lieutenant's memory — she decided it was worth the risk. Without missing a note, she let her voice slide smoothly into the haunting aria. By now the room was almost silent, even Toby had quieted. Jessica did not stop moving or singing; making sure windows were closed against the rain which had become heavier during the morning, checking the stock of bandages,

sheets and blankets in the store cupboard alongside the door —
still she sang.

At some point Isaac returned, moving to stand near Toby,
who had stopped pacing and was watching Jessica, a curious
expression on his face. Jessica took no notice, focused on
sustaining the calm enveloping the room. A few of the men,
who knew the lyrics, joined in; their voices harmonising, the
acoustics in the lofty room throwing their music back in soft
waves. Without warning, Toby began to weep; deep sobs
wracking his body as whatever ravaged his mind finally
released him.

"Jessamine, my Jessamine, oh ma petite Jessamine," his
mournful cry blending with the melody of those singing. Isaac
helped the man to his bed, covering him with a warm blanket
and sitting beside him until he fell into an exhausted slumber.
Jessica finished the song and carried on as though nothing had
happened, even though she was trembling from her effort to
remain unruffled and her insides felt like jelly. Forcing herself
to appear unperturbed, Jessica walked out of the ward and
along to Dr Napier's office, which fortuitously, was empty. She
collapsed with little care for grace, into one of the chairs and,
resting her head in her hands, took deep breaths in an attempt
to settle her nerves.

It wasn't that she feared Toby, or any of the men for that
matter, but to maintain her composure in the face of such
anger had required all her concentration — she felt as though
she had worked a full day and walked Trixie three times round
the park and it was barely lunchtime. As she sat in the tranquil
coolness of the doctor's office, her thoughts inevitably strayed
to Duncan. She had made it a rule not to wallow, so rarely
allowed herself the luxury of thinking about him, except when
on her own in her bedchamber, where his face refused to leave
her thoughts. Toby's outburst today, however, brought Duncan
to the forefront of her mind and she realised how hard he
strived to master his residual trauma — he always seemed so in
control.

A quiet knock heralded Dr Napier who had just returned from a meeting at one of the other hospitals, Isaac, no doubt, having updated him on what had occurred.

"Are you all right, Jessica?" he asked solicitously. She nodded, unable to form words, her throat ached and all she wanted to do was sleep. The doctor continued, "Isaac tells me it was an acute attack. It appears you handled it remarkably well. I believe this has been a long time coming. The breakthrough you saw when last you spoke with him for any length of time has been festering, needing a catalyst. Today something within him fractured allowing him to express his anger and I am sorry you were there on your own. While frightening to witness, it is a vital part of the healing process for, without it he has no hope of facing whatever tortures him. I think this could be his turning point."

Jessica found her voice. "Do you really think so? I am sure whatever torments him is related to this Jessamine person. He still calls me by that name, I do not know whether I resemble her or whether my own name sounds similar, but whatever the reason, I seem to remind him of her. Maybe if I spoke to him in French it might draw him out some more. I speak only a little, but do you think it worth a try?"

The doctor mulled this over for several minutes. "I think at this point everything is worth a try, but only when I am with you. I do not want you to cope with such an outburst on your own again."

"Dr Napier, while I admit it is challenging to face such things on my own, you cannot be with me every minute of every day. Toby's outburst came out of the blue; the room was quiet, with nothing to indicate anything was amiss. I do not fear these men, or their terrors and none would deliberately hurt me. I knew what I might have to deal with when I took on this work. 'Tis good experience; I am learning so much and although I have never seen Dun…Mr Barrington in the throes of an episode, at least now I have some knowledge of how to deal with it should the occasion arise. You cannot coddle me. It would make your day more arduous than it already is." Jessica grinned at the doctor's expression, which hovered somewhere between frustrated and resigned. "Come now, Isaac or Charlie are usually only a shout away, if not there with me. Trust us. If you are not in the ward when Toby needs you, we can find you quickly enough."

Dr Napier gave up, knowing she was correct. Any of the men could suffer a similar attack without warning, he could not be present all the time. Yes, his job — over and above the obvious — was to monitor and safeguard both patients and staff, but he was only one man in a large hospital with many under his care.

Jessica diverted his concerns by asking him about the new prostheses he was working on. Along with several other doctors across London, Dr Napier was involved in the development of more functional artificial limbs. The recent wars had highlighted a desperate need and currently most devices were heavy, ungainly and generally very uncomfortable, strapped on in a way that made it more difficult to move with the prosthesis than without. Many of the veterans at St Bart's eschewed such options preferring a crutch or, in the case of missing arms, just didn't bother with anything, alleging the artificial devices harder to cope with than the loss of their actual limb.

Intrigued by a model of a hand on his desk, Jessica asked Dr Napier how it functioned. He demonstrated and, although still quite crude, it gave the young woman the inkling of an idea.

"Do you think it might be possible for me to commission one of these, Dr Napier?" she enquired hesitantly. "As you are aware, my betrothed lost his lower left arm in the war and, since his discharge, has become a highly skilled carpenter. I realise an artificial device would be unlikely to make a huge difference for the bulk of his work; fence posts, cupboard, tables and the like, but he also creates the most intricate carvings, and I believe it would offer him greater stability when he is working on such a piece. I accept it will be an expensive commodity, but I have some savings and am willing to pay whatever the cost. Even if 'tis one not quite perfected, I would wager he would benefit from its use."

Excitement threaded her tones as Jessica realised the potential of such a device, stubbornly refusing to acknowledge the niggle of unease jabbing at her consciousness, aware of how Duncan might perceive such an offering. He had his pride and she didn't want him to think she considered him less of a man because of his disability; hopefully she could persuade him of the advantages without appearing to.

Dr Napier studied her as she talked, her vivid face full of enthusiasm for his project and he wished — not for the first time — he had met her before this other man had stolen her heart. For one still young, Jessica possessed a maturity beyond her years, which along with her friendly disposition and ability to relate to his patients was a gift he would sorely miss. He had read the letter from Theo Elliott outlining Jessica's plans to work for him, including a request for a report on what she had learned and accomplished during her brief stint at St Bart's and whether his friend would recommend her in the capacity of doctor's assistant.

Even though Dr Napier knew Jessica would be more than suitable and would be loved by every one of Theo's patients within ten minutes of her meeting them, part of him didn't want to let her go. He wanted her here at St Bart's; working her own particular brand of magic on his patients and brightening their humdrum lives.

Shaking off so fanciful a sentiment, the doctor brought his mind back to their discussion and after explaining, in detail, how they might go about organising a device for Duncan, along with the costs involved, the pair returned to their respective tasks.

Toby was still asleep and the atmosphere in the ward had returned to its normal serenity. Several men were gathered around the large table playing cards, others were reading or chatting quietly. Jessica continued with her regular chores, while her mind ruminated over how she would broach the subject of the prosthesis with Duncan. The rest of the day was uneventful. When Toby awoke he was reluctant to talk, keeping to himself. The staff was content to leave him to his thoughts, there was no necessity to force the issue, hoping he would talk to them when he was ready.

Once home, and after an evening with her family, Jessica retired to her bedchamber to write to Duncan. Without mentioning her idea, she scribbled enthusiastically about all she had learned that day with regard to artificial devices and how they could help the veterans she worked with. She wrote several pages, folding them together and, sealing them closed with a large blob of wax, dropped a kiss on the front where she filled in his address. It was late and, undressing quickly, she hopped into bed. As she snuggled under the covers, his face rose in her mind, memories of his touch teased at her and she fell asleep, a secret smile on her face.

Chapter Twenty Two

During the next week or so, several things occurred which culminated in a rather disquieting event. When Jessica arrived at St Bart's the Wednesday following Lieutenant Langdon's flare-up, Dr Napier informed her that the soldier had taken to wandering off. None of the patients were restricted to the wards. They could come and go as they pleased and often could be found in the lovely gardens at the rear of the hospital. Some visited family for a day or a weekend; some were escorted into the city if they expressed an inclination to do so. The problem was, Toby would disappear at odd times of the day and night without explanation, and be gone for hours at a time. No one knew where he went; he just left and came back.

Without physically strapping him to the bed frame, something no one had any intention of doing; they just had to hope it was a phase. Had this behaviour come from almost any of the other veterans, Dr Napier would not be concerned, but Toby was vulnerable at the moment, his trauma bubbling close to the surface and, the worry was, something would trigger an attack when he was far from those who understood and could handle it. One or two lads who acted as messengers were dispatched around the neighbourhood with regularity in case Toby ended up in one of the lock-ups.

This day Toby was his usual quiet self; he spent most of it sitting by the fire, reading. Unwilling to disturb him, Jessica completed her chores and made sure any whose wounds required cleaning and dressing were attended to. Meredith was there also, quite happy to undertake any and all tasks demanded of her, the two girls enjoying relaxed banter with each other and their charges. The day flew by and although it was almost time for Jessica to leave, she was chatting with some of the sailors about life on a battle ship, adding to her ever-increasing collection of stories, when Charlie came to find her.

"Jessica, have you seen Toby? Meredith says he was sitting at the table one minute, the next he was gone." Charlie puffed, sounding as though he had run from the other side of London not the other side of the corridor.

"No, not since luncheon," she replied, excusing herself and going to join the orderly. "Are you sure he's not in the gardens?"

Charlie shook his head. "No! I've been everywhere, no one's seen him." Which explained his state of breathlessness.

"There's naught we can do, Charlie," she soothed. "If the lieutenant wishes to leave, we cannot prevent him."

"It's just he was muttering about Jessamine again and I fear he may be trying to find her." They looked at each other, this put a different perspective on things. If he was searching for this woman, he could be anywhere. They weren't even sure he realised he was in England not France.

"Well regardless, there is still nothing we can do save be vigilant. Doubtless he will return soon, but I think we need to get to the bottom of this Jessamine business, 'tis clear it causes him great distress. I wonder who she was?" Jessica mused.

Charlie had no answers and the pair went to find the doctor to report Toby's disappearance.

Unable to do any more, Jessica said her goodbyes and, collecting Meredith the two ladies hopped into the Drummond carriage, trundling away into the spring evening. After dropping Meredith at her house, Jessica was soon home, hoping she would have time to take Trixie for a long walk before dinner was served. Calling a hello to anyone within hearing, she went upstairs and changed into something more suited to tramping around the park. Eager to be in the fresh air, Jessica flew back down the stairs, Trixie at her heels, and was almost out of the door when her mother waylaid her. Mrs Drummond, appearing from the parlour, informed Jessica that dinner would be in two hours, adding that Helena and Hugh had found a house. Exciting for the newlyweds although a little sad for the rest of the family, especially Mrs Drummond, who would miss her son and his wife. Kissing her mother on the cheek, Jessica sailed out of the front door, saying she'd be home in about an hour.

Glad to be outdoors, the last of the afternoon sun on her face, Jessica, with the ever faithful, Trixie strode along the path and into the park. Although a little late in the day for a constitutional, there were a number of people taking advantage of the milder weather and a few carriages trundled along the tracks. Several people whom she had come to know since walking the dog regularly, hailed her and she greeted others. Jessica loved this time of year, the promise of a warm summer tantalisingly out of reach, yet still discernible, and the air, although cool, was laden with the fragrance of new blossoms. Trixie gambolled happily about in the grass, digging up the odd bulb before Jessica could stop her. Finding a sturdy stick, Jessica spent much of their walk tossing it, watching the energetic creature chase after it, tiring her quite effectively.

The daylight was almost gone when, a little more than an hour later — thoughts of a hot meal spurring her on — Jessica became aware she was being followed. Tightening Trixie's leash until the dog was by her side, she turned slowly, startled to see Toby, no more than ten steps behind her.

"Lieutenant Langdon, what brings you to this part of town?" she forced herself to sound chirpy. Toby smiled, and stopped alongside her.

"My Jessamine, finally, I have found you. I needed to ensure you were safe." He moved closer and Trixie growled deep in her throat sending a trickle of unease down Jessica's spine. The street was quiet and she was still a distance from home.

"Well, do come along then, you realise 'tis nearly time for our evening meal." She encouraged briskly, hoping he would do as she bid.

"You have enough to share?" he looked puzzled.

"Of course, and where else are you going to find food at this hour?" she countered, glad her voice was firm. She waited until he joined her then they walked back to the Drummond residence side by side. Jessica chatted artlessly about the weather, hoping Toby was distracted enough not to bolt. Trixie continued to growl, her displeasure at this human's intrusion obvious, but Toby didn't even seem to notice the dog's presence.

They reached her home at the same time as Hugh and Helena arrived. Jessica heaved a sigh of relief, but before she had a chance to introduce her companion, he shot off along the street and vanished around the corner.

"Who was that?" Hugh asked in astonishment. Jessica told him what had happened, explaining Toby's trauma. "And now he knows where you live? Jessica what were you thinking?" he chastised.

"I was thinking if I could get home maybe you or Nick could take him back to St Bart's," she expostulated, annoyed at Toby for running off and her brother for his lack of faith in her judgement. "Do you imagine I invited him to meet me?" she demanded sharply.

"Let us go inside," Helena intervened before the siblings became cross with each other. Hugh still tended to treat Jessica as though a child. "This is not a matter to be discussed in the street."

Hugh glanced at his wife who sent him a silent message pleading with him to curb his irritation. Taking a deep breath, he forced himself to calm down, noticing Jessica's pale face and tightly clenched jaw, and that Trixie was still growling.

"I beg your pardon, Jess. I…'twas just a surprise, is all." He pulled his sister into a hug. "I didn't mean to make the situation worse." As he felt Jessica relax against his tall frame, Hugh was reminded of the times she sought him out after their father had died, when things overwhelmed her, and she didn't want to bother their mother. A simple hug, yet Jessica always said it gave her comfort and security and Hugh was secretly gratified he still had the ability to make her feel safe.

"It's fine, I'm sure he will find his way back to the hospital, it's only he seems to think I am this Jessamine, whoever she may be and I can't get him to accept I'm not her.

Both Hugh and Helena looked at each other, perturbed by this revelation, understanding more than Jessica realised. An emotionally unstable man, and an ex-soldier to boot, who believed Jessica to be some mysterious French girl, one whom he seemingly knew well, had followed her home. Hugh made a mental note to ask his domestic staff to be vigilant, and inform him should a stranger appear to be watching the house.

Saying no more for now, Helena ushered the other two inside where, over a tasty meal, she and Hugh were pressed for details of the house they had found.

The next day, Jessica was at Trentams, to Hugh's relief — here she was under his protection. He did feel moved to ask whether she intended to inform Dr Napier of Toby's visit, but she just shrugged and said she would think about it, the incident almost forgotten now some time had elapsed. Jessica had assured her brother Toby didn't seem inclined to hurt her, that was the last thing she expected of him and the more she thought about it the more he just seemed lost and alone.

Hugh pursed his lips at what he considered his sister's cavalier disregard for her own safety, but decided to keep his opinion to himself, knowing her dislike of being coddled. He was determined, however, to keep an eye on her, and considered sending a missive to Dr Napier, apprising him of what had occurred.

The following Friday, after a relatively uneventful week, by which, as Jessica commented to Clare while they were making the beds, meant nobody had run away, or caused chaos. Even Toby hadn't left the ward since his encounter with Jessica on the street. Jessica had finished collecting her stories and had, over the past few nights, closeted herself in the Drummonds' study, painstakingly copying them out in her precise script. Now complete, she was determined to find a print house that would be willing to collate them into some form of booklet so she could show Dr Napier and let him decide whether it was worth further publication.

Towards the end of the afternoon, after all their main chores had been done, Jessica shooed Clare off home. Her family was expecting visitors that evening and she wanted to be home in time to change.

"Go, there is little left to do. I will begin the stock-take of the store cupboard. 'Tis unlikely I will finish today but I should like to do what I can, so there is not as much for Meredith on Monday. There is nothing for which I need to rush home. Mama is going to the theatre and then onto dinner with friends and the others are out. I believe Helena and Hugh are attending a ball with Tabitha and Stephen, so I would be home alone anyway. This way I can fill in more time and there are always hackneys to hail."

Clare hesitated, knowing Jessica's capacity for becoming so engrossed in something she forgot everything else around her.

"Go, I promise I will not stay too long, an hour at most." Jessica assured her.

"Are you sure?" reluctant to leave her friend with so mundane a task.

Jessica grinned at Clare. "I am certain, get away with you. Your Mama will not be pleased if you are late. Truly, I will be done in a jiffy." Confirming they, along with Meredith would meet on Sunday afternoon at Gunther's, Clare hurried out of the ward and along to where the stairs took her to the front entrance.

Jessica chuckled quietly at Clare's madcap dash and, turning her attention to the task at hand, walked along to the far end of the corridor where the store cupboard was situated. Starting with blankets and sheets, she counted everything carefully, before moving on to the pile of cloths and bandages — sorting, folding and more counting.

Completely absorbed by what she was doing, time slipped away and it wasn't until she became aware the light had faded to such a degree she could no longer distinguish bandages from shelves, that Jessica realised she had stayed far longer than intended. Quickly jotting down the number of bandages from the latest pile she had counted and noting where she had got to, Jessica closed the door and was halfway to the ward, checking her sheet, when she heard footsteps coming towards her. Presuming it to be a staff member, probably Charlie or Isaac, she looked up, a ready smile on her face.

It wasn't Charlie or Isaac, it was Toby.

Jessica came to an abrupt halt and bit back a groan.

"Lieutenant. May I help you? Is there something you need?" Toby stared at her.

"Lieutenant Langdon, can you hear me?" Toby said nothing, just continued to stare.

Unnerved, for it was quiet and dim along this corridor now, the daylight almost gone. Jessica waited.

After a few minutes, she tried coaxing him again. "Toby come with me, your comrades will be wondering where you are. You know they play poker on Friday evenings. I think I heard Charlie mention beer. You surely don't wish to miss the fun?" It was as though she hadn't spoken, Toby offered no response at all.

"Well, I cannot stand here chatting with you all night. I must get home; my family will be holding dinner for me." Jessica, whose excuse sounded weak to her own ears, made to walk past the soldier but he grabbed her arm.

"No, you cannot go that way, 'tis dangerous," his voice rough and low. He ducked his head. "Keep down, or they will see you."

Jessica tried to disengage his hand from her arm but he merely tightened his grip.

"Lieutenant Langdon! Unhand me, sir," she spoke with firm authority to no avail. Toby began to pull her the way she just come — back towards the storeroom — muttering about tactics and stupidity of army generals and how all these people would die for nothing. Jessica began to panic, there was no one else around, but she yelled anyway

"Orderly, I need an orderly!" she called as loudly as she could without actually screaming. The store cupboard, as on every floor throughout the hospital was situated well away from the main ward, deliberately so. Each ward had its own smaller cupboard; these storerooms were exactly that, purely for storage, from where the orderlies collected their supplies. The secluded position meant unless anyone chanced along, Jessica was quite alone.

She called out again, but her cry was swallowed into the depth of the passageway.

"Hush, do not draw attention. You must hide, do not follow me again." Toby spoke in a strange mix of French and English, "*Les soldats bâtards sont partout.* They will kill you for helping me. Please, my Jessamine, go with ta mère, *c'est elle qui s'occupera de toi.* Please do not follow *mon amour, mon petit cœur,* I will find you when it is safe. *Croyez moi.*"

Jessica understood he was begging Jessamine, who, quite clearly now was his love and his sweetheart, to go with her mother who would keep her safe from the bastard soldiers who were everywhere. She concluded Toby thought himself in France presumably not long before whatever caused his trauma. She responded in her limited French, softening her voice to that of a plea.

"Toby, *mon amour! Je te supplie de me trouver. Ne me laissez pas ici, j'ai très pour.*" "Toby, my love, I beg you to find me. Do not leave me, I am very scared." Although probably far from correct, Jessica hoped it would be enough to convince him she was Jessamine and maybe she could work out what was going on. He drew her into an embrace and, although he was gentle, Jessica had to force herself to relax. He murmured sweet nothings in her ear and kissed her cheek. It was all she could do not to shudder.

"Go now, *ma petite, je veux que tu sois en sécurité.*" He wanted her to go somewhere and stay safe. Confused, Jessica faltered, unsure what he meant.

"Where should I go?" she whispered, still speaking French.

"That way." He pointed towards the storeroom door. "It will lead you through to the other side of the bridge." He glanced around furtively, before pushing the door. It creaked on its hinges, the noise eerie in the gloom, and before Jessica could make a sound or even think of running, Toby shoved her hard into the darkness and locked the door behind her.

"You will be safe, follow the path," his words died away and then there was only silence.

Jessica stood in shock, waiting for Toby to come back and let her out.

"Surely, he is playing games," she mused out loud. After standing for long moments, however, with no sound of returning footsteps, Jessica started banging on the door and shouting for help. She banged and yelled until she was hoarse and her hands were sore. "Oh, this is just great," she groused, trying to think of ways to attract attention that didn't involve screeching like a banshee or breaking her fingers. She looked around; it was completely dark save for a tiny window high in the wall.

Wondering whether it might open, Jessica hitched up her skirts and tried to use the shelves as a makeshift ladder to reach the window. She had only managed two levels when the whole thing began to shake underneath her.

"Oh for goodness sake. They can hold all these blankets but the minute I try to climb them, they start to collapse. Dr Napier needs to organise sturdier shelves for instances such as this." Blithely ignoring the fact, it was unlikely this was a common occurrence.

Huffing in frustration, Jessica tried shouting again, but it was no good. She couldn't keep calling out, on the possibility someone might walk to this end of the corridor. Unless one of the wards used up all of the blankets, sheets and cloths from their particular cupboards she would be locked in until morning. Then she remembered it was Friday. Everything was different over the weekend. From the few hours she had spent at the hospital during those occasional Saturday afternoons, she knew — other than dressing wounds for those who required it — the men were left to themselves. Several of the veterans visited family and others were taken out for some part of each day; the ward monitored only by a skeleton staff, all regular chores adjourned until Monday morning.

Jessica leaned against the shelves, ruminating over what she might do. Would anyone think to come and look for her, and if they did would they try this end of the corridor? If she was stuck here for three days, would she have the strength to shout? She just had to hope Toby would remember what he had done and come back to release her.

Chapter Twenty Three

Meanwhile, several miles away on a quiet street in a far more fashionable corner of London, a carriage rolled up to an elegant residence. It was mid-evening and the gentleman therein was weary from two long and miserable days of travelling. The weather had been inclement and they had been obliged to stop several times to dig the wheels out of the mud. The thought of a long soak in a hot bath and change of clothes was almost irresistible but he longed to see Jessica more. Thanking Jake, who indicated he would wait to convey his passenger to Winchester House where he would be staying, Duncan Barrington climbed the steps and was about to knock on the front door when it opened and Mr Rogers peered out.

"Oh Mr Barrington, sir, I heard the coach and thought it was Miss Jessica. She's rare late tonight." Duncan frowned at this; flipping the fob watch she had given him, noting it was coming up on half after eight.

"Is this typical, Mr Rogers?" Duncan asked.

The butler shook his head. "No, sir, she's usually home by six; occasionally half after, never this late. She knows her Mama worries if she's out after dark. Mrs Drummond is out this evening, otherwise 'tis likely there'd already be a search party going up and down the streets."

"Was Miss Jessica at St Bart's today?"

"She was that, 'tis one of her regular days at the hospital," affirming Duncan's supposition.

"I think I will go and check. It cannot do any harm. I admit to feeling concerned for her safety so late at night. She hasn't perchance accompanied any of her friends to their home, or a gathering?"

"I doubt it, sir. Had that been the case, she would have come home to change."

Duncan saw the sense in this and, saying he would return once he'd checked the hospital, trudged to the carriage, asking Jake to drive to St Bart's as quickly as possible. Twenty minutes later he was striding briskly up the stairs of the hospital to the floor where Jessica worked. Poking his head through the doors of both wards, he noticed all was quiet but of Jessica there was no sign. Spotting Major Vaughan, Duncan asked him when last he had been aware of Miss Drummond on the ward. The Major mulled the question over for several minutes before saying he thought it had been late afternoon. He had heard Jessica and Clare chatting as they tidied the room.

"I presume they both left around that time, I have not heard either since," he concluded.

Duncan thanked him, and went in search of an orderly, coming across Charlie in the ward opposite.

"It's Charlie isn't it?" The young orderly nodded at the query. "Good evening, Charlie, I'm Duncan Barrington, Miss Drummond's betrothed. Is she still here?" Charlie looked surprised.

"I don't think so, sir, she normally leaves about half after five. Mind, now you mention it, she didn't say goodbye, which is unusual. Why?"

Duncan explained that she wasn't at home and no one appeared to have seen her during the evening. Charlie's surprise turned to concern.

"'Tis unlike her, sir. What could have happened?"

"I don't know, Charlie, but we need to find her. How does she normally get home?"

"I think on a Friday she hails a hackney. There's always plenty out front of an afternoon. What about Clare, Miss Raleigh? She was here today also, maybe Miss Jessica went home with her."

"I'll arrange for someone to check, I have no idea of her address. I've only just arrived this evening from the country. Presumably someone at the Drummond residence will know. Thank you, Charlie. Please, if you hear anything, send a message to Jessica's home. This doesn't sit well with me."

Charlie agreed and said he would mention her disappearance to the other staff.

Duncan hurried out of the great building, apologising to Jake for the delay. The Winchester's driver clicked the horses and they rattled away through empty streets, pulling up in front of the Drummond residence barely an hour after they left.

Mr Rogers provided Duncan with the Raleigh's address, but upon on his arrival, Duncan was informed the family were out for the evening; although their butler was able to confirm Miss Drummond definitely hadn't accompanied them. Duncan was perplexed, it was as though she'd vanished into thin air and, much as he wanted to keep looking he had no idea where to start. Returning once more to her home, he advised Mr Rogers of what he had learned, asking him to inform the family as soon as possible adding he was staying at Winchester House, where he could be contacted at any time.

Duncan could see Mr Rogers was now as worried as he; it was probable the retainer had known Jessica most, if not all, of her life and concern over what might have befallen her would doubtless play on his mind.

It was a long night. Mr Rogers updated the rest of the Drummond family as to what had transpired when each arrived home and none felt able to rest. Duncan was too anxious to sleep, and spent the night pacing the floors, trying to work out where Jessica might be and who he could contact to help look for her. The only person who did manage any sleep at all was Jessica herself. Locked in a dark room, there was little else to do, so she created a bed of sorts with blankets and sheets and, although on tenterhooks, hoping someone would come and let her out, eventually just before dawn, fell into a fitful doze.

The next morning, Hugh contacted Lucas Withers, his friend and a gentleman who handled all manner of investigations. The two called upon Duncan not long after breakfast, gathering as much information as they were able, which turned out to be very little. The three men spent fruitless hours visiting every place they thought Jessica might be but, by midday, it was clear she was not and had not been at any of them at any point during the night. None of her friends had heard from her, and late in the afternoon, they finally caught Miss Raleigh at home. Clare mentioned Jessica had said she might begin checking the stock but only intended to stay a little longer.

"I don't suppose it was much after I left, when Jessica finished. Once evening draws in, it's too hard to count anything because you need decent light." Clare reflected. She stared appraisingly at the tall man who was asking her all these questions. "Are you by any chance Mr Barrington?" she enquired. When Duncan nodded. Clare smiled knowingly.

"Well, I can certainly see why," she murmured, not altogether lucidly, to which Duncan raised a quizzical eyebrow. Clare did not elaborate however, simply tapped her chin as she tried to think where Jessica might be. No one was able to suggest any rhyme or reason as to why Jessica had not gone home the previous evening. Lucas and Hugh had checked all around the locale and even the hospitals in case she had been involved in some kind of accident.

Another day slipped away. Lucas had drafted in several of his men, who along with Hugh and Duncan, conducted the most exhaustive search, from the shipyard, through the parks, around the hospital and everywhere in between.

Jessica was nowhere to be found.

By now, Jessica was starting to feel quite peculiar, unable to recall exactly long she had been locked up and despite sporadically banging on the door and shouting, it seemed she was probably stuck in the store cupboard until Monday morning. She knew she hadn't eaten or drunk anything for quite some time, but her stomach was no longer rumbling, and although she didn't know whether that was good or bad, she was glad it had stopped. She had also been rather concerned about what to do should she need to use a chamber pot, but oddly no longer had the urge to do so. Her legs felt a bit wobbly and her head seemed sort of floaty, as though there was too much air in it. That thought made her giggle, as her mother often told her she had more air in her head than brains when she forgot to do something.

As darkness fell for the third time, Jessica could no longer fight her fatigue, so curled up on her not very comfortable bed and hoped to sleep through the night, doing her best to ignore the scrabbling noises which seemed to be going on all around her. Working in an office on the docks, Jessica was used to mice, rats and spiders and was not frightened of them; she just did not relish the idea of being considered something worth nibbling on while she slept.

While Jessica was trying to avoid becoming fodder for hungry rodents, her family, Duncan, and Lucas were still trying to fathom her whereabouts. Oddly, despite Clare's comments, no one thought to check the main stockroom, presuming she referred to the store cupboard within the ward. Lucas had taken detailed notes, but there was nothing within them providing any indication where she might be or have gone. Lucas was becoming convinced she had been kidnapped but was loath to articulate this, for most kidnappings he investigated, ended with the death of the victim. Duncan and Hugh were also aware of the probability, neither mentioning their suspicions for the same reason as Lucas.

For Duncan, the thought someone might be hurting Jessica for whatever reason was unconscionable and he was having difficulty accepting it was even a possibility, but the longer she was missing, the harder it was to persuade himself there was any other explanation. Hugh couldn't think of a reason why anyone would kidnap his sister. The only person with an axe to grind, business-wise, had been killed the previous year. He did, however, recall the odd behaviour of a certain Lieutenant Langdon, which niggled him enough that he went back to the hospital to check on the veteran's movements. Toby was, as usual, sitting by the fire, reading quietly; Isaac confirming he hadn't left the hospital in at least three days.

The whole thing was mystifying.

As the night wore on and unable to sleep, those gathered at the Drummond residence tossed ideas back and forth, until

Helena was moved to speculate whether Trixie might be of help.

"How could Trixie help?" asked Hugh, sounding more than a little sceptical.

"If we give her something with Jessica's scent on, like a glove or one of her cloaks, there's a possibility the creature might be able track her. Dogs do this when they hunt prey; it stands to reason they should be able to follow any kind of trail, animal or human. I know Trixie isn't a scent hound and it has been two days since Jessica was seen but we do know *where* she was last seen. Don't you think it worth a try? If they will allow Trixie into St Bart's, we might at least have a starting point or a direction."

They looked at each other. Despite having little faith in Trixie's ability to track Jessica — or that there would be even anything *to* track — at this stage they had nothing to lose and everything to gain.

"May we go now?" begged Duncan, the slightest hope they might find her, lending urgency to his tones.

Lucas nodded. "I think we must. The longer we delay the less likelihood there will be anything for Trixie to follow."

Helena went to find something her sister-in-law used often, returning with the pair of shabby gloves Jessica wore when walking Trixie, along with a wool scarf, as well as Trixie herself who had been moping in her mistress' bedchamber.

"These should be enough. Jessica wears these ratty old gloves every day and this is her favourite scarf." Duncan thanked her, putting on his own glove before taking both items from her, careful not to add his own scent to any residue of Jessica's. The three men, and a very excited dog, climbed into the carriage as Tom, the Drummond's driver, pointed the horses towards St Bart's.

Despite the dearth of traffic on the streets, the journey seemed interminable, expectancy heightened for the success of what seemed so improbable an experiment. It was after midnight when the carriage trundled to a halt in front of the imposing building, the hulking shadow only alleviated by the occasional glow of a candle in one of the innumerable windows. Duncan led them up to the wards were Jessica worked.

Fortuitously, Charlie was on duty and they found him at his desk immersed in a pile of medical notes. He glanced up as the door creaked open, his jaw dropping when he saw the three men, not to mention an ungainly looking dog.

"You do realise it is well past visiting hours and you cannot bring a dog in here." He chastised them in vexed undertones. "What brings you here so late?" Then he recognised Duncan and his tone changed to one of astonishment. "Please, do not tell me Jessica is still missing?" he appealed.

"We have not found hide nor hair of her these past two days and we wish to try something." Duncan went on to explain about dogs capable of tracking by scent, and their hope Trixie might be able to pick up Jessica's trail, since it seemed there was not much foot traffic on these floors during the weekend.

Charlie, an astute young man, quickly understood what Duncan was talking about. He had heard about dogs used to search for injured soldiers in the war, and others who seemed able to find the dead.

"We do not think she is in the wards anyway, so if, and it seems a big if, she is within the hospital, it will some isolated area rarely frequented by staff or visitors, otherwise someone surely would have found her by now."

Charlie saw the sense in this and stood aside to let Trixie do what she could.

Duncan held the gloves and scarf close to Trixie's nose, the dog sniffed, whimpering at the familiar fragrance. She paced this way and that, wuffling at the ground and around the desk before wandering the length of the ward, earning a pat or two from those men who happened to be awake. For a while it appeared a waste of time, then all of a sudden she growled deep in her chest and shoved her nose against the hallway door. Hugh opened it and, as Charlie handed Duncan a candle, Trixie shot off along the passageway, her head sweeping back and forth over the floor. She doubled back on herself twice, before continuing along the corridor and, just when all three men thought they had come to a dead end, Trixie began whining and pawing frantically at a door in an alcove. There was a key in the lock and Duncan turned it as Charlie came along with a second candle. He pushed the door cautiously, but it flew open as Trixie launched herself at a small bundle on the floor.

Chapter Twenty Four

Nothing happened, no sound and no movement, but Trixie continued to scrabble, emitting peculiar little mewling sounds. Uncertain of what they would find, Hugh got hold of Trixie's collar, dragging her aside as Duncan bent to remove the layers of blankets covering the huddle. Despite their optimism, all four men were astonished, nevertheless, when the last blanket was lifted to reveal a familiar face. Duncan's legs nearly gave out from under him, his relief was so great. Jessica looked to be fast asleep, but her face had an odd grey cast and, as Duncan ran his finger over her cheek, her skin felt very dry.

"Jessica, sweetheart, wake up, we've come to take you home." No response. He tried again, nothing. Charlie leaned forward raising the candle in order to study her in better light.

"I think we'd best take her onto one of the wards," he said. "She looks as though she may've slipped into a stupor." Duncan stared at the orderly in shock. Charlie shrugged. "'Tis no surprise, sir, if she's been shut in here without water for some time, her body may have begun to shut down. We need to introduce small amounts of fluid into her system at regular intervals to encourage the blood to flow properly again and replenish her. Hopefully we are in time to prevent any long-term damage." The other three men gaped; it seemed unfair to have finally found Jessica only to be told she could be seriously ill. Duncan bent his knees, scooping the inert woman into his arms, pressing a kiss to her overly warm forehead.

"I don't suppose there is anywhere on this floor that might be suitable?" Hugh asked, "I think she would prefer to be treated by Dr Napier.

Charlie ruminated for a moment before nodding and led the way back along the corridor to a tiny room adjacent to Dr Napier's office. Spartan in comparison with the main ward, it contained nothing but a bed, a chair, and a narrow shelf under the window, on which Charlie stood the candle.

"We use this sometimes if a patient disturbs the others or needs isolating owing to infection." Charlie explained. Hugh started to speak, but the orderly interrupted. "Do not fret sir, 'tis always prepared and everything is scrubbed clean between occupants."

Hugh offered an apologetic smile and Charlie grinned. "I understand your concern, sir, she is your sister." Hugh inclined his head, watching as Duncan placed Jessica carefully on the cool sheets. "Now please step outside and let me attend to her. Lucas and Hugh did as they were bid, but Duncan refused to leave, obliging Charlie to work around him.

Halfway through Charlie's examination they were rewarded with a slight movement and a sharply indrawn breath, but nothing more. After he had made sure there were no obvious injuries, Charlie fetched a jug of water, pouring a minuscule amount into a cup. Lifting Jessica's head, he managed to get her to swallow a few sips.

"I'll try again shortly," he said to Duncan, leaving the room again, this time returning with a large bowl of water and several cloths. "I think she might feel better if we rinsed away some of the dust and grime," he encouraged Duncan, handing him a damp cloth. The two men did what they could; bearing in mind their charge was fully clothed. Despite their ministrations, Jessica didn't rouse, increasing Duncan's anxiety.

"We must try to wake her," he insisted. "If for no other reason than she will realise she is safe. The mind can play evil tricks and if her subconscious believes she is still locked away, it too will close down. Trust me, I have had some experience with this."

Charlie agreed and the pair talked themselves hoarse trying to get a reaction. At some point Hugh and Lucas took over, but alas nothing worked.

Much later, after Hugh had left to inform his household Jessica had been found, Lucas had seconded Charlie's desk to make notes on the events of the evening and Charlie himself was doing his rounds, Duncan was sitting beside Jessica, talking about anything that came into his head, when a cold wet nose brushed against his hand. Trixie, who had been lying under the bed, decided it was high time her mistress got up and took her for a walk. She leaned over the pillow and resting her head on Jessica's shoulder, started nudging her. This went on for several minutes, Trixie adding quiet yips to her plea, until finally, fed up with this appalling lack of response, licked Jessica's face, long tongue slurping right across the young woman's nose and mouth.

"Trixie, no! Settle, girl,"

Duncan's head shot up as he heard the muttered words. Had he imagined them? Running his eye over her features in the dim light from the only candle, he discerned her lips appeared to have regained some colour. He waited. Trixie, on hearing the familiar voice, wagged her tail, in fact her whole body wagged and she licked Jessica again. A hand lifted from its position on the bed to wipe over the spot where the dog's tongue had left a wet trail.

"Pleurgh...phnerph...Trixie that's horrible." There was no doubting it this time.

"Jess, can you hear me? 'Tis me, Duncan." Eyelids flickered and he held his breath. The same hand reached out, catching his knee. He let his own hand cover hers and felt a tremor. "Jess, please wake up."

A long sigh, "Duncan...?" her voice trailed off, whispered tones disbelieving.

"I'm here, sweetheart."

A frown creased her forehead, but her eyes remained closed. "Really?"

"Truly," He lifted her hand and placed it on his chest. "Can you not feel my heart?" A smile tugged at the corners of her mouth.

"I love you."

"I love you too, please open your eyes for me."

"Too tired."

"I know, but I have travelled a long way to gaze into them, please just for me."

Jessica shuffled restlessly under the covers, but just when Duncan thought she was sinking back to sleep, her eyes fluttered open, seeking his.

Hours earlier, while everyone continued their search for her, Jessica was snug and warm, hidden under plenty of blankets determined not to let any of the critters she was certain were in the vicinity, use her as a nest. Falling asleep quickly despite the alarm circling her mind, she was enjoying a very satisfying dream — which involved Duncan and his sublime kisses — when it was rudely interrupted by a huge spider looming over her, its great hairy legs pinning her to the ground. Not overly fond of spiders, and this one was monstrous, Jessica tried to fight it off, to get back to Duncan, but he was no longer there. Her strength failed her and her body refused to follow her silent screams to run.

Without warning, Jessica felt herself being lifted; terror roiling through her, as she feared the spider was carrying her to its lair, which although sounded preposterous in her head, seemed the only plausible explanation. Then all went quiet and her panic dissipated as slumber lurked, its seductive melody drawing her back into darkness. She felt herself slipping away, but voices began calling to her, insinuating themselves into her subconscious and refusing to let her sleep. Why couldn't they just leave her alone? Didn't they know she was tired? Jessica did her best to ignore them, but they insisted, pestering her to wake up. They floated around her and seemed familiar but she couldn't quite place them.

Something was shoving at her shoulder and just as she was about to demand it stop, a slurping, wetness plastered itself over her face, ugh it was most uncomfortable. Unbidden, an image of a large, floppy and exuberant dog, rose in her mind, along with a name.

"Trixie, no! Settle girl."

The bed rocked and the wetness came again. She tried to shove it away, with little success.

"Pleurgh…phnerph…Trixie that's horrible."

As her arm fell back to her side, a rich, deep voice spoke next to her ear, entreating her to wake up. It couldn't be him, he was miles away. She stretched out her hand and it came into contact with something — a leg perhaps? A large hand closed over her cold fingers lifting them against a warm body where she could feel the steady beat of his heart and she breathed the question, willing it to be true. His answer still confused her, unsure whether she had fallen back into the dream or he was indeed here beside her, clasping her hand.

He was pleading with her to open her eyes, it was such an effort, but she couldn't resist. Giving in to temptation, she raised her lids, her gaze colliding with a pair of the bluest eyes watching her from an anxious face. It was really him! He was here in London, in…wait, where was she? Glancing around the room — which wasn't wholly unfamiliar, but definitely not her bedchamber — and fearful she was hallucinating, Jessica tried to get up. The hand enclosing hers released its grasp and moved to her shoulder.

"Rest sweetheart, I'm here and you are safe."

A shudder ran through her as a tear trailed down her cheek. "Don't cry, love we'll have you home soon." A cup was held to her lips. "Might you sip a little water?" The cool liquid made her aware of a raging thirst and she tried to gulp the contents of the cup.

He wouldn't let her, "You can only take a little at a time; too much and you will become unwell."

"Hold me, please hold me," she pleaded, her voice little more than a whisper. Everything was becoming hazy again and she couldn't tell what was reality and what her overwrought imagination might be conjuring up. She felt the bed shift as he settled his bulk next to her and he lifted her into his arms as though she was no more than a child. She cuddled against him, head nestling in the crook of his neck, one arm draped over his waist. Duncan drew the blanket over both of them and Trixie jumped up, slinking along the bed until the full length of her body rested against Jessica's legs. Jessica patted the dog absently, fondling her silky ears, glad of the extra warmth, but most of all she relished being held by Duncan and, secure now in his strong embrace, drifted back to sleep.

Sometime later, Charlie popped his head around the door to check on his patient, closing it again quietly when he saw the couple wrapped together and deeply asleep. Despite it being unconventional he didn't wish to disturb them.

Lucas had departed, none the wiser as to who was behind the incident, commenting that he would need to interview some of the staff and patients on the morrow. Charlie had his suspicions but wanted to discuss them with Dr Napier before he made any official statement.

The next morning, the sun pouring through the window woke Jessica. Blinking in its brightness, she wondered why had she left her curtains open, as Trixie padded up the bed and licked her face.

"And a very good morning to you too," she chuckled, fragments of memory filtering through. She was alone, in a strange room, one she vaguely recalled from a dream. Puzzled she made to get up, but her legs felt shaky. "Where the dickens am I?" she asked the dog, who tilted her head in an amusing fashion and yipped, for all the world as though she was replying. Then Jessica recognised the blankets, they were the same as the ones she used on the veterans' beds and the ones she had been counting when…everything flooded back. Being locked in the storage room, panicking that she'd be stuck there the whole weekend. Someone must have found her or had Toby let her out? No, surely, she wouldn't have ended up in a hospital bed if Toby had let her out, she would likely have run all the way home.

She was trying to fathom exactly what had happened when the door opened and Duncan peered round. He looked exhausted, but his smile sent tingles all the way through her and she beamed when she saw him; she hadn't imagined it, he was actually here.

"Oh, 'tis really you, you're here. I thought perhaps it was all a dream," she said willing him to kiss her, then deciding it maybe wasn't such a good idea, her mouth felt dry and most unpleasant.

"No dream, love. How do you feel this morning?"

"Sticky, achy and my mouth feels as though it's been stuffed full of dust. I don't know whether I'll ever feel clean again and I desperately need to brush my teeth, or at least rinse my mouth with something refreshing." Jessica ran her fingers through her tousled hair as Duncan handed her a glass of cold water in which someone, wise to such things, had added a drop of mint. "Oh, how did you know?" She swilled it around her mouth and swallowed, immediately feeling less unkempt.

"You'll have to thank Charlie, but I doubt you're the first person to feel uncomfortable after such an experience. Once we get you home, you'll be able to indulge in whatever luxuries you women enjoy for as long as you please." Duncan assured her, coming to sit on the chair beside the bed. "Can you remember what happened?"

"Oh yes, it was Lieutenant Langdon," calmly stated. "He thought he was saving me." Furrowing her brow in concentration, Jessica told Duncan the curious tale. "It's so strange, he honestly believed we were in France and that he was helping me escape some soldiers but whether they were French or English I have no idea." Duncan listened, aware of how trauma could manifest unexpectedly.

"So, we have to assume this Jessamine was important to him and something happened which prompted him to rescue or save her. Do you know where his regiment was?" he asked. Jessica ran her mind back over their discussions, recalling Toby had fought in the Battle of Toulouse, and was at the taking of the bridge at Croix d'Orade.

Duncan mused over her answer. "It was such a waste that battle, had they but known it, Napoleon had already surrendered; all those men lost for lack of a speedy messenger service."

Jessica waved her hands excitedly. "*That's* what he was taking about! He kept railing on about the idiocy of those in charge and such like. Oh, Duncan, do you suppose this Jessamine was hurt somehow...?" she gulped, "...or worse and, because Toby found out later that the fighting took place after the surrender, he believes the military are to blame for whatever happened to her?" She tapped her chin, thinking out loud. "That doesn't explain why he keeps calling me Jessamine though."

"Maybe you remind him of her, perhaps your features are alike. I suppose your names are not wholly dissimilar, especially if distorted by the fog of trauma." They couldn't come up with any other explanation and needed to discuss it further with Dr Napier and maybe Lucas — he might have government or military connections who could shed more light on the matter.

"I'm not certain it's a good idea for you to continue working here until this is cleared up though, love. You can't keep getting locked in storerooms. It was only by chance Helena thought of using Trixie to find you, otherwise 'tis likely you would still be there. Who knows how long it would have been before something was needed from that room?" Jessica could hear worry in Duncan's tones and she was torn. Half of her agreed with him, the other half believed she was still of use, even if only for the last few weeks until she left to be married.

"I don't know Duncan, I love helping here and I think I'm useful. Oh, I know Clare and Meredith are perfectly capable, but what else would I do? Hugh is talking with Sybil Miller and Lynette Collins in the hope one or both might be able to take over my job at Trentams, so other than to show them what's required — and that will take me less than half a day — I'm no longer needed at the shipyard. I will go mad if I have to sit around all day and partake of ladylike pursuits."

Her plaintive wail and doleful expression caused the ghost of a grin to flicker across Duncan's tired features.

"I'm sure you have plenty to do planning our wedding, well your part in it anyway — I do believe Billie has everything so well organised at Whiteoaks, no one dare move for fear of upskittling something," he chuckled at the memory of Billie's affronted response when he'd suggested, maybe less than tactfully, they didn't need such largesse.

"'Duncan Barrington, Jessica deserves the best we can provide, don't you ever forget it,'" her vexed tones shooing him off in exasperation.

Jessica giggled as he mimicked this snippet, commenting she would never stand in the way of Billie's schemes and assumed he, Duncan, would know better than to attempt it.

"You've known her for some time now, haven't you? What prompted you to question her plans in the first place?" Duncan shrugged his shoulders saying it must have been a mental aberration and he'd never think to do so again.

Jessica was quiet for a moment, ruminating over Duncan's comment about largesse, then she ventured hesitantly —

"While I appreciate everything Billie and Giles, not to mention my family, are doing for us, I admit a large wedding is rather intimidating. That said, I have no mind to suggest a more intimate celebration would be preferable, for both Mama and Billie are in their element and I would not wish to upset them. Billie, especially, has been so generous and kind, but I do worry it will be overwhelming." She bit her lip, uncertain of Duncan's reaction. She believed him to be in accord with her sentiments, but he could yet surprise her. She was relieved, therefore, when he replied,

"My love, I confess to being uncomfortable in large groups of people. Such gatherings tend to make me feel somewhat claustrophobic. But Billie is correct, 'tis our wedding and you *do* deserve the best." He dropped a light kiss on her forehead. "Besides, what are a few hundred guests when later, I get to have you all to myself?" he said, a wicked gleam in his eyes.

Jessica blushed and snuggled against him, as he distracted her from her qualms most effectively.

Chapter Twenty Five

They became engrossed in all things wedding related until, a little later there was a knock on the door and Dr Napier poked his head around.

"Jessica Drummond, now what have you been up to?" He twinkled at his patient, coming into the room and greeting Duncan. "What happened?"

Dutifully Jessica repeated all she could remember, Duncan filling in the rest.

"Dr Napier, Toby honestly believed I was Jessamine. We must get to the bottom of whatever happened to her, otherwise his odd behaviour will likely continue and who knows what else might happen." Jessica entreated in defence of the man's actions.

"It's in hand Jessica, I have some experience in these matters." The doctor replied, his smile taking the slight rebuke out of his tones. Jessica clapped her hand to her mouth, blushing fiery red.

"I do beg your pardon," she apologised. "I forgot my place." She bit her lip; mortified she had overstepped her boundaries.

Dr Napier chuckled. "Do not take on, Jessica. I'm glad you are so concerned about our veterans; especially in light of your recent…err…adventure. I think, when Lucas Withers returns, we may have to put our heads together and come up with a strategy not only to monitor Toby, but also to uncover everything we can about what happened to him in France, now he has revealed some of his story. At this moment, however, I would like to check you over if you would be so kind as to allow it." He raised an eyebrow and Jessica nodded, her colour still rather high. Duncan muttered something about going to see whether either Hugh or Lucas had arrived and left the doctor to his examination.

A little later, satisfied Jessica exhibited no adverse effects, Dr Napier joined Duncan and Isaac — who had relieved Charlie several hours previously — and the three deep were in discussion about Toby, when the rest of the Drummond family arrived. Duncan showed Mrs Drummond to the little room and left mother to care for daughter, while the doctor updated the others. Finally, everyone who needed to be was fully apprised of the facts, not that there were many, but at least they knew who was behind Jessica's disappearance and some of why it happened.

Dr Napier took the floor. "I will endeavour to keep a watch on Toby, but we do not have enough staff to monitor him all the time. We all have jobs and situations taking us away from the ward at any given moment, neither is this place a prison. Much as it is unnerving, Toby has not committed a crime; he is a simply a troubled soul who needs our help. Although I have yet to discuss this in more detail with Jessica, it is my hope she agrees it would be detrimental to resort to more restrictive measures, on the off chance of a recurrence of his actions three nights ago. Before we go any further, I think we need to establish whether he even recalls it." He glanced around the desk receiving nods of agreement from all who were listening. "I also think it is important he sees Jessica,"

Duncan started to interrupt, but the doctor waved him to silence, "I will not leave her alone with him, do you think me addled, man?" Duncan smiled sheepishly, Dr Napier grinned and continued, "Jessica said Toby wanted Jessamine to get to safety. If he still thinks Jessica to be Jessamine and sees her walking into the ward, it might ease his mind."

The others could see the sense in his argument, Helena merely commenting that Jessica would need to be comfortable with the suggestion.

Taking over from the doctor, Lucas informed them he had sent a letter requesting an audience with the office of the Secretary of State for War and the Colonies, the government department dealing with all matters pertaining to the Army. He was hoping they could be persuaded to provide more detailed records, or at least offer assistance in accessing them. Lucas Withers was held in high regard among senior ministers, his discretion when handling sensitive issues well known.

Helena left them to it and went to see Jessica. Her sister-in-law being alternately berated and cosseted by her mother who declared her hair would be whiter than snow if her family didn't learn how to avoid life-threatening situations. Both Jessica and Helena grinned self-consciously, aware neither could claim innocence in that regard. Helena diverted the conversation by asking about wedding plans, to the relief of Jessica who mouthed a grateful 'thank you' out of her mother's line of sight.

A tray of food appeared for Jessica who devoured it with little care for manners — so hungry she reckoned she could probably eat a horse or several. Shortly thereafter Dr Napier suggested her family leave her to rest and return at day's end to take her home.

"I would like to keep an eye on her a little longer just to be sure."

Duncan, as expected, stayed with her, the couple relishing time alone together. At some point in the early afternoon, Jessica, hoping her recent internment engendered a sympathetic ear, broached a subject she had steered away from for fear of upsetting her betrothed.

"Duncan, I wondered perhaps whether you might allow me...it's just I haven't and I..." Jessica paused to get her contrary tongue under control. "Duncan, please may I see your arm?" her petition came out in a rush. Duncan stared, perplexed and she hastened to elaborate. "I know it seems an odd request, but you keep it hidden away, your sleeve always tucked neatly around it. We are to be wed, I trust I will be privileged to see all of you, preferably without clothes," blushing as she heard the words fall from her lips. "Errr...anyway, please might you...would it be too..." she faltered, unsure how to phrase her desire to stroke her fingers over the damaged limb, to kiss the scar, to prove she wasn't affected by his disability. She hoped he already knew, but it bothered her that he kept his arm hidden from view. Even when she'd seen him in shirtsleeves in his workshop his left arm was covered. Duncan was silent and Jessica felt a flicker of dismay. "Oh, Duncan, I'm sorry, forget I asked. I didn't mean to…I just thought…" Duncan hushed her by dint of kissing her thoroughly.

"Don't apologise for asking questions, love. We *are* to be living together soon, I don't want there to be anything you are afraid to ask me. I only hesitate because my arm is…" he searched for a polite way of saying it, "…rather unsightly and I have no wish to offend you."

Jessica stared him, flabbergasted.

"Nothing about you could ever offend me Duncan. I love you, everything about you, all of you, especially those parts you deem less than perfect. Now may I?' she raised an eyebrow as her fingers reached for his sleeve. He nodded, tensing a little, preparing for her horrified exclamations when she saw the ugly scarring. He supposed it was better she saw it now; it might prove too abhorrent, prompting second thoughts.

As ever he underestimated Jessica, who already seemed to know what was going on in his head.

"Duncan Barrington stop thinking like that. When will you get it into your thick skull, you're stuck with me forever!" Taking the initiative and untucking his sleeve, she rolled it up to reveal the maimed limb, which was all that remained of his lower forearm. To be scrupulously fair, the military surgeon had performed the amputation as neatly as possible, given it was carried out in a makeshift hospital on the edge of a battlefield in less than sanitary conditions. The arm had been severed about halfway between Duncan's elbow and his wrist, the scarring irregular and quite knotty. Jessica felt tears forming. Did this man — this man she loved beyond reason — this powerful and virile man believe, what was to her mind, so small an infirmity diminished him in her eyes? She ran cool fingers up his arm, bending her head to brush her lips over the scar, her tears trickling onto the disfigured wound as though they might miraculously heal it. Without conscious thought, she lifted his arm, pressing it against her heart; the steady beat resonating through him, as she raised sorrowful eyes to his.

Duncan's heart clenched as he reached out and stroked her cheek. "Jess love, don't weep for me I am used to it now. I was angry for a long time, but eventually I learned to let it go. Yes, my army career was ruined because of it, but I am alive, I survived and I found you. What more could any man want?"

She hiccuped, striving to swallow her sobs. Uncaring how inappropriate it was, Duncan sat on the bed, enveloping her in his embrace, kissing away her tears, before pressing his lips to her forehead, her cheeks and her nose. He felt Jessica relax, a gentle sigh escaping her lips and, unable to stop himself, captured her mouth with his — their mutual fears and anxieties of the past three days melding with their ever-burning passion as Duncan kissed his love until neither could remember where they were.

It was quite some time before they came back to earth, senses in complete disarray.

"I love you," Jessica murmured. "I love you so much I fear I may burst with it."

"Well that would be a shame," grinned Duncan. "You'd be no fun to kiss if you were spread all over the walls and ceiling." Jessica giggled and nudged him in the shoulder, his comment effectively diverting her and the couple resumed their easy conversation, chatting about what they had been doing since last they met.

As evening drew in, Dr Napier pronounced Jessica well enough to go home. Before she left however, she wanted to see Toby. Before she did so, the doctor spent a little time discussing the matter with her, explaining what he felt to be the appropriate response to Toby's actions and how she wanted it dealt with. Without hesitation, Jessica declared she had no mind to demand any measure of reproof; all she wanted was for Toby to come to terms with whatever haunted him.

Satisfied her reaction was genuine and, as he had assured her family earlier, Dr Napier — along with Duncan — accompanied Jessica onto the ward for which she was thankful, unable to quell, completely, the unease threading through her. She entered the room to a riotous welcome from the veterans who were aware of her misfortune, although Toby's involvement had not been disclosed.

She walked along the ward chatting with each one, catching up on their day, laughing at their jokes and affirming she felt fine. Toby was sitting with two or three others around the fire, still needed, for even though they were well into spring, the evenings remained cool. Jessica didn't single him out, instead simply included him in the light banter she enjoyed with the other men. Toby smiled and offered a few words, but didn't seem inclined to converse beyond pleasantries. Jessica left him alone, she couldn't force him to admit what he'd done if he even remembered doing it. Saying she was looking forward to seeing them the following week, she took her leave, thanking Dr Napier and Isaac. The latter two advising her to get some rest and not rush about too much. Duncan shook his head, knowing neither suggestion would be heeded, but adding his thanks for the care Jessica received.

Soon, Jessica was home, her family welcoming her as though she had been away for months rather than only three nights. Even Nick, not given to gestures of affection, pulled his sister into a tight hug and begged her never to frighten him like that again.

Jessica grinned up at her brother, his normally grave countenance flushed in his agitation.

"I'll do my best," she promised, hugging him back. "I didn't ask to be locked up you know." She winked at him squeezing his hand as he released her.

Duncan, presuming the Drummonds would prefer a night with just family, made to depart, only to have Mrs Drummond, knowing his time in the city was limited, ask him to stay. He accepted gratefully and they all enjoyed an uproarious evening. Good food, comfortable surroundings and lively conversation — staying well away from recent events — helped restore everyone's rather shaky equilibrium.

The next few days sped by and all too soon Duncan had to return to Whiteoaks. Still, as he whispered in Jessica's ear the night before he left, while his hand stroked over her slender body, it was only a month until they would be wed, never to part again. Jessica shivered under his touch, her body clamouring for more, so much more.

"Don't talk, talking means you're not kissing me," she muttered darkly, hearing laughter rumble through his chest.

"You will be the death of me, Jessica Drummond." He replied, suppressing his mirth with difficulty.

"Just kiss me." She demanded, unbuttoning his waistcoat, tenacious fingers seeking and finding the gap at the neckline of his shirt. Duncan groaned and gave up the argument; praising all that was holy they were alone and unlikely to be disturbed, thanks to Helena suggesting an evening at the theatre.

"Wait," he strode over to the door of the library where they were currently ensconced, turning the key. Jessica's eyes widened at his audacity, "I prefer not to be disturbed," he growled, his deep voice sending thrills up Jessica's spine. "I recall a request made by a certain Miss not too long ago, and now seems the perfect opportunity to fulfil her wish." Jessica's brow creased, then a wicked smile curved her lips, remembering to what he referred.

"Well, it would be discourteous of me to hinder so gallant an inclination," hooking a finger into the waistband of his trousers, she drew him close, fingers resuming their exploration. Duncan cupped his hand along her neck, his thumb stroking down her throat. He touched his lips to hers, briefly, tantalisingly. Jessica tilted her head, standing on tiptoe to kiss his jaw line, the shadow of stubble, rough under her lips.

They moved apart, watching, the air around them seemed to crackle, as though a storm was brewing.

Chapter Twenty Six

Senses heightened, Jessica felt as though she was on the edge of a chasm, and to fall would be the most incredible experience of her life. She tried to speak, but the words lodged in her throat.

Duncan's heart overrode his head, which was shrieking at him to stop before it was too late, sweeping Jessica against him and kissing her until she could no longer stand. Lifting her into his arms, he carried her to the ornate chaise, his lips never relinquishing hers. Reclining now, one arm locked her against him, as the other began searching under all the frothy nonsense until he was rewarded with the silkiness of her skin. As his hand ghosted up her leg, he could feel her trembling, exultant he could affect her so.

While Duncan stirred her into a dizzy spiral, Jessica began pushing up his shirt, scattering butterfly kisses over his chest and running her fingers through the smattering of hair, loving his sharp intake of breath as she did so.

"Jessica," he gasped as her fingers slid down over his waist, coming to rest on the fall of his trousers. "I know I started this, but we really mustn't."

"I know! Our behaviour is most incautious, but you haven't yet achieved your aim and I am loath to let you leave until you have." Came her considered reply — in breathless spurts, her eyes glowing like topaz in the firelight. Duncan could not have argued with her even had he wanted to, his power of speech robbed as the last of his buttons fell to her quest, her fingers claiming their prize.

"Jess, much as I desperately want to…" his voice ragged with longing, control and coherence rapidly deserting him. "…not here, not yet. I want to … urghhhhh…" her light touch almost torture. Giving up the battle, in the hopes of winning the war, Duncan chased his own treasure, finding her centre, pushing her relentlessly to the brink until she would have screamed his name had his mouth not stolen her breath in yet another scorching kiss.

Sure she would die, or at the very least faint from the multitude of emotions roiling through her, Jessica considered, abstractedly, whether her head was detaching itself from her body as finally he flicked her over the edge. She plunged, but it felt more like flying, soaring on a wave of pleasure she could never have imagined existed.

Gasping for breath, Jessica drifted back down from the heavens, aware Duncan had smoothed her skirts, was still kissing her and her body was now lacking any substance.

"You … you … how … oh…" was all she managed, words refusing to form.

"I did warn you," he murmured, kissing her ear lobe.

"Hmmmm … yes, I believe you did." She wriggled in his embrace, getting comfortable, her head resting on his shoulder. "Do you have to go?" fiddling with the buttons on his waistcoat.

"I'm afraid I do. Not much longer to wait now though, love." They remained like that for quite some time until Duncan realised Jessica had fallen asleep.

He turned the beautiful woman in his arms so he could study her; tousled hair curled around a face still flushed from their fervent encounter. He had to leave, yet he didn't want to say goodbye. The depth of love he had for Jessica was frightening, liberating and humbling all at the same time. At the back of his mind, Duncan still had a niggling suspicion he would lose her, that she would wake up to his many faults and shortcomings and realise he wasn't the man she believed him to be. That she loved him in the first place never failed to astound him.

As though she heard his thoughts, Jessica awoke, momentarily disoriented, before realising where she was and in whose arms she was wrapped. Gazing up at him, eyes cloudy with sleep, she smiled and everything else, all his doubts and fears, fell away.

"I really have to go, love," he whispered.

"If you say so," she murmured a drowsy reply.

"Unfortunately, and with great regret, I do say so. Come, you should be in bed too; you're back at St Bart's tomorrow. Let's hope Lucas has heard something." Referring to that gentleman's latest missive informing the Drummond family he was awaiting several reports from the War Department. Jessica nodded, letting Duncan slide her off his lap and onto her feet. She swayed, so tired she could barely stand. Duncan made sure they both looked the picture of respectability then, remembering to unlock the door, rang for a maid.

Emily appeared seconds later.

"I think Miss Drummond is about asleep on her feet. She may need a little assistance." Duncan kissed Jessica on the forehead whispered his love for her and said goodbye. He wasn't entirely certain Jessica heard for she just stared at him. As he reached the door, however, her gentle voice arrested his steps.

"Never forget you have my heart, Duncan. Keep it safe." Echoing her previous farewells. He spun on his heel and, uncaring that Emily was right there, took two strides and gathered Jessica into his arms, kissing her most satisfactorily, then vanished into the night, before he changed his mind.

"Oh my..." was Jessica's only response to such a delicious adieu. Emily merely grinned, escorting her mistress upstairs and helping her undress, Jessica fast asleep before her head touched the pillow.

The next day, while saddened Duncan was gone, Jessica was back at the hospital and soon far too busy to dwell on his departure. It was precisely a week since Toby had locked her in the store room and Jessica had no intention of going anywhere near that section of the corridor alone, ever again. Toby had never broached the subject, and Jessica didn't think it wise to remind him, hoping it would all come out in the fullness of time. It was clear his trauma was bubbling close to the surface and maybe wouldn't require much to trigger another episode, but so far, he hadn't shown any signs.

Sometime during the afternoon, Lucas Withers appeared with a sheaf of papers. Dr Napier was with another patient in the ward opposite, so while they waited for him, Clare went to organise hot drinks, while Lucas, Jessica and Charlie chatted about this and that. Shortly thereafter, the doctor appeared looking his usual harassed self, his hair sticking up all over, the others grinning at his rather rumpled state. He glanced down at his attire.

"I had to wrangle an obstinate patient," he explained, his face crinkling in amusement, making himself comfortable and sipping the now lukewarm coffee. Clare offered to get him a fresh cup, but he declined. "Thank you, Clare, this is cool enough to drink now. I guarantee if you make me another coffee, I'll get called away before I have the chance to take a single sip. Now," he turned his attention to Lucas. "What can you tell us?"

Lucas shuffled his papers and contemplated his audience. "Some of what is in these documents is confidential, for it relates to military campaigns and their strategies. I have been given permission to share what I think pertinent only with those who cannot perform their work without the information contained therein. It took some persuading, but when I mentioned the veteran is so disturbed by his memories he locked a staff member in a store room, I got their attention."

He paused, flicking through the sheets until he found the one he was looking for.

"It seems Jessamine and her mother, Madam Pelletier, had been loosely connected to the allied forces for some time. There is mention of a French medic, Étienne Pelletier who, for reasons unknown, assisted English and Spanish military doctors. We can only assume Jessamine and her mother were daughter and wife respectively. Étienne was killed in 1812, but the women remained with the troops. Maybe both had gleaned enough medical knowledge to be useful. Whatever the reason, they followed the army when it moved into France. Jessica said Lieutenant Langdon froze when he was telling her about the Battle of Toulouse, so I asked them to check whether there was any record of civilian casualties and, although not as comprehensive as the military accounts, I can confirm both Jessamine and her mother were on the list of those killed. There are no other details so I cannot tell you where or how, but it is no great leap to believe it must have been during the battle. There were an horrendous number of losses during the offensive which, unfortunately, included civilians. There is one other important revelation I think you need to be aware of. Jessamine is not listed under Pelletier, rather under Langdon…"

He paused, and Jessica gasped, the full impact of what Lucas was saying like a punch to her stomach.

"Lucas, they were married?" her question an anguished cry.

Lucas nodded, "…and as far as I can tell, it was legal. This surely explains his distress and why he keeps trying to 'save' Jessica. I suspect he either witnessed their deaths or found them in the aftermath, blaming himself for not getting them to safety sooner."

"It is the most plausible explanation." Dr Napier concurred. "So, now we have somewhat of a starting point and we know Toby's current state of mind, maybe we can get him to tell us what happened. It may require Miss Drummond's delicate touch…" he winked at Jessica, who blushed, "…but we must ensure either myself, Charlie here or Isaac are within hearing range. After last week's incident, I am uncomfortable leaving any of my volunteers alone with the lieutenant, at least until his mind accepts that what occurred in France, while horrific, happened long past, not something which recurs over and over again in his present."

Lucas agreed and suggested Dr Napier ask one or two of the veterans to keep an eye on things whenever Jessica was going to be on duty.

"I imagine Captains Maynard and Everard, along with Ensign Shepherd would be prepared to aid our endeavours and there are one or two others I would gladly include." The doctor mused, glancing around the ward as he spoke, noting those soldiers whom he knew to be dependable, their injuries physical rather than psychological.

"When would you like me to try talking to him again?" enquired Jessica, feeling less anxious now they had a plan of sorts. She still didn't believe Toby would hurt her deliberately, but neither did she want to be alone with him, the experience having taught her just how unaware some of the veterans were of their own actions. Jessica trusted the men for whom she cared, believing they had built up a rapport over the preceding months but was far happier knowing there would always be a guardian close by when she was working.

"Maybe leave it until next week when you come in, rather than try this afternoon, it's getting late now and this is not something we can rush." Dr Napier suggested, the others agreeing and shortly thereafter, the meeting broke up, each going their separate ways. As they concluded their chores, Clare and Jessica who, along with Meredith had already arranged to see each other the following afternoon, chatted excitedly about the art exhibition they were to attend.

The weekend flew by. In between art galleries and gossiping, Jessica had a fitting for her wedding gown and the several new dresses Mrs Drummond deemed appropriate for her daughter's trousseau. Jessica did try to persuade her mother since she would be living in the country and working for a doctor, that plainer more serviceable attire would be preferable, but her loving parent was adamant. No daughter of hers would be wed without sufficient gowns to suit any occasion, not to mention an inordinate amount of underclothes, gloves, hats, shawls, shoes, slippers and boots.

It was all rather overwhelming and Jessica experienced a moment of panic, worried Duncan would think her frivolous. Helena assured her he would think no such thing, contending with so many outfits, she wouldn't need to attend the modiste for years — something Jessica suffered ungraciously at the best of times. That was enough to convince her and she braved being tucked and pinned, and tugged and pinched until her mother, Helena and the modiste were satisfied. Jessica had to admit it was fun choosing colours and materials and she *loved* her wedding gown, which she believed somehow made her appear far less average than normal. Privately, Helena commented to her mother-in-law that Duncan's eyes would likely fall out when he saw his bride, both agreeing Jessica looked astonishingly beautiful in it, but also knowing the bride-to-be would pooh-pooh such a notion.

Wednesday arrived in the blink of an eye and Jessica was nervous; this day could prove a turning point in Lieutenant Langdon's overall recovery. She knew that even if they had a breakthrough, it would be a long haul. Toby had refused to acknowledge the trauma, which had closed his mind for so long, accessing his memories could have adverse consequences and regression was a distinct possibility. They had to take the risk, he was too unstable and no one wanted to see him in any more distress.

Jessica arrived at St Bart's the same time as Meredith, the two walking upstairs to the ward together. Dr Napier had apprised Meredith of their plan and she had expressed an interested in observing the process. Jessica heard an unexpected tone in Meredith's voice as her friend talked about the doctor and made a mental note to do some observing of her own.

Chapter Twenty Seven

The ward was bustling, all the usual tasks to be completed before any other therapy could be considered. Jessica was of a mind to let the discussion with Toby unfold naturally rather than have the lieutenant feel as though he was being singled out, something she mentioned to Dr Napier, who agreed. Thus, she carried on as normal and it was not until mid-morning, her chance presented itself.

As she was handing out cups of coffee, Jessica noticed Toby was missing from his preferred chair by the fire. He tended to read the paper at the same time every day, but today he wasn't to be seen. Puzzled, Jessica glanced out of the window, spying the veteran sitting in the hospital garden. It was a lovely day, bright and sunny and the garden was sheltered. Informing Isaac of her intention, Jessica, slung her cloak around her shoulders and grabbing two cups of coffee, hurried down the stairs and out into the sunshine. The spring air was redolent with the scent of blossoms and the neat garden beds were full to bursting with a riotous profusion of flowers. It was a peaceful space, and one Jessica hoped might be just right for a man to unload his terrors.

"Lieutenant," she called, cheerfully. "I've brought you your coffee. Isn't it a glorious day?"

Toby nodded and thanked her for the drink, sipping the brew with obvious pleasure. "Oh, I do love coffee," Jessica said confidingly. "Whoever invented it deserves high praise indeed."

"I believe it was first consumed in Ethiopia but I think coffee, as we recognise it, came from the southern regions of the Arabian Peninsula." Toby stated diffidently

Jessica gaped at the veteran. "How do you know that?" she demanded. Toby explained how he loved history and it was something he came across when studying the history of the Arabs. Jessica was riveted and asked plenty of questions, amazed at Toby's breadth of knowledge. "I never consider how big our world is until I hear stories from lands afar." She mused. "It sounds very romantic; exotic peoples, so far removed from our mundane existence we would be lost, unable to comprehend a single thing about their lives or their culture."

Toby grinned in agreement, but added that seeing the world from another's perspective, while intriguing is not always the idyll it is made out to be. Jessica twisted on the bench and, reading his face, guessed he was withdrawing again. Sending up a prayer for help, she took a leap of faith and simply asked the question, the answer to which they all wanted to know.

"Toby, might I be so bold as to ask what happened to Jessamine?"

The soldier made a reflexive movement, and in a gesture of comfort, she rested her hand on his knee.

"Please don't go Toby, I know this is hard for you; you have trusted me with your story, but you have only told me half of it. I believe you need to tell me how it ends. I think once you do, you will feel better, you have held your hurt inside for so long you cannot function properly anymore. Do you know you locked me in the storeroom?"

Toby goggled at her in confusion, shaking his head. "Surely not?"

"I'm afraid, you did, but you thought you were protecting me from French soldiers. You thought there was a path I could follow which would lead me to safety. Toby, you believed me to be Jessamine." Toby just stared at her, but she could see him ruminating on her words as clearly as though he spoke his thoughts out loud. Calming her nerves, Jessica continued, "I know Jessamine was your wife and you must have loved her very much, doing everything you could to get her away from danger. What happened that night at Toulouse?"

Silence fell between them as Jessica realised Toby was fighting some inner battle; she took his hand, stroking over his fingers, which clenched and unclenched. Out of the corner of her eye she spotted Dr Napier and Meredith and, almost imperceptibly, shook her head hoping they would stay back. They understood, and went to sit on another bench across the garden, apparently engrossed in conversation. Toby still hadn't spoken but as she watched him, Jessica noticed a change in his countenance, as though a veil had fallen away and she knew he was about to unburden his heart.

"I met Jessamine not long before we marched from Spain into France. Her father had been one of the medics but he was killed trying to rescue a wounded soldier. They were alone and vulnerable because of their connection to the allied armies. Also, Jessamine had picked up much from her father and knew how to treat basic wounds. Madame Pelletier, her mother, had always helped the army cooks, her food far more palatable than the slop usually served. Jessamine was beautiful; tall, with flaxen hair and eyes, the colour of molten brandy, that could see into a person's soul." He smiled at the memory. Jessica shifted, uncomfortably aware he might have been describing her. It certainly explained his obsession with calling her Jessamine. She dragged her attention back to Toby who was still speaking.

"Toulouse was a total waste of lives, Napoleon had surrendered, but the message didn't reach us until we lost countless soldiers. There was the debacle with the bridge at Croix d'Orade, then when we launched the main offensive on the city, Marshall Soult had it well defended and we suffered a catastrophic number of casualties. Battle lines shifted and I was terrified Jessamine and her mother would become trapped. The night before what proved to be the final onslaught, I tried to persuade them to leave. There was a little-known track leading away from the city, into the countryside where they should have been able to hide out until the fighting was over. I thought they had done as I asked, but the way was cut off and they were forced to double back." His voice dropped and Jessica realised he was, once again, seeing that night when everything he loved was torn from him. She squeezed his knee; he patted her hand, absently, as he gathered his thoughts.

"She found me just before dawn. I begged her to go, to get as far from the battlefront as possible, saying I would come and find her when it was safe to do so. I couldn't go with her, and I assumed she'd done as I asked. I refused to let myself worry about her, I had to focus — my unit, along with two other

219

divisions were making our way along the west bank of the Hers, our goal, the Heights of Calvinet. The weather was atrocious, turning the ground into a quagmire, delaying us, confusion reigned and in the ensuing affray Jessamine and her mother were killed. They shouldn't have been there, it was my fault, Jessamine wanted to stay close and her mother would never leave Jessamine." His voice cracking in despair. "I presumed they had found a way to get to safe ground but, much later when we checked for causalities, we came upon them. She looked so peaceful lying there, an angel asleep in the mud, but 'twas clear her wounds were grievous. All I can pray is that she didn't know; that she died instantly. I cannot bear to think she suffered, because she loved me."

Toby keened, words of sorrow and regret tumbling from his mouth in a mix of French and English, tears falling, his chest heaving with sobs. Jessica did the only thing she could think of and wrapped her arms around him, rocking him gently and crooning a lullaby, her own tears mixing with his. Dr Napier moved then and, after sending Meredith to fetch Isaac, went over to where Jessica and Toby were sitting, joining them and speaking in measured tones, calling Toby back from his heartbreak.

Isaac arrived, the two men helping the distraught veteran back inside, escorting him to the same private room Jessica had slept in not two weeks previously. Jessica was exhausted and elated; this was what they needed, this might be the start of the healing process! She hoped Toby would come to accept it was not his fault Jessamine died. Yes, she was a casualty of war and her death may well have been preventable, but she had chosen to stay, knowing the dangers. Her love for Toby stronger than her compulsion to flee, and Jessica had faith the young lieutenant would find solace in that.

It was early afternoon before Dr Napier came to find Jessica. She was chatting with Major Vaughan about her booklet of stories, which was now compiled and, to her delight, currently with a printer. Asking whether he might borrow Miss Drummond briefly, the doctor gave her an update. Toby was upset but still talking; the details he was providing filling in the many gaps around the cause of his catalepsy.

"I don't think it will be the only time we revisit this conversation. He needs to talk about it frequently until it becomes part of his memory and no longer ruling his everyday existence, but I do believe this was what we were waiting for. Thank you, Jessica, you have been a great help in this regard." Jessica shrugged genially, unwilling to take credit, her cheeks growing pink.

"It was my pleasure and honour to assist, Dr Napier, but you and the rest of your staff have been working with Toby for years. I think because I happen to resemble Jessamine, I just helped the last little piece fall into place. I wish I could witness his continuing recovery, but alas, marriage calls and soon I will be swallowed up in the wilds of Hampshire."

Dr Napier chuckled, Jessica's words completely at odds with her smile, bright enough to light the whole hospital.

"We will miss you, my dear and I am endlessly glad you met a man whose disability prompted you to seek us out. His gain will be our loss."

By now Jessica was fiery red and she twiddled with her dress, not quite knowing what to say. Dr Napier took pity on the young woman and diverted her by mentioning the prosthetic she had commissioned was ready for her approval. This did the trick and Jessica was excited to see the device, which was astonishingly lifelike. Dr Napier explained recent developments in the technology they employed to create such things was advancing rapidly and this particular piece was modelled on a prototype they hoped to manufacture on a much larger scale once they secured funding.

"Maybe if the booklet is popular some of the money from it could be channelled into this endeavour." Jessica suggested eagerly, the two discussing the possibilities with enthusiasm, Dr Napier promising to talk to the printer before Jessica left for her wedding.

The next couple of weeks disappeared in a flurry of preparations. Jessica handed over her work at Trentams to the two women Hugh hoped might undertake the role — Sybil Miller and Lynette Collins. Canny women, Sybil and Lynette had shown themselves highly competent and quite capable of shouldering Jessica's tasks. They decided to share the workload as both had commitments at Sanctuary House the women's refuge where Helena also worked. Jessica found leaving her job at the shipyard harder than she expected. She hadn't been there very long, less than a year, but it had been lovely working with her two brothers and the knowledge she wouldn't see them every day, brought the reality of how different her life was going to be, into sharp focus. Nevertheless, she was excited at the prospect of working with Dr Elliott, never mind the thrill of marrying Duncan, a dream she had almost thought might never come to fruition.

Before Jessica had time to ponder the great changes she was about to face, it was the night before she was due to depart for Whiteoaks. Her wedding would take place two weeks hence, but Billie had invited her and her mother to come prior, giving Jessica the opportunity to spend a little time with her betrothed and the two could organise any last-minute details in a more relaxed time frame. Helena — who along with Hugh and Nick would travel the following week — came to see Jessica as she was preparing for bed.

"May I come in?" she asked peering around the door. Jessica nodded, trying to brush out her recalcitrant hair, which always seemed to be knotted. Helena took the brush out of Jessica's hand and began to untangle the shiny locks. After a moment or two she asked. "How do you feel? Are you sure this is what you want, what your heart desires more than anything else?"

Through the mirror, Jessica stared at Helena in confusion, wondering why she was asking such a question, after being instrumental in bringing them together.

"'Tis only that this is a big move for you. You are giving up everything for Duncan. I know you love him, but is that enough? Will you be happy so far away from the rest of your family?" Helena elaborated.

Jessica let an image of Duncan alongside one of her family roll around her head. In her mind's eye, she switched between the two, and although she loved her family dearly, she knew she loved Duncan more.

"Yes, Helena, 'tis more than enough. I know this may sound odd, but I only feel half-alive when he is not by my side. 'Tis as though he and I are two halves of a whole — a whole I didn't know I was looking for, or needed, until a scrap of a dog got stuck in bushes the day after your wedding. I acknowledge it hasn't been an easy courtship and I accept 'tis likely there will be times when we argue, when he has dark moods, or when I am irritating, but we have fought hard to be together. I love him more than my own life and if I try to imagine a future without him in it, all I see is grey mist. Whatever happens, whatever life throws at us, as long as I am with him, I have faith we will handle it."

Helena smiled and took Jessica's hand reassuringly. "I already knew this, I just wanted to be sure you did. I am very happy for you and I also have faith this is how it is supposed to be. Duncan needed someone to lift him from himself, to make him realise he is a man who can love and is worthy of being loved in return. He has been a trusted friend all of my life and I am so very glad he found you; he deserves the best."

Jessica felt tears pricking her eyes, blinking furiously she held them back and leaning forward kissed Helena on her cheek.

"Thank you," was all she said, but her fingers curled around her sister-in-law's hand and squeezed gently, the gesture telling Helena how much her sentiment was appreciated.

Chapter Twenty Eight

Two days later, a carriage drew up outside a beautiful house, its warm red brick welcoming, in the amber glow of the setting sun. Two tired people and a rather dishevelled looking dog were assisted down, and greeted with warm hugs from their hosts. Billie and Giles Trevallier ushered their guests inside Whiteoaks, while willing hands took care of the mountain of luggage. After settling into their chambers, indulging in a proper wash and a change of clothes, the two guests were soon enjoying a hearty meal with the Winchesters, gossiping as though they hadn't seen each other for years rather than the two months it had actually been.

Jessica wondered where Duncan was, but didn't feel it polite to ask, only to be surprised when he appeared, at the end of the meal, his smile when his eyes alighted on her enough to send her thoughts into disarray.

"I beg your pardon for the interruption, but I wondered whether Miss Drumm ... Jessica, might be agreeable to a brief stroll in the garden. The moon is bright and the night clear."

Jessica inclined her head and, in a voice not quite steady, asked her hostess whether she might be excused.

Billie grinned her assent and Jessica fair flew through the door to fetch her wrap and call Trixie.

Moments later, the couple were meandering along the pathways, hands entwined, chatting; Jessica's momentary shyness obliterated by Duncan's very satisfactory method of saying 'hello.' Trixie was bounding about, glad for the chance of a proper leg stretch after two days confined in a coach trying to be well behaved.

"Less than two weeks, goodness, I can't quite believe it." Jessica said, her tones pensive. That their wedding was almost upon them still seemed unreal, and she was beset by the occasional flicker of unease that it was all too good to be true. What if Duncan was revisited by the notion he was not the right man for her? She knew he loved her as much as if not more than she loved him — if that was possible — but she also accepted he had his insecurities, and that the demons she knew tormented him from time to time, might overwhelm his common sense.

Determined not to let him sense her fleeting disquiet, she smiled and came to a standstill in front of him.

"Duncan Barrington, I don't think you will ever know how much I love you." She lifted up on the tips of her toes and brushed her lips to his, feeling a tremor run through him.

"I think I might have an inkling." His arms came around her and abruptly all doubts were banished to the far reaches of her mind as he kissed her, taking it deeper and deeper until she was only aware of him and those magical lips that could transport her to the edge of the universe.

For Jessica, the days before her wedding were some of the happiest and most difficult of her life.

The day after her arrival at Whiteoaks, Duncan took her and her mother to his home, Briar Cottage. 'Cottage' was rather a misnomer as the property was not small, sporting six bedrooms, one of which Duncan was in the process of transforming into a dressing room. He, along with several of his friends, had knocked a wall through, joining two rooms into one.

Since their betrothal, he had spent most of his free time building new wardrobes, a chest of drawers and a dressing table all in the same wood, all highly polished, with an intriguing yet delicate pattern carved into the front of each. When Jessica studied it closely, she realised it was a 'D' and 'J' entwined, but so cleverly done it looked merely a random design. Surreptitiously grasping his hand, she squeezed his fingers, her heart swelling. That he cared enough to create such beautiful furniture nearly reduced her to tears.

The carving of Trixie took pride of place on the mantel in the study-come-library; a most comfortable space where Jessica imagined ... hoped ... they would spend their evenings. There were the usual domestic quarters; Duncan had Maggie, Dinah and Miles — cook, maid and butler/groom respectively, but Billie had organised another maid, a gardener and a dedicated groom, freeing up Miles to continue as butler.

Coming from a household without too many luxuries, Jessica was worried they wouldn't have enough to keep so many people occupied but Billie assured her those she had engaged constituted the bare minimum. Once they had been introduced to one another, Jessica couldn't have let any of them go anyway, as all were delightful, and excited to have gainful employment.

At the back of the house stood a stable with an adjacent field, abode of Orion, as well as Duncan's two carriage horses. Jessica was reluctant to spend long there, still discomfited when in proximity to the huge creatures. She knew she would probably have to overcome her nervousness; here in the country it would be far quicker to get around on horseback, but that was something she would deal with if and when it proved necessary.

Billie, and Grace Elliott, along with the female staff, had gone through the house from top to bottom, replacing the soft furnishings as required. Briar Cottage had been in Duncan's family for generations and Grace had been heard to murmur she believed some of the furniture might well have been there since the first Barrington took possession. With Duncan's permission, the women created a brighter more welcoming aspect using lighter fabrics and colourful cushions. Duncan had been astonished when he saw the result, three days before Jessica arrived, amazed his home could look so cheerful, thanking his self-appointed decorators profusely.

While Mrs Drummond inspected the small garden, which was beginning to blossom with a multitude of flowers, Duncan and Jessica enjoyed a few moments to themselves.

"So, do you think you might be happy here, love?" Duncan queried of his betrothed.

"I declare myself utterly enchanted." Jessica pronounced. "Briar Cottage is charming and I already feel as though 'tis my home." Tucking her arm through his as they wandered about the rooms, windows open to allow the fragrant air to waft through. Jessica sighed,

"Is something wrong?" Hearing her, Duncan had a moment of panic — had he forgotten something?

"Nothing at all, I was just thinking in all my life I have never experienced such contentment. I believe I am the luckiest woman in England." She was drawn against him, his lips brushing her hair.

"Well, I've considered myself the luckiest man in the world for several months now," he murmured in her ear, the timbre of his voice making her spine tingle. Jessica fitted herself to him, lifting her face for his kiss which he bestowed willingly, uncaring how many people were milling around the house. "A week Friday cannot come soon enough for me," he growled.

Jessica gurgled with laughter at his salacious expression.

She nudged his shoulder. "Come, we should join Mama. If she is left too long in a garden, matters not whose, she cannot help but dead-head flowers or trim bushes." Indeed, they found Mrs Drummond, chatting with Bert — the new gardener — about the plentiful varieties of rose from which he was currently clipping straggly stems.

Jessica begin to explore the surroundings of what would become her home, nestled on the edge of the Winchester's vast estate. She accompanied Dr Elliott — or Theo as he insisted she call him — around the village, meeting the locals, listening to their litany of woes; surmising, correctly that many liked to see the doctor, and now his new assistant, just to have someone with whom they could chat. Jessica wasn't in the slightest perturbed that she would be more likely to spend her time with folk who were lonely rather than unwell. Her sunny and naturally affectionate demeanour endeared Jessica to the somewhat isolated community and, by the end of her first week at Whiteoaks, she felt as though she had been more or less accepted. They seemed especially interested in her romance with Duncan, as most of the villagers presumed him a confirmed bachelor. Unwilling to share such intimacies, Jessica discovered, however, a soupçon of detail was enough to keep them happy and she didn't mind, such care for one of their own, heart-warming.

One morning, a week before her wedding and, following several days of entertainment organised by Billie and Giles, to which any number of guests had been invited, Jessica was strolling over to the workshops to see whether Duncan might have a moment to take a break. He had been unusually quiet and, if she was honest, maybe a little preoccupied the last couple of days — although the shift was probably indefinable to all but her. As she reached the door raised voices could be heard. Hesitating, and knowing she didn't want to interrupt, Jessica was contemplating whether it would be better to return later, when the doors burst open and Nate stomped out cursing every man and his dog.

Spotting Jessica, he apologised for his language, adding, "If you can make him see sense, please try. There's no talking to him today." Tossing his head towards the interior of the workshop.

Concerned, Jessica offered an understanding grin and, knowing she would have to deal with the darkness that still occasionally tormented Duncan, sooner or later, took a deep breath and stepped inside. Duncan was facing one of the benches, leaning on his outstretched arm, head bent, his hair falling about his ears, as though he'd been yanking at it; it looked shaggier than Trixie's coat. She walked over and touched his shoulder. Duncan jerked away, then, realising who it was, raked his fingers through his hair, which now looked as though he'd been dragged through a hedge backwards

"Jess, sorry, I…that is…I didn't…" his face twisted.

"It's all right Duncan, don't apologise. What's happened? Has something upset you, or do you just feel out of sorts?"

He stared at her, and she could see his mind warring over whether to tell her to mind her own business, or give in and share his frustration.

"Just a bad morning, is all. We had some furniture that should have been finished, but we've suffered an unexpected delay and 'tis an annoyance I didn't need."

"Was the delay Nate's fault," she dared to ask.

Duncan shook his head. "'Twas nobody's fault," he grumbled. "Nate just happened to be here and I vented my frustration out on him," grouchily. "I'll apologise."

Jessica slid between him and the bench, stroking cool fingers over his jaw. "Are you sleeping? Do you want to talk about what's bothering you?"

"Much the same as ever, and nothing's bothering me." His attitude was slightly brusque.

"So, not enough then?" she smiled, stretching up to kiss his cheek.

"The only time I've ever slept well was the night you fell asleep on my knee, oh and the night we found you at St Bart's. Seems I can only get a decent rest when you are beside me." Duncan's stance relaxed a little as he spoke, and his expression softened.

"Well, you should be looking forward to Friday evening then?" Jessica responded, dropping a sly wink.

"I sincerely doubt there'll be much sleeping that night, love." He promised. He held her gaze for a moment, before moving her gently aside. "Much as I'd love to spend hours kissing you, I have to get this finished." The warmth disappeared from his voice, and his tone became detached.

Jessica frowned. "Are you sure you don't want to talk?" She kept her voice carefully bland.

He shook his head. "'Tis naught to bother your pretty head about." He threw over his shoulder, already engrossed in his task.

Jessica walked slowly out of the workshop, tutting at his rather patronising 'pretty head' comment — good job she loved him. Spying Nate nearby she joined him. "How often does he get like this, Nate?"

"Not as much as he used to. 'Tis rare now, 'specially since you and he…" Nate left that dangling.

Jessica's lips curved, but didn't quite form a smile.

"Most times 'tis the smallest thing, usually something unimportant, sets him off. He was grumpy when I arrived this morning. Maybe 'tis all the festivities." Nate realised what he'd said, as Jessica bit her lip, colour draining from her face. "Oh no, Miss Drummond, Jessica, I beg your pardon, don't listen to me...I didn't mean...oh the devil." He rubbed his hand over his chin, mortified by the implication of his words

Jessica forced a bright note into her voice. "Don't fret, Nate, I understand. Mayhap you are correct, 'tis all rather exhausting. I'm not used to such revelry either. I'll let him be for a couple of days, give him some space." She smiled, rather sadly Nate thought, and headed into the main house. Going up to her bedchamber Jessica sat for a long time, thinking about what Nate had said. Why had she let things become so — well — big? Neither she nor Duncan was comfortable in large groups. She had let the excitement of the wedding take over from the joy of being married — ignoring twinges of uncertainty, pushing aside the belief a quiet ceremony with just their families would have sufficed. They had no desire to be swamped by all the flummery; they had only ever needed each other.

She kept herself busy until the following evening by which time she had come to the conclusion that if they were going to share their lives, they had to be able to talk about things, however awkward, uncomfortable or downright difficult they might be. What was the point in agreeing to love and honour each other if they couldn't have a meaningful conversation when either was troubled? After the evening meal, a meal Duncan hadn't attended, to Billie's well-concealed consternation, Jessica sought him out. He was where she expected him to be, but he wasn't working, he was just sitting, absently polishing a piece of wood. As she approached, she noticed it was another carving of Trixie, this time curled up as though asleep.

"We missed you at dinner, Duncan. Do you have a moment?" she asked quietly, unwilling to disturb the peace. Standing, his face in shadows, Duncan shrugged carelessly and her heart clenched.

"What is it, Jess?" Weariness laced his tones. She stayed where she was and, in a voice that sounded far steadier than she expected, apologised for allowing the plans for the wedding to get out of hand, adding that a quiet ceremony would have been preferable and she didn't want him to think it was her idea, or that he was about to leg-shackle himself to a flighty chit with a pretty head, who only cared to be entertained. Her deliberate use of less than polite phrasing lending a harshness to her words.

Unable to read his expression, Jessica forged ahead. "I know something bothers you. If you refuse to talk to me I cannot help. I might not be able to help anyway, but at least I am here and I will listen. We used to talk all the time, what's changed?" She paused; he just stared, making no move towards her. She waited, still nothing. She cocked her head and, smiling gently, took a step forward, reaching out to stroke her fingers against his shirt. "Well, you know where to find me," and before he could draw breath, vanished into the gloom.

Duncan frowned. Now what was all that about? He ran her words over and over in his head until it hit him like a sledgehammer. She thought he wanted out of their wedding; that what bothered him was being married, was a life with her. That even though he had been the one who did not want to delay, now the wedding was mere days away, he had realised it wasn't for him and couldn't find a way to tell her. He slammed his fist against the table. Jessica wasn't wholly incorrect in her assumptions; he *was* finding all the celebrations rather difficult to deal with. Essentially a private person, Duncan struggled to cope with the constant barrage of well-wishers and parties. Yes, it was tiring, but none of that was Jessica's fault, she had only arrived a week ago. All he wanted was her. The rest wasn't important, but even though he had accepted all this frivolity was part and parcel of the wedding, he never expected it to affect him in so adverse a manner.

Vacillating over what to do, he decided to leave it 'til the morrow — best to talk about things in the light of day after both of them had, hopefully, managed a few hours of sleep.

Chapter Twenty Nine

The next morning, Jessica was awake early; in fact, she hadn't slept much at all. Her thoughts continued to spin around and around, coming back to one thing — Duncan loved her, she never questioned that, but something was amiss. In spite of his assurances to the contrary, his odd behaviour during the last couple of days had allowed the vague suspicion he preferred to keep their relationship at arm's length, to solidify. As she was dressing, another thought struck her and, reaching for the box she had packed so carefully, Jessica lifted out the cleverly crafted prosthesis, wondering in light of everything else going on, if and when would be the right time to present it to her betrothed.

It was clear something troubled him, Jessica's enthusiasm and excitement for her idea dampened by her increasing apprehension at his reaction. She pondered what to do while she finished dressing, finally determining it was better to give it to him sooner rather than later. Even though Jessica acknowledged there was a chance her gift might offend or worse, anger Duncan, she hoped he knew her well enough to trust she wasn't questioning his ability, or his value, or his love for her.

Decision made, she hurried through breakfast and, collecting the box, made her way to the workshop, Trixie at her heels. As it was still early, Duncan was there alone. Gathering her courage, she walked in calling a cheerful 'Good morning.' Duncan smiled and was about to speak when Jessica interrupted.

"Before you say anything. It wasn't my place to beg you to tell me what bothers you. I know you will do so, if and when you feel able."

Duncan looked at Jessica in surprise; this was the last thing he expected her to say.

She rushed on as though nervous. "Further, I have a gift for you, well more something I believe might prove efficacious in your work. I commissioned Dr Napier to make it. I hoped it might help, but I don't want you to think…" She babbled on, her words tumbling out too fast for intelligibility.

Eventually, unable to make head nor tail of her ramblings, Duncan, held up his hand. "Jess, love, what are you talking about?"

She handed him the box. Intrigued, he opened it, pushing aside the cloth wrapping, his eyes falling on the artificial hand. Duncan looked at Jessica, down at the hand and back at Jessica. He rubbed his forehead, questions brewing in his mind. Why had she given him this? He thought she loved him as he was. Did she need him to seem whole and undamaged? He stared at the woman he loved and despite the trepidation in her face, he could feel black fury building, blinding him to everything else and try as he might he could not hold it in.

"Why have you given me this? You think me a cripple?" he roared, humiliated Jessica thought him so inept he required an artificial hand. "Look around you, I have never needed one before. What makes you think I should start now? Is it that you can only love me if I look whole?"

Jessica flinched, distractedly picking up the carving of Trixie — so lifelike she expected it to bark or sit up and beg. She turned it around and around in her hands, as though the repetitive action would help her to stay calm, but Duncan's rage, while not wholly unexpected, prompted her own anger to flare. All her niggling fears bubbled to the surface, and never one to curb her temper, Jessica let her fury fly.

"I wouldn't care if you were a blind, deaf, mute with no limbs, I will love you until the starts fall from the sky! When will you *ever* get that through your thick skull? I organised the prosthesis because I'll hazard you would like to feel more stable when you are carving, have something to rest against, or to grip your more complex pieces while you work on them. I thought to make your life easier, but 'tis clear you would rather continue as you are, because your stupid pride won't let you accept any assistance. You would wallow in self-doubt and misery rather than give happiness a chance. Well you go ahead, Duncan Barrington, you enjoy being pathetic, you hold onto your grief and your torment, 'tis obvious you do not wish me to help share your burden." She paused her breath coming in painful bursts, her anger and distress threatening to choke her.

Jessica's anguish had Duncan's outrage evaporating as quickly as it escalated. He took a step towards her but she moved out of his reach, raising her palm like a barrier, determined to say it all.

"Stay back, let me finish. I was assured you were a brave soldier, they tell me your courage in battle was an inspiration to the men who served under you. Your friends, of whom you have many by the way, have sought me out; eager to tell me you are a man of honour and a gentleman. I already knew that. I also believe you love me, but I am starting to wonder whether you know what love is, even when it's right here in front of you, all but smacking you in the face. So, you were dealt a blow; those men at St Bart's are far worse off than you. Some unable to speak for their trauma, those who struggle simply to walk the length of the ward, or whose nightmares haunt them while they are awake. Their courage reduces me to tears because even though they cannot see any end to their ordeal they still try, they still hope. You are surrounded by loving family, supportive friends and a woman who loves you beyond measure yet still you think yourself undeserving."

She spat the words, wrath bristling out of her, tears pouring down her face, her hair spilling over her shoulders like warm honey and her eyes blazing orange flame.

"If you truly wish to marry me, to share a life with me, you *cannot* keep shutting me out. Your darkness is my darkness, your pain mine. Never once since we met, have I *ever* considered you anything other than whole. Your disability only makes you stronger, your black days mean you embrace happiness with an intensity few can appreciate, you just need to stop being so bloody stubborn, and accept that, to me, you are and always have been perfect. Here, does this make you feel better?" Seizing the device, she hurled it into the fire before storming out of the workshop and across the courtyard, Trixie bounding after her.

Duncan was rooted to the spot; he felt as though he had been flayed, her words tore at him, shredded him. Jessica was right, she had said as much before but he hadn't been listening. She had given up everything — her life in London, her work, her family and friends — to move here to be with him, never once expecting him to give up anything for her. Much as he loved her, he had forgotten how to share the deepest part of himself, drawing her close but never quite letting her all the way in. What was wrong with him? He leaned against door jamb of the workshop, his life crumbling before him, stunned that he'd let her go — again. No, not this time!

Hooking the charred prosthesis out of the flames and dumping it into a vat of water, he inspected the damage. To his relief, it was salvageable. He was aware how costly such artificial devices were and realised Jessica must have paid for it with her own coin. Biting down on a rather crude expletive, Duncan strode out over the stone flags and through the open back door of the main house into the kitchens.

"I do beg your pardon..." he began.

It was clear on the faces of the domestic staff within that they had heard something of Jessica's rant.

Duncan spread his hands, "I know, I know, I deserve to be dropped down the nearest well, but please tell me, did Miss Drummond come this way."

Sarah Haskett, Whiteoaks' cook, pinned him with her gaze. She had known all the men from Oak Stanton since they were boys and never let them get away with anything. Even Giles, the Earl of Winchester quailed before her.

"'Tis a shame you are so tall for I would be happy to put you over my knee and spank you." She wagged her finger at him. "Duncan Barrington, you should know better. No, Miss Jessica didn't come this way, she likely went out towards the Great Park, she often walks that way."

Duncan thanked them and turning on his heel, hurried around the building. Shielding his eyes against the sun, he gazed out over the gardens to the park beyond; there was no sign of Jessica or Trixie. Frowning he tried to work out were else she might go. Into the village perhaps? He pondered his options for a few minutes then decided to saddle Orion; he could cover much more ground that way.

In the meantime, shaking with reaction, Jessica stomped around the house and into the library through the elegant French doors, the ambience of the room, overflowing with all those beautiful books calming her ire somewhat. As she was making her way upstairs, Thomas handed her a letter delivered that morning. Puzzled, she turned it over to see who had sent it before sliding her finger under the seal and unfolding the page. It was from Dr Napier. Intrigued, Jessica leaned against the bannister and began to read.

Apparently, Toby Langdon had disappeared from the hospital. They had no idea where he was but the doctor had a suspicion he might make his way to Whiteoaks, he had been asking where she, Jessica, was and why she had left. It was not inconceivable someone might have informed him she was getting married at the Winchester Estate. The lieutenant seemed unable to separate Jessica from Jessamine, and France from England in his mind, and they were concerned he still imagined Jessica to be in some kind of danger. The doctor did add he realised how fanciful it sounded, but they had no other explanation for Toby's actions and wanted her to be aware of the possibility, however improbable.

Jessica folded the letter tapping it against her chin as she mulled over its contents. She would have to tell the Winchesters, she was a guest in their home with no mind to place anyone at even the slightest risk, and she believed Giles would know what to do. Then there was Duncan — he had witnessed Toby's behaviour and understood such neurosis more than most, but she found herself unwilling to return to the workshop so soon — their quarrel still rankled. Returning to her bedchamber, Jessica sat for quite a while, considering the situation, before grabbing her wrap, and going to find Billie. Thomas directed her to the herb room, where Billie was working with her beloved ointments and balms, baby Max asleep in his cradle next to her.

"Billie, I apologise for intruding," she said quietly, "but I think we might have a problem," explaining what Dr Napier feared. Always practical, Billie washed her hands, scooped up her sleeping son and made her way to the kitchens. She asked Sally to watch Max, placing the baby in another cradle tucked in a corner, away from all the hustle and bustle, uncaring how unusual it was for a countess to leave her son, and heir to the earldom in a kitchen. Billie advised Thomas and Will, who both happened to be there, of their problem, asking them to find Giles. Then flinging her own wrap around her shoulders, bustled Jessica out into the courtyard.

Halfway across the cobbles to the workshops, they were disturbed by the sound of a coach. Billie peered along the driveway and gasped as she realised it was Hugh, Helena and Nick.

"Goodness, they must have driven like the wind, I did not expect them to arrive so early in the day. Jessica, I must greet them. Go and tell Duncan." Reading Jessica's expression correctly. "Yes, I am aware he's been out of sorts lately. You know he suffers the occasional bad day and I expect all this excitement has been difficult for him to cope with — he's not one for parties."

Jessica flushed at her hostess' perception, relieved Billie hadn't heard about her own outburst. She went to find her betrothed, only to find the workshop empty save for Nate.

"Nate, where's Duncan?"

Nate shrugged. "No idea, Miss Jessica, he's been gone a time. I thought he was with you."

"No, we...errr...had a slight altercation and I haven't seen him since," she replied, evasively.

Nate chuckled. "All's I'll say is you'll have a lively marriage; you two are well matched. Don't fret, he'll come back when he's walked off his temper."

Despite the growing worry, Jessica felt a grin tug at her lips. Nate was right, they were well matched. While she didn't like arguing, she did enjoy spirited debate and to make up afterwards…the thought of that made her tingle all over. Suddenly desperate to see Duncan, she rushed back around to the kitchens, almost knocking Will over in her haste.

"Will, have you seen Duncan?"

The young man shook his head and was about to say something else when Jake stuck his head out of the stables and called over

"Orion's gone, if that helps." Will and Jessica stared at each other for a moment, then Thomas appeared and mentioned Duncan had been looking for her earlier.

"Did he not find you, Miss Drummond?"

Jessica shook her head. "No, I took the long way around through the gardens before coming in through the library. He must have just missed me." For no reason she could think of, Jessica felt uneasy. What if Toby had already arrived in the area? What would he do if he found her and his mind was unbalanced again? If he believed her to be Jessamine and saw her with another man — never mind they were estate staff — how would he react? She expressed her concerns to the three men standing with her, all understanding her misgivings.

As they were about to split up and look for Duncan, Hugh and Helena appeared, followed seconds later by Nick, each drawing Jessica into a warm hug as they joined the little group. Although glad to see them, Jessica brushed aside the usual niceties and promptly informed them of Dr Napier's suspicions. As Jessica was talking, Hugh's brow creased, and he mentioned overhearing someone asking about the Winchester Estate at the inn where they had stayed the previous night. He hadn't thought it important until now, as so close to Whiteoaks, he imagined such queries wouldn't be unexpected — tradesmen, supplies, all manner of people would likely visit the estate during any given week.

"Can you recall what the man looked like?" Jessica pressed her brother.

Hugh shook his head, "Not really. I only registered it because he mentioned Whiteoaks. I really didn't take much notice of who was speaking."

Even after Jessica described Lieutenant Langdon, Hugh wasn't sure.

"But you saw him, that night outside our house," Jessica argued. "Surely you must remember! What about at the hospital?"

"I did not meet Toby at the hospital, there were several veterans on the ward when we were looking for you. I don't recall any of them particularly. As for the evening outside our house, it was for a split second and the light was failing. I am sorry, Jess but I cannot confirm the man I heard last evening was one and the same. Mayhap he was simply a tradesman." Hugh spoke gently, hoping to calm his sister's anxiety.

"Perhaps, but I think we must accept there is a chance it was the lieutenant and that he may be here. What shall we do?" Jessica beseeched them.

"I think all we can do is be vigilant. This is a huge estate; we cannot possibly check it all. Don't go wandering off on your own, Jessica and keep Trixie nearby, I believe she'll protect you."

The dog, upon hearing her name jumped about and yipped excitedly, presuming a walk was in the offing.

"Later, Trixie," Jessica rubbed Trixie's ears absently.

Just then there was the thundering of hooves and Orion galloped towards them — riderless.

Chapter Thirty

The group in the courtyard fell speechless with shock as Orion, ears flattened and eyes wild, slithered to halt, stamping in agitation. Will grabbed the flailing reins and tried to calm the creature, leading him into the stables, where Jake took over.

"Where's Duncan?" Jessica exclaimed, her voice rising several octaves in her panic. Trixie barked, unsettled by the commotion, making Orion neigh, the sounds echoing around the buildings and adding to the tension.

"We should find him. If Orion's unseated him, Duncan could be hurt, he wouldn't send Orion home on his own," stated Will bluntly. Agreeing, they divided up into groups, Will yelling for Jake, Matthew — one of the footmen — and Nate. Horses were saddled and, all save Jessica who still couldn't bring herself to ride, set off in different directions, hoping to cover as much ground as possible. Needing to distract herself from the riotous thoughts clamouring in her head, Jessica sought out Billie and, as she was informing her hostess of this latest development, Giles, along with Henry, one of his stewards, happened upon them. The two men, once apprised of the situation, hurried to join the search party.

"I have to help, but being on a horse…I…and on foot, I would be useless." Jessica muttered in an agony of uncertainty. Billie laid a comforting hand on her friend's arm.

"Jess, I think you know in your heart you can do this. You have more courage than you realise. Go on, find Duncan. Take Orion, he will likely lead you to his master."

Jessica stared at Billie. "I'll never manage to ride that creature, he's enormous," she objected, a twinge of fear adding to her panic.

"Of course you can," Billie soothed. "Come on, I'll go with you. Trust me, Orion might be big but he's quite gentle." Sceptically, Jessica followed Billie to the stables, where Orion had his head buried in a feed basket. Billie talked to the stallion, stroking slender fingers up his black nose, scratching at the little white blaze below his forelock, bright against the dark hair. Orion nickered softly, clearly at ease with the petite countess, his distress dissipating with each stroke. Opening the stable door, Billie slipped the reins over his head, handing the saddle to Jessica.

"We'll need to put this on outside, I can't reach." Leading the horse out into the sunlight, Billie walked over to a set of stone steps. Climbing them, she motioned for Jessica to pass the saddle and once hoisted into place, the two women buckled the straps and shortened the stirrups.

"You'll have to ride astride," Billie said.

Jessica nodded distractedly — riding astride was currently the least of her worries, for regardless of how unladylike it was, she preferred this style anyway. She hesitated and moments ticked by as she tried to quell her trepidation at the thought of getting back into the saddle. Then she remembered Duncan and how he battled his fears. He needed her, she could do this. She had no right upbraiding him, if she could not find it within herself to conquer her own phobia.

Taking a deep breath, Jessica tucked up one side of her dress and mounted the great stallion who stood calm now, letting his rider settle into the saddle. She felt the horse shift beneath her, ready to run and, pushing aside her nerves, gripped her knees against Orion's flank. Leaning forward she stroked his neck and whispered in his ear.

"Come on, let's find Duncan." Calling for Trixie, Jessica clicked the reins and the three trotted out of the courtyard. Once around the rear of the domestic buildings, Orion cantered towards the Great Park and, presuming the horse would simply take her to his master, Jessica slackened the reins letting him have his head, Trixie streaking along beside them. They cantered steadily for a good fifteen minutes, beyond the briars where she had found Trixie and on towards the denser woodland surrounding that part of the estate. Slowing their pace, she circled, unsure of the pathways through the trees. Trixie bounded up beside them and Jessica paused, listening intently. All was peaceful, save the buzz of insects and the chirping of birds.

"Trixie! Seek," she instructed the dog. She had nothing of Duncan's for the dog to scent, but maybe, just maybe Trixie was clever enough to work without one — she had nothing to lose, unknowingly echoing the thoughts of her family not so very long ago. Trixie shot off along a shady path. Dismounting Orion, Jessica followed the dog into the wood; the track was narrow but passable. She couldn't think why Duncan would come this way, but she had to check.

A couple of hours earlier, Duncan was riding across the estate, puzzled as to where Jessica might be. He had checked the paths she usually followed when out walking, as well as the herb garden, the vegetable garden and the orchards. She seemed to have vanished. It didn't occur to him she would return to the house for he knew she found a brisk walk the best way to calm down. Also, there was no sign of Trixie, adding to his belief Jessica was somewhere in the grounds.

He came to the rise at the fringes of the Great Park, taking several moments to scan the gently rolling landscape around him, willing a small, angry figure and an ebullient dog to pop into his line of sight. *Nothing.* Frustrated, he urged Orion on. Contemplating whether she knew of the pool under the waterfall at the end of the path to his left, Duncan decided to investigate, pushing ahead along the trail. It was a popular place for the locals in summer, especially the estate workers, its shadowy coolness offering a respite during the long hot days, but they were only in late May and it would be another month or so before they began to venture this way, making it a lonely spot.

Despite his head telling him Jessica would have no idea about the waterfall, Duncan's heart insisted he check anyway, for its tranquil seclusion offered the perfect restorative. He rode slowly through the wood, the thick canopy of new leaves colouring everything in shades of green, and it wasn't long before he came to the waterfall — in full spate, following recent rains — the spectacle quite stunningly beautiful. Iridescent rainbows arced over the cascade, droplets of water spraying up from the base, catching the sunlight like tiny crystals. Any other time, Duncan would have been mesmerised, today he barely registered it, and of Jessica, there was no sign. Patting Orion on his neck, Duncan turned the horse and was about the retrace his steps when an angry voice halted him.

"How *dare* you?"

Duncan peered around the pool and through the surrounding trees, seeing no one.

"Who goes there?" he demanded. "What right have you on Winchester lands?" He heard a muttered response but didn't catch it. "Who goes there?" He repeated in stentorian tones. A figure emerged from the shadows, one who seemed vaguely familiar. His gait was that of a soldier and, as Duncan watched his approach, something about the man's face tweaked a memory.

"Lieutenant Langdon, Toby?" his tones incredulous, as the veteran's name fortuitously popped into his head.

Toby stared at him, his expression one of deep-seated anger.

"Lieutenant, do you remember me? I am Duncan Barrington, Miss Drummond's betrothed. We met in London, at St Bart's. Are you visiting locally?"

The soldier glared, muttering in a strange mix of French and English, and all Duncan could discern was how furious the man was with his commanders and the bastard French.

"How dare you?" he accused again, his voice throbbing with hatred. "You imbecile, 'tis your fault my Jessamine is dead. You are never going to win, we had the upper hand, you are an incompetent fool and now you must pay!" The last sentence lifted on a shriek as Toby launched himself at Orion, swinging a large branch. There was nowhere for the horse to go; Toby was between the stallion and the path. Orion reared, pawing the air, the unexpected action jolting Duncan from the saddle and, although he scrabbled to hang onto the reins, they slipped from his grasp and he felt himself sliding off the great horse, landing on his backside with a very ungainly thump, the wind knocked out of him.

Orion, relieved of his rider, fled into the woods, leaving nothing between Duncan and a man seemingly intent on his destruction. Toby stalked towards him, still swinging the branch. Duncan, smarting from the heavy landing, caught his breath and struggled to his feet, glancing around to see whether there was anything he could use to defend himself, spying and grabbing a likely looking branch of his own from the undergrowth.

"You think yourself an emperor?" Toby spat. "You are naught but a coward, sending innocent men to die brutal horrific deaths while you sit on your gilded throne." As the man heaped vitriol upon him, Duncan gawked, trying to comprehend what trauma the soldier had experienced, which made him think not only he was in France but also that he, Duncan, was Napoleon. Then he remembered — he was wearing his dark blue riding coat into which his sleeve was tucked — replicating an affectation employed by Napoleon as a way to proclaim his calm, resolute and stable leadership. Dear Lord, the poor man was hallucinating. How the devil was he going to extricate himself from this pretty pickle? No one knew where he was — any chance of help non-existent.

Keeping his voice steady, Duncan explained who he was, where they stood and that Jessica would be so pleased to see him, if only they might make their way to Whiteoaks. Pausing in his tirade, Toby seemed to listen, letting the branch dip to the ground, leaning against its bulk, his chest heaving in enraged breaths. Behind Duncan, the thunder of the waterfall enveloped them, effectively cutting the two men off, any other sound swallowed in the constant deluge. Even if anyone passed close by they wouldn't hear. Duncan's only hope was to talk the lieutenant out of the dell and back into the Great Park, where there was a chance of estate staff happening upon them.

Duncan negotiated until he was hoarse. Toby countered with accusations of ill-intent and inadequacy, of wasting lives and sending men to their deaths on fruitless missions. Of killing innocent civilians and leaving a trail of devastation across Europe. Try as he might Duncan could not convince Toby he was not the French Emperor. There was nothing for it, he had to risk passing him and glanced towards the tree line, thinking he had more chance dodging between the trees than sidestepping Toby.

Hoping to distract the veteran, Duncan began skimming flat rocks across the pool, watching them bounce while he talked. The rhythmic action diverted Toby who watched curiously, fascinated by his adversary's skill. Duncan waited several more minutes until he thought he could chance it. While Toby was fixated on a larger than normal stone effortlessly hopping over the water, Duncan shot off through the trees his tread loud in the undergrowth. Toby realised what he was up to and, snarling in frustration, sped after him. Both men were fit, but anger lent speed to Toby and he soon caught up, launching himself at Duncan, the pair clashing in a confusion of limbs. Toby's determination to finish his enemy once and for all spurred him on. Duncan put up a good fight, landing several well-timed punches, but his attacker had the upper hand from the start.

"I am not Napoleon," Duncan gasped, cursing the loss of his left hand — a second fist would have been most welcome right at this moment — his strength failing. "Jessica would not marry a French Emperor. Be sensible man!" He pleaded as he tried to avoid Toby's furious onslaught. The veteran, however, was beyond reason, shoving Duncan hard against the trunk of a tree, punching him as he did so. Duncan's head snapped back and, as his world exploded in agony, he sent out a silent apology to Jessica, presuming Toby intended to finish him, sorrowful he would never see her again.

Then everything went black.

Jessica made her way along the path. As she ventured deeper into the green dimness, she heard the oddest sound, reminding her of when she found Trixie. Standing still, she listened; it was coming from her right. Releasing Orion's reins, she made her way cautiously towards it, keeping Trixie at her side. Seconds later, she came upon a most distressing scene. Duncan was slumped against a tree, blood pouring from his nose, one eye swollen and his clothes torn. Next to him,

245

huddled in a heap was Lieutenant Langdon, weeping copiously and apologising. Unsure who to tend to first, Jessica hurried back to where Orion waited patiently, leading him out of the wood, she slapped him on the flank and yelled

"Home!" She watched, until she was sure the animal understood her command. Orion neighed and galloped away, up over the rise, disappearing out of sight. Trixie came up behind her, whining.

"Come on girl. Let's go save our man." She ran her fingers down the dog's back, ruffling the silky fur. Trixie nuzzled her mistress's leg, following her into the shadows. Back in the tiny glade where the two men lay, Jessica checked to make sure Duncan was breathing, pleased to note his chest rose and fell steadily. Unbuttoning his waistcoat, she pulled his shirt free from his trousers, running a relatively practiced eye over his skin, noting where it was darkening as bruises began to blossom. Not daring to move him, she tore a strip from her petticoat, using it to staunch the blood still dripping from his nose. Another strip bound a laceration on his arm, presumably caused by a branch or stick during their scuffle. Unable to do any more for now, she turned her attention to Toby. Kneeling alongside him, she drew the weeping man against her, stroking his hair, and spoke softly.

"Toby, Lieutenant Langdon, 'tis me, Jessica. What happened?"

He shook his head, continuing to apologise, his sobs not abating. Without a proper examination, she could not tell whether the man was hurt but, although battered, he seemed to have avoided serious injury. Trixie made herself a bed in the undergrowth as, without conscious thought, Jessica began to sing. She sang lullabies, hoping to settle the distraught soldier, eventually trying the one she had sung at St Bart's — *au clair de la lune.* Half way through the folk-song, Trixie bounded off, whimpering excitedly and, as the last notes died away, there was a rustle through the trees and half a dozen men loomed over her, stunned into silence at the scene before them.

"Praise every God in the existence of the world," Jessica muttered; Orion had done his job. "I think there's been a bit of a fracas." With that understatement, she attempted to stand, her legs stiff from crouching so long. Nick took her arm and, hooking his around her waist, helped her up and out into the afternoon sunshine. "Nick, Duncan! I don't know how badly hurt he is. Please tell them to be careful with him."

Her brother sat Jessica on an old log, telling her not to fret and to wait there, before going back into the woods to assist the others. She took a moment to compose herself. It was so peaceful; several horses stood in a loose circle, chomping on the lush grass and a light breeze lifted her hair, the scene completely at odds with the brutality whose aftermath she had just witnessed.

Chapter Thirty One

It was quite a while before the men reappeared and by now Jessica was hopping about, desperate to know what was taking them so long. Four of them carried Duncan, the remaining two escorting Toby. Giles said he was going to fetch the carriage — it was the only way they could get Duncan back to Whiteoaks safely — while dispatching Jake to find Theo Elliott.

As the two men rode away, Jessica fell to the ground where Duncan, still unconscious, had been laid; taking his hand and talking to him, while smoothing his unruly hair off a face greyer than ash. Unable to help herself she kissed him, blinking against a rush of tears. Hugh pointed out Duncan had received a bash to the head, which explained why he had not regained his senses.

"Don't you dare die on me, Duncan Barrington, I haven't finished shouting at you yet," she ground out fiercely. "You promised to love me, you promised always to be there for me, you promised never to let go. Don't you even think about reneging on your promises. If you give up, I'll never forgive you." She leaned close whispering in his ear." You cannot die while you hold my heart." The hand she held suddenly gripped hers and she jerked backwards, raising her eyes to his face. His eyelids flickered and opened, blue colliding with tawny, and she held her breath.

"If you say so." His voice weaker than normal, the effort of speaking sending pain lancing through his skull.

"I most definitely do say so." She responded, a tender smile curving her lips. He smiled back and untangling his hand, reached up to stroke her cheek. She pressed her hand against his, relief coursing through her. "I love you, Duncan, please don't ever scare me like that again."

"I love you too my beautiful Jessica. I promise never to confront another demented soldier as long as I live. Ooof, my head hurts." On that note, he turned away from her to be violently and unceremoniously, sick.

"Hush, don't try to talk just rest. Giles has gone for the carriage, we'll have you home soon."

"How did you find me?" He choked out.

"Orion led me to you," she didn't elaborate and Duncan's head was too befuddled to register the import of that statement, content just to let her voice wash over him. Jessica talked quietly about nothing of any consequence until the carriage rattled towards them nearly an hour later. The journey back to Whiteoaks was, by necessity, slow. If they tried to go quickly, the motion of the coach over the rough ground made Duncan cry out in pain and he was sick twice more. Jessica sat with him — one of the other men leading Orion — dabbing the blood away from his nose, continuing to distract him with mundane chatter and, before too long, they came to a halt in the courtyard.

Willing hands assisted Duncan, who tried to convince them he was perfectly capable of walking, belied by his inability to put one leg in front of the other. They ignored him anyway, depositing him carefully in one of the many bedchambers, as directed by Billie.

"You have enough guests to worry about, I should go home."

Billie tutted, shushing him and told him to let Theo examine him; they would worry about where he might sleep later. A hint of a grin pulled his lips, but before he could say any more, Theo shooed everyone out so he could work in peace.

Downstairs, Giles and Hugh kept an eye on Toby, who had reverted to his usual reserved self, confused as to why he was in Hampshire in a house he didn't recognise. Jessica explained what she thought had happened, her words stirring, what seemed to Toby, more like a distant memory than a recent occurrence. Recollection slowly seeped back, however, and the poor man was mortified by his behaviour.

"I cannot be trusted not to repeat my actions, what am I to do?"

Concerned his distress might send him over the edge again, Jessica told Toby what Dr Napier had suggested in the weeks after his last upset. That he needed intensive counselling, probably every day for an extended period until he learned to recognise the triggers and, eventually, the hope was that the dissociative nature of his attacks would lessen until they became a thing of the past.

"Even though it was important for you to accept what happened to Jessamine and that it happened years ago, it brought the trauma to the forefront of your mind and you have had to learn to deal with it all over again. But now we know its cause and surely 'tis better to know and have something to work with than have no idea why your mind behaves as though you cannot control it. Dr Napier knows of some doctors who specialise in what ails you and he trusts they can help you come to terms with your experiences in Toulouse," she paused regarding him steadily. "Toby, do you think you might be able to tell me what happened today?"

Toby studied Jessica, noting there was no censure in her placid demeanour, her encouraging smile and relaxed posture inviting his confidence. He glanced nervously at the two men sitting beside her, but neither appeared to bear him ill will. He began to talk, hesitantly, at first, but soon words bubbled out, almost too quickly for comprehension. As suspected, he had heard Jessica was to be wed and, in his mind, this became twisted into an image of her being taken against her will, by the French. He had made his way to Whiteoaks and had slept in an old disused barn not far from the Great Park. He had seen Duncan riding out and had mistaken him for Napoleon — Duncan's military bearing and the tucked sleeve becoming muddled in his poor tortured head. Fearing, not only for Jessamine's life, but also the lives of his comrades in arms, Toby admitted he just wanted to rid the world of the lunatic Emperor, in the hopes this would end the war. It wasn't until he saw Duncan unconscious and bleeding that he realised he had tried to kill the wrong man.

Despite the sickening nature of the attack, the very fact Toby recalled it all, showed marked progress and was as much a breakthrough as his revelations a month previously. Not that it was much consolation to the distraught veteran right at that moment.

"You have no idea how terrifying it is, to recognise what was absolutely clear seconds before is no more than a figment of your imagination. By Jove, I could have killed him, I could have killed him…" Toby's voice trailed off and he dropped his head into his hands. Jessica looked at Hugh and Giles.

"What happens now?" She whispered.

The two men had no answers, not yet. They would need to talk with Duncan. If he decided to press charges, Toby would be required to face the local magistrate, who just happened to be Giles.

"Let us see what Duncan says. I do think however we need to consider a guard to watch over Lieutenant Langdon for all our safety, especially his own."

"I worry I may dissemble again, lock me up if you have to — whatever it takes." Toby agreed, his dismay obvious.

Jessica laid her hand on his arm, squeezing it lightly. "Toby, we will do everything we can to help you heal. Will you trust us?"

Toby smiled shyly and nodded. "Thank you for your patience and kindness, I doubt I deserve either." Was all he said, warmed by the concern in the faces of the three in front of him.

"Now, I'm going to find out what Theo has to say, then I intend to sit with my betrothed. We have a discussion to conclude and he needn't think just because he has a sore head that I will forget about it." Jessica winked at three men and, leaving Giles and Hugh to arrange a watch for Toby, made her way back to the guest room where she hoped the doctor had completed his examination of Duncan.

Tapping softly on the door, she was admitted by Theo, who affirmed he was finished.

"Except for a rather nasty gash on the back of his head and some fairly severe bruising, your betrothed will be fine." Theo grinned at Jessica. She huffed her relief and asked whether she might be permitted to sit with him. Theo had no problem with her request, saying he would let Billie know. "'Tis likely he will suffer from an outsize in headaches for a couple of days, and he will be stiff from the beating he took, but I suspect it won't prevent him from getting up on the morrow. I have instructed Billie to administer some of her remedies as required and then, 'tis merely a matter of allowing time to work its magic Now, I'm going to examine our lieutenant and, if he feels so disposed, have a quiet chat with him. I believe he may need an understanding ear." The doctor's comment reminding Jessica that he was not unaware of the effects of trauma.

Patting Jessica on her shoulder, Theo took his leave, saying he'd be back the next day to see how Duncan fared.

Pulling the chair closer to the bed, Jessica studied Duncan's craggy features. The greyish cast had left his face, but he was still pale, in stark contrast to the dark purplish bruising beginning to form around eyes that were closed. Presuming him to be asleep, she resisted the overwhelming temptation to stroke his cheek or run her fingers over the stubble on his chin and down his throat to where his open shirt revealed a smattering of dark hair. Sometimes the strength of feeling she had for this man scared her. The thought she might have lost him made their earlier, and totally ridiculous, argument seem trivial. Nonetheless, it needed to be resolved. Swallowing a sigh, she smoothed the bedclothes around him, settling back into the chair and tucked her hand into his.

The hand tightened around hers, Duncan's lids lifted and he turned his head, eyes searching for hers.

"Jess," he held her gaze and she gulped at the emotion in those fathomless blue depths.

"Hello, I thought you slept. I didn't mean to disturb you. I just needed to touch you." She explained, blushing.

"I wasn't asleep."

Then both spoke at the same time —

"Duncan, I'm sorry I yelled at you. I should have been more sensitive of your feelings."

"I'm sorry I bawled at you. The last few days were…trying…and my thoughts have been a little troubled but I should not have taken it out on you."

Jessica offered a tentative smile and, before her courage deserted her, asked the question uppermost in her mind. "Duncan, are you sure you wish to marry me? 'Tis not too late…I…if you have reservations…maybe it is too much…?" She stopped, gathering her thoughts and spluttered, "I would gladly be your mistress if marriage brings me too close."

Duncan's jaw dropped, her words bouncing around his aching head. "I beg your pardon. I do not think I heard that correctly. Please would you be so kind as to repeat it?"

Jessica did as he asked, her cheeks fiery red at how brazen it sounded.

"Jessica Drummond, what on earth makes you think I don't wish to marry you, or that I would *ever* ruin your reputation by taking you as my mistress? The very thought…" words failed him and he pulled her closer.

"No, your poor head! Have a care. You'll make yourself sick again." Jessica tried to extract her hand but he refused to let go.

"Come here, wench," he growled, low in his throat.

"Wench? Excuse *me*, sir, I am *nobody's* wench." Indignantly.

"You are my wench and I am never letting you go." The reply rumbled through him as he succeeded in trapping her against him.

"B-but y-you changed, then l-last evening and this m-morning, the argument. It seemed…I thought mayhap it was…you didn't…" Now it was she who couldn't find the words and despite her best intentions a tear rolled down her hot cheeks. Duncan groaned and, ignoring the hammering in his skull, shuffled up on the multitude of pillows to cradle her in his arms.

"You are correct. I was withdrawn, and I should have talked about it with you. My behaviour was ill-considered and hurtful."

Jessica tried to squirm away, but he merely hugged her tighter.

"Jess, I do not cope well with lots of attention and I struggle when in large groups, for they make me feel confined — imprisoned almost. I know I am an adult and should be able to handle such things and if 'tis the odd occasion, I can and I do.

Unfortunately, I failed to recognise how badly these last two weeks would affect me, for seemingly they were too much and my reaction was deplorable. I do not deserve your gift, which after due consideration, I think will prove most beneficial." Dropping a kiss on her nose before continuing —

"Please believe me when I say it was not my intent to upset you or have you believe I do not wish to marry you. Until we met, love and marriage were not something I contemplated; but you blew into my life with your bewitching eyes and your kissable lips and a body that turns my head to mush, managing to tip my neatly organised world on its head. I cannot wait to marry you, to have you in my life, my home, and most especially my bed every day and night for the rest of our lives." Tilting her chin with his finger, he kissed the tear away, feeling her tremble against him as her breathing quickened. "I love you, Jessica Drummond with a love so profound it brings me to my knees."

"Well, 'tis fortunate we're to wed in three days good sir, otherwise you may have even more trouble staying upright." Jessica smiled, her signature carefree smile, which lit her face and sent heat spiralling through the man in whose embrace she remained.

"Oh, God, Jess," uncaring that he felt as though he'd been run over by a carriage — twice — Duncan bent his head, capturing her lips and kissing her until the room seemed to rock and all cares had fled. His kiss was love, laughter, togetherness and joy and, finally, they believed this was their destiny. Yes, it would probably be a tumultuous union, they would likely still argue — both had fiery temperaments — and there was nothing wrong with healthy disagreement and debate, which for them, would strengthen rather than diminish the love they shared. A mystifying, inexplicable, immeasurable and unquenchable love, and unexpected though it may have been, was no less devoted.

Chapter Thirty Two

After all that had transpired, Jessica suggested they delay the wedding until Duncan's injuries healed properly, but her betrothed wouldn't hear of it. Frequent application of Billie's special ointment, although pungent, had worked wonders for, despite some lingering discomfort, Duncan felt almost human again, and was very thankful his eyes looked more shadowed than bruised. Nothing was going to prevent him from marrying Jessica, even if it meant he had to be carried into church, glad that hadn't proved necessary. Moreover, Oak Stanton was a close-knit community and so, even though the unfortunate incident was common knowledge, all were caring enough to pretend naught was awry.

Thus, they were married four days later surrounded by family, friends, well-wishers and a very excited dog. Jessica was determined Trixie should be included, she was, after all, the reason Duncan and she met.

Helena and Mrs Drummond were correct — Duncan could scarcely believe his eyes when he saw Jessica walking towards him down the aisle of the tiny village church. Her dress, shimmering in shades of bronze and burnt amber flowed around her as she moved. Threaded through with ribbons matching her gown, her hair swirled around her head in an intricate style — one he looked forward to unravelling later — and her eyes shone like tawny gemstones.

Hugh, in place of her father, walked beside her proudly until it came time to relinquish his guardianship.

Leaning close he muttered. "Are you sure?"

Jessica grinned up at her tall brother, and nodded, "Absolutely," she affirmed a little louder than she intended, eliciting a ripple of laughter from the congregation.

The couple pledged their lives to each other, Duncan sliding a simple gold band along the third finger of Jessica's left hand, brushing his lips over her knuckles as he did so — causing all the women to sig in delight. To Duncan's surprise, Jessica kept hold of his hand and, before he realised what was happening, slipped onto his third finger, a slender signet ring into which his initials had been engraved.

"Mayhap this will keep us balanced," she grinned. He squeezed her fingers gently and, as they were pronounced husband and wife, Duncan stroked his hand along her cheek, kissing her tenderly and for so long, the vicar was heard to murmur he hoped they remembered not only were they still in church, but also that air had proved somewhat essential in sustaining life and they might like to partake of a gulp or two, making the newlyweds blush to the amusement of their guests.

Later, after they had enjoyed the wonderful meal and entertainment so generously organised by Billie and Giles and, presuming no one noticed their quiet departure, Duncan led his wife away to the coach waiting in the courtyard. Percy, the Barrington's new groom, clicked the reins and they trundled through dappled lanes to Briar Cottage. Telling Percy he could return to the festivities, Duncan secured the front door and the couple strolled, arm and arm, through to the cosy library where they found a decanter of red wine and a plate of tasty looking cakes left by their thoughtful staff.

"I don't think I'll need to eat until next week, although a small glass of wine would be welcome," Jessica said, flopping into one of the large wing back chairs and groaned, holding her stomach in mock discomfort. "Billie certainly knows how to entertain in style." Sipping at the wine Duncan had just poured, she ruminated over the day — the sumptuous celebration would doubtless keep the gossips happy for weeks. Glancing at her new husband, admiring his upright stance and rugged features, unbidden, she recalled his comments four days previously. "Was it too awful?" Her expression was solicitous.

Duncan grinned and came to sit next to her. "No, love. That was exactly the right amount of awful."

Jessica gaped at him in shock, only to feel her lips curl at the devilish twinkle in his eyes.

"I speak in jest. I believe it was the most wonderful wedding I have ever attended. Did you see the bride? She looked exquisite; the man she married is surely more fortunate than any man in Christendom. Of course, I may be ever so slightly biased."

Jessica giggled. "You are exasperating," she chastised, stretching out to smooth her hand along the dark grey of his jacket, feeling the fine wool under her fingers. Duncan took a long sip of his wine, then placing the goblet on the platter, stood drawing his wife out of the chair and against him.

"Thank you." He murmured lifting a long ringlet of hair, kissing the creamy skin underneath. Jessica shivered in anticipation.

"What for?" she whispered, as unconsciously, she arched her neck, needing more. He obliged, scattering kisses over her throat.

"Saving me."

Jessica pulled away and studied him, her head cocked to one side. "Saving you? I didn't save you; you didn't need saving, you needed loving. Although to be clear, that is exclusively my purview — if another woman decides she might like to try loving you, the consequences will not be pretty."

Duncan chuckled, "My hands are full with the woman I have, I do not think I have the energy for any more." Jessica started to splutter about his intentions should an unexpected wave of superfluous stamina engulf him, at which point he shut her up most effectively.

Several minutes later, heat coiling through them, restless ardour ignited, he reluctantly broke their kiss.

"Jess, I love you more I can ever say but..." he stroked a finger along her jawline, "...maybe I could show you how much?" He hesitated, the afternoon was barely over. Was it too early to think of making love to his bride? Apparently not, for Jessica moved against him, slipping her fingers under his jacket and started to unbutton his waistcoat. "Not here, I know a far more comfortable place." Swinging her up into his arms and striding out of the room.

"And there was I thinking the library quite congenial for such things," Jessica grinned, unknotting his cravat and kissing the v of skin at the open collar of his shirt.

"Jess, do that again and I'll drop you. Have you any idea what that does to a man?" He heard her gurgle of laughter as he carried her into their bedroom.

"Well, I was hoping it would prompt him to make passionate love to me. Do you know of anyone who might be interested?" Pertly.

Duncan deposited her carefully on the bed and let out a bark of mirth.

"Jessica Barrington you are most definitely a wench."

"If you say so."

"I do say so."

Jessica knelt on the bed, and reaching for him, finished unbuttoning his waistcoat, pushing it, along with his jacket off his shoulders, the fine wool and heavy brocade crumpling as they hit the floor. "I should probably pick them up, they'll crease..." she muttered absently as she plucked his shirt free from his trousers. Her fingers teased over his heated flesh, endlessly searching, tracing his muscles. Stretching up, she murmured "...but since I'm your wench not your housekeeper, they'll have to wait. First, please kiss me."

Still amused by her sauce, Duncan didn't need asking twice, crushing her lips with bruising intensity, while seeking and finding the tiny buttons hidden cleverly under a ribbon of satin down the back of her gown. As each button fell to his inquisitive fingers, the silky layers began to slither onto the bed, pooling around Jessica, glimmering like aged whisky. Unlacing her stays, he trailed kisses down her throat and over her shoulder to the rise of her breast, hearing her breath catch. Chemise and petticoats followed and, completely entranced by Duncan's intoxicating kisses, Jessica was naked almost before she realised it.

"Oh…errm…" Hot colour bloomed over her cheeks as, flustered, her arms dropped from around Duncan's neck to shield herself.

"Oh, love, you have no need to be modest with me." Duncan breathed hoarsely, running appreciative eyes over her willowy body. "You are more beautiful than I could ever have imagined, and trust me, I've done a lot of imagining."

Jessica felt a giggle bubbling up.

"Have you now? You, sir, are a rake." One hand on her hip, she wagged a finger at him, her hair beginning to unwind from the ornate style, long strands rippling over her skin in honeyed rivulets. Duncan was rendered momentarily speechless as he gazed at her; still dumbfounded she actually loved him.

"Jess, my God woman, you are perfection."

Abruptly, laughter fled as longing whispered through her and she fisted his snowy white shirt, pulling him to her.

"This has to come off," she tugged at the cotton, somehow managing not to rip it as she dragged it over his head. "Duncan!" she breathed, his defined physique a revelation. Here and there, scars marred the tanned flesh, remnants from his time on the battlefield. Taking her time, Jessica stroked her fingers over each one, following with a kiss, until Duncan was fairly certain he might burst into flames from the fire scorching through him.

Reaching the fall of his trousers, Jessica made short work of the fastenings, but then hesitated, her hands trembling; she had to let Duncan shrug out of them, as her knees turned to water. Sinking back onto the rich coverlet, she gulped as her husband stood before her, supremely masculine — at least she presumed he was, being the only man she'd ever seen without clothing. His need for her was evident and even though her body begged for his touch, she found herself inordinately shy.

"Have you…did you…is this your…? Jessica, form a sentence for goodness sake," she admonished herself out loud. Duncan chuckled and, taking her hand in his, lifted her onto her knees.

"I have, but rarely. 'Twas years ago, and although I cannot say there was no affection, it was never with love." He admitted, kissing her cheek.

Jessica held his face. "Oh, Duncan, while my head is saddened that you have never before known love, my heart is warmed, for I get to be the first and to have that love returned is the most precious gift."

Duncan sucked in a sharp breath. "'Tis you who are precious, my love." He tucked her against him, fitting her to his shape, hearing her sigh as their bodies melded. Wrapping one arm around her, Duncan ghosted light fingers across her skin; learning her as though each part of her body was a page in a favourite book, to be read over and over and over again.

Jessica simply stopped thinking — it was pointless trying, nothing made sense anymore —succumbing to the potency of his touch. Everything was heat and fire and passion and Duncan.

As his lips beguiled her, his fingers traced a tortuous path over her breasts, swirling around them until she quivered, arching into him, needing something, anything to ease the ache within her, the ache only he could assuage. Whimpering softly, Jessica's hands followed their own quest, trailing over Duncan as though the curves and planes of his body composed a map known only to her tenacious fingertips. As her journey led her unwaveringly down to his trim hips and around to the soft skin at the top of his thigh, Jessica sought and encircled the muscle, now rigid against her stomach, wrenching a guttural groan from Duncan, at the same moment as he found her centre, his fingers drawing her to what seemed an insurmountable peak. The ache intensified until she cried out and, just when she thought her heart would stop, he tipped her off the precipice and she was falling, falling, sensations roiling through her so fast she didn't know when one finished and another started, unaware she'd uttered a plea until his whispered words penetrated her consciousness —

"I have you, I'll never let you go."

Breathing coming in shudders, Jessica tried to hold on, wanting to savour every moment of this astonishing experience.

"Duncan...oh...goodness...how...what..." she could only manage staccato bursts. She felt a chuckle rumble through him as he lay her on the bed, joining her there, kissing her tenderly and languorously, letting the passion build once more.

"That was only the first course, love," he whispered in her ear as he gently bit the soft lobe, his own breathing less than steady.

"It gets better?" she gasped, wriggling against him, revelling in the feel of his body against hers. "Oh, you have the most irresistible body." Her fingers were already snaking up over his back and chest, feeling the rapid tattoo of his heartbeat. "I cannot stop touching you."

"Go ahead, I have no intention of preventing you." He grinned, lifting himself up onto his elbow, grazing a gentle finger from the hollow at her throat, through the shadow between her breasts and over her stomach, down to where her desire burned hottest. Even under so slight a touch Jessica's skin tingled and pulsed as, involuntarily, she raised her hips towards him, the ache returning.

"So..." the word almost a purr, causing Duncan to raise an eyebrow. "What's the main dish?"

"Why *you* of course." Stealing her giggle with his mouth, tongues tangling, bodies entwining, Duncan continued his seductive sorcery, coaxing her towards the zenith until she was writhing under him, her hands weaving their own magic, making his body thrum with need and he knew he was close.

"Jess, love."

She paused, fingers resting on sensitive flesh and looked up at him. Her hair was delightfully dishevelled, errant strands splayed across the pillow; the golden afternoon sunlight streaming through the window caught the sheen on her skin, and her eyes, hazy with longing, glowed with hidden fire. Duncan didn't think he'd ever seen anything so beautiful.

"What's wrong?" she lifted herself to kiss him, burnished locks streaming behind her. His breathing hitched and it was all he could do not to bury himself in her right then, but he had to take this slowly.

"Nothing, nothing's wrong, I...it's just...I need to..."

Captivated by the expression of boundless love on Jessica's face, Duncan was held motionless, lost for words.

"Duncan?" She cupped his face, her entreaty breaking the spell and he clarified what was about to happen as quickly as possible — his ability to maintain any form of control vanishing like mist under a hot sun — before resuming his heart stopping kiss. As Duncan carried her to the edge of the abyss, Jessica lost herself in the maelstrom of emotions and feelings he was inducing and as the ache within became almost unbearable he claimed her, as gradually as possible, until he was swallowed in her arousal. Jessica felt a sharp stab of pain, immediately quenched as, instinctively, their bodies began to move together until the world blazed with white light, and they were consumed by the waves of ecstasy crashing through them.

Much later, as heartbeats and breathing became somewhat less erratic, Jessica snuggled against her husband. He was still kissing her and it was utterly divine.

"Well that was the tastiest meal I've ever eaten," she volunteered, her voice a little husky. Duncan chuckled as he tucked a wayward ringlet behind her ear and kissed her nose.

"Oh, I'm sure there are other dishes just as tasty. Shall we take a look?"

Sitting up, Jessica swatted him on the chest, a mischievous grin tugging at her lips. "Why, Mr Barrington, I am astonished you could even think of another meal so soon after the last one."

"Oh, Mrs Barrington, you would be amazed at my appetite," making her squeal as he swung her on top of him and proceeded to demonstrate just how hungry he was.

Epilogue

The next few days disappeared in a blur of blissful happiness. Jessica and Duncan chose not to leave Briar Cottage — except for the, very, occasional constitutional — savouring private time together and enjoying getting to know each other intimately. They had talked before and already knew much about the other but being alone with no call on their time, allowed them the luxury of discussing all manner of things, even those, which may not be easy to confide. Since their argument and the events that followed, the couple realised how easily things can be misunderstood if neither was prepared to listen with a sympathetic ear.

They were also sensible enough to accept their hot-headed personalities would always make for a spirited relationship and their marriage would never be dull, but that disagreements should never be allowed to fester. As Jessica maintained, she didn't want perfection, she had only ever wanted Duncan and Duncan was wise enough to know his dark days would recur, but with Jessica by his side, he hoped they would lessen, his life no longer empty.

Duncan had no mind to press charges against Lieutenant Langdon; both were veterans and both suffered debilitating flashbacks to a greater or lesser extent — help was what Toby needed not incarceration. Thus, the veteran was escorted back to London and assessed at St Bart's before going to stay at the specialist facility Jessica had mentioned. It was an old rambling manor house set in acres of lush green fields, a tranquil place for healing. It took some time, but eventually Toby learned to recognise how and when the demons haunting him might be triggered. Concern for Toby's recovery led Jessica to follow his progress with sporadic letters and she was gratified to hear — several years later — he had met and married a young widow who lived on a smallholding, the couple settling into farming life with aplomb.

Soon enough, it was time to get back to, or in Jessica's case begin, their regular lives. It didn't take Jessica many days to become familiar with Dr Elliott's routine and soon she was shouldering the more mundane aspects of his work. The villagers and those working on the Winchester's estate warmed to her cheerful nature, and Jessica loved it. Duncan did, belatedly, recall Jessica's comment about Orion, realising she had braved her fears in order to find him. He suggested they ride together around the estate, her on a more suitable mount, allowing her to regain her confidence in the saddle with a companion. Truth be told Jessica loved the freedom of riding, admitting she regretted not confronting her aversion sooner. It was far more convenient when she was visiting the out-lying farmsteads, much quicker than walking, or waiting until there was a spare carriage, for it would have taken her twice as long to do her rounds.

Dr Napier, Clare and Meredith kept Jessica updated on the goings on at St Bart's, including the exciting, but not altogether unforeseen news of the doctor and Meredith's betrothal. Although she loved to hear from them, Jessica was surprised to find she didn't miss it as much as expected. She was pleased to learn, however, her booklet was selling steadily, the money going towards the development of prosthetics, and other small luxuries which helped ease the life of those reliant on St Bart's for their ongoing welfare.

Her life was here now, in the small village of Oak Stanton, with the man who would forever hold her heart — oh and the rascally dog who brought them together

Three Years Later

A tall man, with a military bearing, strolled down a leafy lane, enjoying the light breeze cooling his face. It had been a long but satisfying day; the several large items of furniture he and his staff had been working on, finally complete, along with one, much smaller, yet very special piece currently tucked in his pocket. He had spent hours on it and was a new direction for him; he hoped the recipient would be happy with the result.

Swinging through a gate nestled in a gap in a low hedge, Duncan Barrington called a 'Hello,' trailing his hand through the lavender bushes lining the path to his front door, breathing in the heady fragrance. Miles opened the door, welcoming the master of the house, informing him Mrs Barrington was in the garden. Duncan grinned his thanks, amused by the fact that it didn't matter how many times both he and his wife had begged their staff to call them by their given names, formality, it seemed, was ingrained.

Making his way through the library and out onto the terrace, Duncan was met by a sight that always lifted his heart, even on his darkest days, which were seldom now. In the middle of the garden, under the shade of a huge copper beech tree, lay a colourful rug on which Jessica was curled, reading to a small child cuddled onto her lap, while a scruffy looking dog lay asleep beside them. To one side stood a cradle and he could just make out two small fists pumping the air, a sure sign a demanding squall was in the offing. His footsteps on the stone flags caught Jessica's attention and she turned, smiling the way she did just for him.

"Duncan, you're home!" Standing the child on her feet, Jessica pointed her finger and Duncan was rewarded with an ecstatic shriek, waking Trixie and probably the rest of the neighbourhood. The little girl wobbled her way unsteadily to her father as Trixie bounded alongside. Duncan lifted his daughter into his arms, and fondled Trixie's ears as the excited creature wound herself around and around his legs whining in delight.

"Papa." Katherine Dorothea Barrington, or Kate, as she was known to all and sundry, squeezed her father's face between her chubby hands and planted a sticky kiss on his mouth. At just over two years old she was the apple of her father's eye and knew it. Jessica joined them, stretching up for her own kiss, loving the tingles fluttering through her as their lips met. Duncan settled Kate into the crook of his arm, bringing Jessica close with his other, fingers stroking up and down her back.

"I missed you today," smiling his customary greeting.

"I missed you too. I spent the morning sitting with old Mrs Fotheringham; bless her she thinks she's suffering from all manner of ailments yet she must be near ninety and healthy as an ox. Still she has some good stories and loves Kate." Jessica occasionally took their daughter with her on those house visits where she knew the occupant was lonely rather than unwell, the child often having a more beneficial effect than any conversation or medicine. She chuckled in recollection, but before she could add any more, a familiar wail reached them. "All right, Freddy, I'm coming." Rolling her eyes at her husband, she hurried over to the cradle, scooping up her tiny son.

Not quite four months old, Frederick Arthur Barrington had the lung capacity of a seasoned town crier and saw fit to practise his abilities to the full extent of his vocal range whenever possible. He fussed at her clothes until she allowed him what he wanted, his cries softening to satisfied grunts as he suckled.

Jessica made herself comfortable on the rug, leaning against the trunk of the tree while her son drank his fill, admiring her husband's powerful body as he swung Kate up in the air making her chortle with glee.

In the three years since they wed, her love for this man had only deepened; they still clashed, but less so now than they had in the beginning. Their lives, their souls, so closely intertwined they could anticipate a thought or a word often before the other even knew they were about to think or say it. He never failed to set her heart racing with a gentle smile or the briefest caress and their private time together was something she cherished.

Freddy had fallen back to sleep, replete for now and Jessica was tucking him back into his cot, re-arranging her clothes, just as Nesta, one of their maids, came out to get Kate ready for her bath. Jessica thanked her adding she would follow shortly. Taking advantage of a few peaceful moments, Duncan shrugged out of his coat dropping it on the rug and drew Jessica into his arms.

"Come here, wench, I haven't said hello properly yet." Crushing his mouth to hers, he kissed her until her legs started to buckle.

"Well, hello to you too," she gasped when he finally relinquished her lips. "I trust you don't greet all your women friends in so congenial a manner?"

"'Tis by far the best way to get their attention," he twinkled down at her.

"You are incorrigible," she giggled, elbowing him gently in his chest. "Now please do it again."

He readily obliged, and for long moments the rest of the world faded into insignificance.

"Do you think anyone would mind if I made love to you under this tree?" he growled.

Jessica spluttered with laughter. "I for one have no objection; however, the rest of our staff might be somewhat surprised should they come upon us, and I'm supposed to be helping Nesta bathe Kate."

"I do believe I am willing to risk it, and I'm sure Nesta can manage for once." He continued kissing her and somehow, they ended up lying side by side on the rug, under the leafy canopy. Duncan's fingers roamed over Jessica's slender frame, seeking her curves and her hollows, teasing along her throat and to the swell of her breasts, skimming over her waist and under her gown. All the while, his lips sending her into a paroxysm of passion, until she didn't care about anything except the mastery of her husband's touch as he took her to the heavens and back.

Much later, lying wrapped in each other's arms oblivious to all else around them, they shared their respective days. Duncan remembered the gift he had brought home, so he sat up, shifting Jessica onto his lap.

"I have something for you. 'Tis not my usual subject matter, I hope you like it." Reaching for his coat, he slipped his hand in the deep pocket, withdrew something wrapped in soft cloth and handed it Jessica. Peeling back the material, Jessica stared at the offering within. It was a carving of her, their two children and Trixie. She was at the centre, sitting on an old log, Kate leaning on her knee, Freddy tucked into her shoulder and Trixie lying in front of the group. Fashioned from aged oak, it was astonishingly beautiful. He had captured the essence of each of them, from the tilt of her head, to Kate's cheeky smile, from Freddy's dimples to Trixie's puppy grin.

"Duncan, goodness...how did you...when...?" Tears flooded her eyes, as she stared at him, words — typically, yet not unexpectedly — failing her.

"I've been working on it since Freddy was born. It's taken a little longer than usual, for 'tis the first time I have carved people." He looked at her, dubiously.

"My darling husband, I am...this is..." She traced the rich wood, sensing the love that had gone into the carving. "You could not have given me anything I will treasure more. 'Tis exquisite," she whispered, three tears sliding down her cheek. About to wipe them away — she refused to cry — she was halted as her husband's lips did it for her.

"I love you, Jessica Barrington. I love you more every day. You took my melancholy heart and filled it with joy. I am forever thankful a tiny puppy saw fit to get entangled in a thorny bush, for without you, my life would be as a barren wasteland."

She cupped his face, bringing his head down until their foreheads touched. "I love you too, Duncan Barrington. I am so glad 'twas you who stole my heart, for had we not met it might still slumber, its beat, quiescent. Now, with no more than a glance, you compel an untamed rhythm, yet one which is always in harmony with you." Jessica brushed her lips to his. "Duncan, my life began, truly began, the day you came upon me in the snow, grumpy with the silly chit from London who refused to get on a horse. We didn't make it easy for each other and I know we made mistakes, but I never once doubted our love.

"Doubt thou the stars are fire, doubt that the sun doth move, doubt truth to be a liar, but never doubt I love."

Jessica leaned back as, quietly but with feeling, Duncan quoted from Hamlet,

"I did not know you were familiar with the Bard," she whispered, the beauty of the words echoing in her head and, igniting within her core, a delicious warmth.

"I used to find his words soothing when I couldn't sleep; something I am no longer troubled with," he grinned. "I find this particular phrase fitting. It runs through my mind every time I see you and has done so from the moment we met, although it took my head a little longer to catch up with my heart. Our is a love hard fought and hard won, but it is the stronger for it, deep-burning and..." he paused, searching for the perfect word, "...unquenchable."

Mesmerised by his words and his smouldering gaze, Jessica slid her hand up, cupping her husband's cheek, rubbing her thumb over the soft stubble of his beard and all fell silent around them. Duncan drew her close once more and, as the afternoon sun slowly dipped towards the horizon in a ball of flaming gold, he showed her just how unquenchable their love remained.

Thank you for purchasing this book, I do hope you enjoyed reading it.
If you have a moment to write a quick review on Amazon I would be most grateful.
The synopses for my other books follow.

I hope we meet again soon,
Rosie

You can find me on,

Facebook:
https://www.facebook.com/RosieChapelTheAuthor/
Twitter: @RosieChapel2015
Website: www.rosiechapel.com
Goodreads:
https://www.goodreads.com/author/show/14759605.Rosie_Chapel

Once Upon An Earl
A Regency Romance
Linen and Lace - Book One

When Fate saw fit to intervene in the life of Giles Trevallier, the very respectable Earl of Winchester, by dropping a female — soaked to the skin and with no memory of who she is or how she came to be there — literally at his feet, no one could have predicted the outcome.

The woman eventually recalls that her name is Willow and as Giles begins discreet enquiries, he is shocked to discover that she is rumoured to be responsible for a fire that destroyed her family home, killing her father.

While trying to unravel the mystery surrounding her, Giles realises that he is falling hopelessly in love with Willow, who unbeknownst to him is fighting similar emotions; and as with anything involving the heart, a thoughtless word or gesture has a tendency to thwart even Fate's best-laid plans.

Faced with misunderstandings, whispers of scandal, secret documents and foreign agents, their chance at a happy ever after seems elusive, but fairy tales often happen when least expected, and love — however inconvenient — usually finds a way to conquer all.

To Unlock Her Heart
A Regency Romance
Linen and Lace - Book Two

After being caught in a scandal with a duke, Grace Aldeburgh has been shunned by everyone - family, friends and Society. To shield herself from the trauma she was subjected to, Grace buried her heart away, so deeply that she wasn't sure it could ever be found.

Two years later, with little hope of ever being free of the stigma, relief seems at hand in the guise of a bequest from her Great Aunt. Grace has inherited a house in a tiny village, far from prying eyes and malicious gossips. Once there, she meets Theo Elliott, the village doctor and what begin as a tentative friendship, blossoms into something more enduring. Fearing further censure, Grace knows she must tell Theo her secret, but the doctor is no fair-weather suitor and has already resolved to be the man to unlock her heart.

Just as happiness appears to be within her grasp, her erstwhile tormentor once again stalks Grace. After a failed kidnap attempt, the duke's quest culminates in an acrimonious confrontation with Grace and suddenly the reason for his venal pursuit of her becomes agonisingly clear.

Love on a Winter's Tide
A Regency Romance
Linen and Lace - Book Three

Lady Helena Trevallier is in no hurry to marry, unwilling to allow a man to dictate her life. She has a secret, one that would probably horrify her social set and one any prospective suitor would demand she curtail. Every day, Helena disappears into a world few acknowledge, helping the poor, downtrodden and abused.

Hugh Drummond avoids most of the Society events he is invited to; events stalked by mamas seeking husbands for their daughters. A state of wedded bliss is something that holds no interest for him. Busy managing his shipping line, he sees no need for a wife, whose only joy is dancing and frivolity. If — and it was a huge if — he ever married, he would want a woman as capable as he, not some giddy society Miss.

Then, Hugh meets Helena and despite their resolve, fate, it seems, has other ideas. As their attraction deepens however, treachery threatens to tear them apart. Will they uncover the perpetrator in time or will their love be swept away, lost forever on a winter's tide

A Hidden Rose
A Regency Romance
Linen and Lace - Book Five

After witnessing his mother's grief at the loss of his father, Nick Drummond resolved never to cause someone he loved such distress. Even the happiness of his siblings would not sway him – until he met Rose.

Rose Archer was almost content assisting her doctor father in a tiny fishing village in the north of Yorkshire. To experience the world beyond, a tantalising dream – until she met Nick.

Unexpectedly, the impossible becomes possible, and the renounced – desired above all things, but the shipwreck that brought them together, may yet tear them apart. Will Nick learn to trust his heart, or will his love for Rose remain forever hidden?

His Fiery Hoyden
A Regency Novella

Please inform your master, Sasha is perfectly happy here with me and there is more chance of hell freezing over, than of my brother dancing attendance on his Grace."

A plea for help ignored. A child left to bring up her baby brother.

Livvy has no respect for the nobility; they let her down when she most needed them. Why should she accede to their demands now?

Philip, Lord Harrington, is stunned to discover the young heir to the dukedom lives a stone's throw away in a ramshackle cottage, and resolves to restore the child to his birthright.

They meet in a clash of wills, but just when it seems Livvy might surrender, the victory Philip desires, may not taste all that sweet.

The Pomegranate Tree
Hannah's Heirloom - Book One

Hoping to trace the origins of an ancient ruby clasp, a gift from her long dead grandmother, Hannah Wilson travels to the fortress of Masada with her best friend, Max. Strange dreams concerning a rebel ambush begin to haunt Hannah and following a tragic accident, she slips into the world of Ancient Masada.

A woman out of time, Hannah must rely on her instincts and her knowledge of what will befall this citadel to survive. Will she escape, or is she doomed to die along with hundreds of others as Masada falls – and what does any of this have to do with an ancient ruby clasp?

Echoes of Stone and Fire
Hannah's Heirloom - Book Two

Pompeii - a vibrant city lost in time following the AD79 eruption of Vesuvius. Now rediscovered, archaeologists yearn for an opportunity to uncover the town's past. Some things however, are best left alone - revealing the secrets hidden beneath the stones could prove perilous. Hannah and Max are brought to Pompeii by a surprise invitation to join an excavation team who are trying to uncover the city's long history.

After entering an excavated house that bears a Hebrew inscription, Hannah's two worlds collide and she falls back through time to ancient Pompeii. A place where her ancestor is a physician to gladiators engaged in mortal combat, where riotous mobs run amok and where a ghost from the past returns to haunt her.

Will Hannah and her loved ones manage to escape the devastation she knows is coming, before the town is engulfed in volcanic ash? Will she ever find her way back to Max the love of her life, waiting not so patiently millennia away? Or will echoes be all that remain?

Embers of Destiny
Hannah's Heirloom - Book Three

AD80 - Hannah and Maxentius must embark on a new journey to Northern Britannia. This harsh frontier is far from the comforts of Rome and danger lurks where least expected; a garrison of soldiers, some unhappy with their isolated posting; local tribes, outwardly accepting of their Roman occupier, but who may still resent the seizure of their lands.

Millennia away, Hannah Vallier finds a familiar item while working in a museum near Hadrian's Wall. It is the pomegranate; carved by Maxentius on Masada. Before Hannah can discuss it with Max, disaster strikes! Believing her husband has been killed, Hannah retreats into the past, her soul melding with that of her ancestor, but with little idea of what they could face. Is the risk from the conquered tribes, or much closer to home?

As rebellion threatens to shatter a fragile peace, Hannah's heart whispers that just maybe Max isn't dead and that he is calling her home. Can she trust her heart or will she remain caught out of time, her destiny floating away like embers on a breeze?

Etched in Starlight
Hannah's Heirloom - Prequel

Maxentius - a Roman soldier fresh from the battlefields of Armenia, arrives to take command of the military outpost of Masada, Herod's isolated citadel in the Judaean desert. A seemingly mundane posting after years of warfare, Maxentius finds it more challenging to maintain a focused garrison than to face the wrath of the Parthians across a disputed frontier.

Hannah - a young Hebrew physician spends her days dealing with injuries from street brawls, deprivation, disease and loss. As her beloved Jerusalem plunges into chaos; her brother — who belongs to a band of rebels determined to drive out their Roman occupiers — tells her of their plans to storm a desert fortress and steal the weapons stored there, persuading his reluctant sister to go with him.

Masada - following the ambush, Hannah finds and treats three badly wounded Roman soldiers. In the aftermath and against impossible odds, Hannah and Maxentius realise that they are more than healer and captive, their fate already etched in starlight.

Prelude to Fate

For Lucia, staring into the jaws of an horrific death, escape seems impossible.

Rufius Atellus, a veteran Roman soldier, is appalled when he recognises one of the victims about to be executed. Surely this is a ghastly mistake?

A ferocious she-wolf, anticipating a tasty meal, suddenly finds herself under a human's control.

In an unexpected twist, and as danger threatens, the lives of all three become inextricably entwined. Was it chance brought them together in that theatre of bloodshed, or simply a prelude to fate?

Of Ruins and Romance

While escorting a group of tourists around the ancient Roman port of Ostia, Kassandra Winters bumps into someone she first met in less than auspicious circumstances two years previously. The encounter leads to a job offer - to be the assistant guide for a three-week tour of ancient sites in and around Rome. Unable to resist such an opportunity, Kassie agrees.

Kassie has intrigued Gabriel St Germain since he accidentally knocked her flying outside her university professor's office. Her face haunts his dreams, yet he never expected to see her again. So, he is surprised when she appears, as though destined to do so, in the middle of a ruin, and he concocts a plan to win her heart.

Gabriel's old-fashioned courtship touches something deep inside Kassie and, although struggling to believe someone as handsome as Gabriel could possibly be interested in her, she soon realises she has fallen irrevocably in love with him. However, just as Kassie shares everything of herself with Gabriel, her world comes crashing down. Can their romance survive or will it fall in ruins, like the relics of antiquity that brought them together.

All At Once It's You

When Alex arrives in the small village of Rosedale Abbey, to take up a position as a research assistant for a renowned archaeologist, the last thing she is looking for, or expects to find, is love.

Jake was perfectly happy with the status quo. When it came to relationships, he didn't do committed or long term. He called the shots, and if his current flame didn't like it, she knew what to do. A philosophy, which served him well - until he met Alex.

Romance blooms, but even as the untamed wilderness of the North Yorkshire moors weaves its spell, a long buried secret might yet jeopardise their happily ever after.

www.ingramcontent.com/pod-product-compliance
Lightning Source LLC
Chambersburg PA
CBHW061548170626
46811CB00001B/134